D1502997

Bloggers Can't be Trusted

by

Starrene Rhett Rocque

"I yell too much, get stressed too quick. But the best thing about it, I can change that shit, and still remain who I came down to Earth to be."

Don't Rush Me, Jean Grae

Part I

#EverythingisTerrible

I'd been fascinated by words for as long as I could remember. It wasn't about how big or complicated they were it was about the stories they told. I loved reading and immersing myself in various tales, fiction and non-fiction, about people's lives around the world. According to my parents, I started reading at two and treated my books the way most children treated their dolls and action figures. I cuddled with them in bed, carried them around with me wherever I went, insisted on reading to anyone who would listen and I cried when my books got so tattered from overuse that they were unreadable and barely bound together.

My parents didn't mind that. They appreciated that their Little Brown Dimple Doll—which is what they called me due to my deep dimples, dough-eyes, round face and high cheekbones inherited from my maternal grandmother—who was growing up in Bed-Stuy before the oversaturation of rental bikes, designer dogs, and trendy cafes, would rather immerse herself in literature and the arts than fall into trite traps like drug dealing, teenage pregnancy and other ills that often plagued the denizens of Every Hood USA.

Not every kid from the hood grew up to become a product of that, of course. My parents were successful and gave me everything I needed to succeed. My dad, a corporate finance lawyer with his own multi-services practice, and my mom, the owner of her own dance, martial arts, yoga and Pilates studio, chose not to move to the suburbs because they owned their property and felt the need to stay in order to invest in their neighborhood. I grew up in a brownstone that was inherited from my paternal grandfather, and my parents still lived there, representing what became a line of ownership and tradition in the Barnes family.

My world consisted of school, dance and theater classes, occasional piano lessons, date-days with my dad, attempting to be stage manager to my mom's oft-whimsical productions at her dance studio, and fantasizing about becoming the next Lorraine Hansberry. I knew that my name, Nyela Barnes, would one day hold weight in prose and make an impact on pop culture.

I wrote plays, monologues, and novels for fun—all of which my mom still hoarded and brought up in conversation to whomever would listen when she bragged about my career as an entertainment journalist.

Time spent with my mother meant mulling over the black classics. No child of hers would go out into the world without learning about Black History before slavery, and not being able to recite Langston

Hughes, or recognize Duke Ellington's "Sophisticated Lady" by ear, or not be able to choreograph a Katherine Dunham-inspired routine. Time with my dad was more about being rebellious because he had a different idea of arts and culture. My dad and I often took field trips to restaurants, where we would escape my mother's family-imposed vegan eating, record stores, or to my uncle's house on Long Island, where we'd watch Blaxploitation films and listen to hip-hop. Dad was corporate but he always said, "Don't let the suit fool you!" whenever people were shocked that he could quote everyone's favorite rapper, and even the more esoteric hip-hop lines from the likes of MF Doom or Jeru the Damaja. He and my Uncle Chris, who worked in publishing law, witnessed hip-hop's birth. They often traveled uptown to visit their cousins who just so happened to live on the infamous Sedgwick and Cedar block in the Bronx, where DJ Kool Herc helped birth hip-hop. They were young men then who were there for the block parties, witnessed the battles, the breakdancing, and carried that identity with them everywhere. At Uncle Chris' place, they would stage cyphers where they'd encourage my big cousin C.J. and I to join in the fun. I was a terrible rapper, but those moments gave rise to my self-proclaimed Hip-Hop Zora Neale Hurston phase. During that short-lived period, the stories I wrote combined my inspiration from hip-hop and the Harlem

Renaissance. My goal was to write hip-hop literature and so, similar to Miss Hurston, I was very intentional about the use of dialect in my stories, but of course, my dialect of choice reflected hip-hop culture. Those stories were terrible, but the writing practice was helpful. I was also a voracious reader of Walter Mosley, Octavia Butler, Terry McMillan, Omar Tyree, and even Marvel Comics. My taste was diverse, so my stories varied across genres, but at the core was usually hip-hop, and sometimes even Blaxploitation as my protagonists tended to be badass women like many of the roles played by Pam Grier, Tamara Dobson, and Teresa Graves in the 70s. However, by the time I entered high school in the 21st century, my focus shifted to becoming an entertainment journalist. I used to read *The Source* and *VIBE* magazines, which I always got from my dad's stash, and *Honey*, which my mom got me a subscription to even though I was a little younger than the intended demographic.

I was enamored by stories about hip-hop clubs in Japan, or how some rapper founded a charity to help bring awareness to homelessness in the United States, which I thought was a great way to fight the stereotype that all rappers thrived on nihilistic messages and behavior. That was when integrity in entertainment journalism actually mattered. It was those stories and influences on my life that inspired me to double major in anthropology and journalism, and minor in creative writing in college. I graduated magna cum laude, and eventually worked my way up the ranks and became a respected writer in New York City. That was before people started getting off on the current cult of negativity that I believed was being driven by the Internet. Even when I started at *Spark* magazine, one of the top urban entertainment magazines in history next to *VIBE* and *The Source*, as an assistant editor, the industry was different. I had since been witnessing its decline over the last few years.

Now, people would sell their first born into human sex trafficking just for the sake of getting followers and attention. The more sensational a story was, the better. The big wigs with money that ran a lot of these companies had no real clue about what digital strategy took, what good the Internet could be used for, or even how journalism and digital publishing actually worked, and there was an insane obsession with metrics. Their goal was not quality stories; it was all about numbers and the perception that higher numbers meant more money. I understood that, but there was also a serious lack of balance as a result. Go ahead and count how many celebrity Twitter beef stories you spot in one day, and pay attention to how many "breaking news" stories about nip slips and celebrities doing mundane things like grocery shopping you noticed. Then, ask yourself if you actually learned something useful from it all.

We are living in the age of the spectacle, but I couldn't place all the blame on business and the Internet since we the people have fed this monster for years.

Part of my job as Pop Culture Editor/Music Editor/Features Editor/Dumb Shit Editor/Entertainment Editor/Whatever-the-Fuck-They-Want-me-to-be-that-Day-Because-we're-Understaffed-and-the-Company-is-too-Cheap-for-Competent-New-Hires-Editor for *Spark* magazine required me to monitor the traffic daily, which was why I knew that the aforementioned stuff was what people gravitated toward in droves. Thinking about this was exhausting, but I'd been mulling it over for weeks because I was starting to realize that there was a change in my personality that I didn't like, and it was because of what my life had become.

On paper I looked great, but the truth was that at 27, I was still in the middle of my quarter-life crisis, which seemed to be delayed by a year, but hasn't stopped since. I missed the enthusiasm for my career that I had when I was an intern for the print version of *Spark* during my last year in college and even after graduation. Journalism on the web still hadn't *really* taken off then and social networks were still more relegated to college students. *Spark* had a web component then, but they weren't really focused on creating articles, listicles, or any digital content, and laughed at me any time I suggested that we went there. The economy was allegedly recovering from a major recession not too long after I started, but my industry never really bounced back. There were still massive layoffs and major cuts happening on a whim, which forced people to pick up extra job responsibilities, often with no extra pay. Interns became more like volunteer staffers under the guise of gaining experience and college credit, and actual staffers became more like slaves out of fear that there was always someone waiting in the wings to take their respective spots because the fear of ending up in the unemployment circus, homeless, or worse, no longer getting invited to exclusive events, was *so real*.

I was still naïve and wide-eyed at that time, which also coincided with the magazine's developing need to focus on digital content, once they finally decided to get serious about it, so I happily took on more work feeling like it was a startup project that I could really turn into something amazing. It was my dream job then. Working at *Spark* actually became part of my identity and I didn't mind since I was so driven to one day become Editor-in-Chief. However, these days, there were a lot more R.I.P. moments than V.I.P., but the problem was that the V.I.P. moments could be so addictive that you failed to enact an effective exit strategy, which was quite an emotionally abusive cycle. Perks included access to powerful people, free trips, free products and entry into some of the most exclusive events in the world. With every V.I.P. moment that happened, there was a high that almost made you forget the R.I.P. shit like, writing asinine sensational and exaggerated stories that probably weren't factual, dealing with crappy narcissistic personalities who treated people like shit, lower pay for more work, celebrities trying to fight you because they didn't like something you wrote since you had to hyperbolize it, and much more.

My position was on the mid to higher end of the magazine totem pole, but I still occasionally had to freelance so that I could have some change left over to play with once my bills were paid. This was New York City, after all!

I knew I sounded cynical, and probably whiney too, but I've just been really bored with my life and my job and needed to vent. I missed being excited about...anything.

These days, I edited some feature stories in the magazine *and* oversaw the television, film, and sometimes music content too on the website. I was actually still excited about *Spark's* underdeveloped TV and film content. Cinema had always been another passion of mine, and also part of those field trips I mentioned taking with my dad, but I only recently got serious about the idea of incorporating it into my career.

Perhaps I could shift focus to that screenplay I kept starting then scrapping.

"Hey Nyela, we're waiting for you in the conference room," Patrick said, peering over the partition that divided our cubicles. He was the other more senior editor on staff who worked with me on *Spark's* website.

I got so wrapped up in surfing the web for potential stories and leads that I didn't realize that our weekly content strategy meeting (that really didn't incorporate much strategy) started now.

—

Ideally, the purpose of a meeting at most people's jobs was to discuss ideas and make progress for the business. But that wasn't what was put into practice at *Spark*.

My boss was Tony Walker. He should be filed under crappy narcissistic personality. He was a record executive who hit his peak in the 1990s, and then he became publisher *and* editor-in-chief, which was an oxymoron because there was almost always a conflict of interest when it came to the two roles. Publishers were the money people, E.I.C.'s were supposed to be the ones more focused on content and integrity, but when someone was both, their decisions were always solely about money and maintaining relationships with the magazine, journalistic integrity be damned. He liked to make us feel like shit under the guise of motivation. Most of our meetings involved lectures on everything we didn't do right, and often getting cursed out.

Back in his hey-day, Tony made a name for himself as a notorious, bellicose leader, and once almost went to jail for allegedly hiring a crackhead to stab a man he accused of bootlegging his artist's music, but that was another story.

I used to take his behavior personally, but I learned to tune him out around the end of my third year here. Now I just zoned out and fantasized about all the shit that I *really* wanted to be doing, like writing that screenplay. I even used the time to think of new posts for my blog.

I got settled in to a seat at the end of the conference room table furthest away from Hot Head Tony, as I liked to call him, and prepared for today's vitriol.

"Y'all need to be more like Bossip and stop trying to do all this fancy journalism shit!" Tony said, at a volume most likely on a billion decibels. "The people want jokes!"

We went through this every day. Today he wanted us to be like Bossip, tomorrow it was going to be Buzzfeed and next week it would be TMZ, but we definitely couldn't be any of those when we didn't get exclusive and original breaking news like we used to, nor did we have the amount of staff required for the amount of leg work it took to crank out original gifs and lists at the speed of light.

Like I said, *Spark* was one of the pioneering urban pop culture magazines and had built up a reputation over the years for quality articles, but remember, we were now competing with bloggers who got higher numbers and tended to be friends with all the people they got exclusives from. Also, people really just didn't like Tony. I wished we were able to continue the integrity of our brand, but it was hard when clueless businessmen assumed that the web was magic. They thought that just because you typed something and hit send, people were supposed to flock in droves to read your stuff and that numbers would automatically be off the charts. That was not how the digital space worked. Content was a factor, but you also had to employ digital marketing tactics, not from just *any* publicist or marketer, but one who understood how to promote online. Usually, there was no publicist or marketer in place at all. They wanted the writers and editors to fulfill those roles too. There was also Search Engine Optimization, which could be complicated to explain, but just know that there were people who dedicated their lives to the algorithms of how people searched for information online and anyone who wanted to have a successful website should learn the ways of SEO wizardry so that content, based on certain key words in the copy, headline, and url's on their site, actually showed up in the top five results listed when people searched for it and enticed people to click. Big wigs in my industry also tended to not want to hire SEO Jedi's and analytics gurus to make sense of what content actually worked for their respective brands because they were cheap, that is, unless shelling out extra money involved a first class flight and car service for their personal use, but I digress. So, between the identity crisis copycat shit, and not having the right staff in place for certain positions, we were always relegated to virtual chaos.

"What the fuck is up with these wack-ass headlines? We gotta draw people in and get that hot shit because right now our content ain't shit! Do what you gotta do to get those clicks. I'm talking race bait, sex, and post some misogynistic rap shit so them feminist bitches can go off and blow our shit up from sharing it."

I glanced around the room and noticed that most people's eyes were glazed over, nothing out of the ordinary, but Hot Head Tony was actually pretty tame today.

"Again, it's all about race, sex and politics! That's the shit that gets click throughs. Controversy! We want more posts like that Tall Shawty article Nyela wrote a few months ago. That shit was gold!"

Great, now everyone in the room was staring at me about something that I'd like to forget. Basically, I thought it would be a good idea for us to do celebrity blogs online. We'd call the celebrities of choice—usually rappers or singers, sometimes actors—and have them speak on various topics and then put their words together as an editorial for the site. It did well for traffic so we did it as much as possible. Enter Tall Shawty, a rapper.

At the time, every single website known to man was posting something defamatory about black women. Generally, we were called ugly and undesirable, trifling baby factories, and basically the cause of all the ills of the world, but the most popular dig was deciphering reasons why none of us could find a man and were destined to be single and miserable forever because studies showed this, of course. Every single black woman on the planet was just destined to be ain't shit.

I decided that this was one of many topics that we'd cover and Tall Shawty being the outspoken personality that he was, let lose. In Tall Shawty's world, black women were too sassy and aggressive and needed to learn how to submit or "bow down." In fact, black women's "nasty attitudes," and especially the fact that we were all "gold diggers" was the reason he hadn't dated a black woman since he started making money in the rap game—his words, not mine. Mind you, this was a man with three babymamas, and he was also in the middle of being sued for back child support by at least two of those women.

Within hours of his semi-rant being posted, everyone with an opinion had something to say about it. Feminists, Womanists, misogynists, intellectuals, idiots, pseudo-intellectuals and any and everything in between raged with such fervor that it delivered the most epic traffic that *Spark* online had ever seen. Our server crashed twice.

People talked about the Tall Shawty scandal for nearly two weeks, which was eons in the digital world, and we pimped it too. A majority of our subsequent stories had something to do with that incident. We had other well-known celebrities and cultural critics blog their rebuttals, which helped keep our traffic extremely high throughout that month. At the time, I got @-attacked on Twitter because apparently, I was a tricksy journalist—bitch, trash and negro bed wench were other favorite choice words—who twisted the poor man's words around.

Tall Shawty actually insisted that he didn't say most of what was printed, and there was even a petition circulating among rabid idiot Tall Shawty fans to have me fired. *Spark* obviously didn't fire me because I was good at what I did, and the story did what they wanted. But I released the audio of our interview to make people feel stupid, which helped to extend the life of the story once again. People talked about it to death for a while until they just stopped, and that was that. It was over just as swiftly as it started.

That was one of the many things I hated about the web and I guess, by extension, people too. They claimed to hate sensationalism and drama, yet they were always arguing on message boards, over-intellectualizing negativity, complaining about how the media promoted too much of the bad stuff and generally looked for everything that was wrong with society. Yet when we posted something positive we got nothing but crickets. My World AIDS Day and educational news posts never got comments and not so much as 500 page views on the analytics side of things — which was horrible because our stories usually got a combined total of about 50,000 page views a day. But the minute I posted about some celebrity's new tattoo, a shady tweet, or #ThirstTraps on Instagram, the traffic shot through the roof.

"Look at all the poppin' bloggers and see why they're winning right now. They borrow the same shit from each other *and* they know how to pluck nerves!"

Hot Head Tony was still talking, unfortunately.

"But those same celebrities they piss off can't live without 'em and you see how quick the publicists will send them exclusives and shit!

That's where we gotta be at, like them poppin' sites! Fuck trying to be innovative if that shit don't work!"

I found myself back at my desk after about an hour that felt more like five, of listening to Tony's rambling. I trolled the web, once again, for stories that I could use, but my best friend Reiko broke the monotony with a text message saying she had big news. She could be a drama queen so she kept me in suspense, instead of just texting what it was, until we met up tonight for a boozy-girl-talk session over drinks and tapas.

—

Reiko tackled me as we arrived at Verlaine simultaneously, and screeched, "I GOT THE GIG!"

The gig she was referring to was co-host of the newly revamped Mega Morning Riot Show on Urban 109. Urban 109 had been New York City's top station for hip-hop and R&B for years. The station was regarded as a pioneer in urban radio and was especially noted for its morning show until rival stations started eclipsing its success. Part of the issue was that the station had the same morning show hosts since the late 1980s, but the hosts failed to keep up with the times, got stale, and clashed with station heads on a consistent basis. Finally, the head honchos called for new blood. Reiko, who had been an industry cool kid since our internship days at *Spark,* didn't even have to audition because of her popular satellite radio show, where she already covered urban news, gossip and did celebrity interviews. She was a soloist on satellite radio, but in her new gig she would be one-third of a trio on the Mega Morning Riot. (Side note, I always thought the word urban was a silly description for what catered to hip-hop or black interests, but I was using it here for the sake of clarity. People seemed to understand it better so, whatever.)

"I knew you'd get it!" I said, sliding out of her bear hug and leading the way inside.

I was happy for her, but I was also kind of jealous. She got to have career excitement while mine was rapidly going downhill.

"So, who are your co-hosts?" I asked, hoping my voice was even enough to hide my envy.

"I'll be working with DJ Blackenstein and Cookie Clark."

"Wait, *Cookie Clark?* The video girl that blew the whistle on all her sexual conquests in the music industry?"

"Yup," Reiko replied, rolling her eyes.

I'm glad she was as annoyed as I was.

"She's such an attention whore! I wonder who she fucked or manipulated to get the gig," I said.

"She probably didn't have to sleep with anyone. The hiring decision was also a numbers game. Blackenstein and I had our own respective radio shows that did well in terms of ratings and content, but they looked at social media influence too. Blackenstein doesn't have a blog, but his show ratings combined with his Twitter, Facebook Fan Page and Instagram followers were at about a combined total of 800,000 followers."

"And between *your* actual blog, your radio show, your Twitter, your Instagram #ThirstTraps, and your rapidly growing Snapchat, I *know* you're over a million."

"Something like that. But I also have relationships and get exclusives that the station could use."

"But back to that trick, Cookie. She doesn't have platform built on merit," I said.

"Um, hel-lo! She has a popular blog, vlog, a bigger social media presence than me and Blackenstein respectively, *and* she wrote a *New York Times* bestselling book!"

"Girl bye! You know she had a ghostwriter for that book! She's vapid. She's another pretty face with a fat ass and paparazzi photos with random ballers and actors plastered on *The YBF*! I'm pretty sure someone more deserving and talented could have snagged that spot."

Cookie Clark was a cute girl. She was petite, but curvy even though I wouldn't be surprised if she at least had breast implants. She had been the reigning urban it girl and Instagram model favorite for the past two years, and also did a couple of *Smooth* magazine covers and spreads, as well as *Playboy*. But what she was *really* known for was sleeping with anyone with a penis and some clout in the entertainment business. The book she wrote, based on a blog she started to share her industry escapades, skyrocketed her popularity. She shared all the sordid details about her conquests with some of the industry's biggest names under the guise of female empowerment. She has slept with married men, took credit for a few celebrity divorces and there was even a rumor, which she neither confirmed nor denied, that Kanye West dumped Amber Rose for her before getting serious with Kim Kardashian. Again, she allegedly started her blog and wrote the book so that impressionable young women could learn from her mistakes. I read the book and it really just seemed like glorified bragging, but whatever. People seemed to like simple shit, and that was exactly what she put out into the universe and managed to get rewarded for.

"You know what they say. Hoes be winnin!" I said.

We laughed as the waitress arrived with our drinks and to take our orders.

"You know what, though? I'm going to give her a chance," Reiko replied.

"What! You're supposed to be on #TeamCookieHaterade like me!"

"But we have to work together. It would make for better chemistry if we actually got along. Besides, you know how much shit people talk in this industry. Who says she isn't a nice homewrecker? And she has connections too. Hell, I may be able to collaborate with her on some networking shit."

"Just be careful, girl. You know she's an equal opportunity saboteur."

"You already know who you're talking to. I survived *The Bad Girls Club*. Remember?"

Reiko did a stint on *The Bad Girls Club* a couple of years ago. I liked to pretend it never happened, although I was still occasionally reminded whenever we went out. The Reiko I knew was feisty but cool; she had a B.A. in English Lit and a M.A. in Broadcast Journalism, and only pulled out the wicked bitch card when provoked. But the *B.G.C.* version of Reiko showed out for the cameras. She became the house manipulator, and engaged in a lot of fighting, bickering, and random mastermind plots to get other women kicked out of the house. I always knew that Reiko liked attention—she was gorgeous, outgoing and smart, so she was used to it—but she sometimes used negativity to make a name for herself and unfortunately, it worked. It put her on the map socially and financially in a way that her internships, her party promoter phase, her model phase, and stylist phase, never did.

"So what the fuck is up with *you* lately?" Reiko said. "You've been depressed as hell and it makes *me* want to slit *my* wrists."

"It's not like this is new news, but I hate my fucking job. My hatred for my job is an intense force that consumes me, and it grows stronger every day. Speaking of the force and hatred, the entire staff got cursed out again today by Darth Maul." I took a sip of my lychee martini then continued. "And I also haven't spoken to Sincere in weeks."

Sincere was the other major source of stress in my life, and he was inevitably going to come up because that's what girl's time was about, right? The last time Sincere and I spoke, we were boyfriend and girlfriend, but considering that he had been missing in action with no communication for at least two weeks, I guess that was a moot point. I was obviously a smart girl, but sometimes, I did the dumbest shit when it came to men, like assuming that Sincere's ghosting didn't necessarily mean a break up.

"No texts, emails, or anything?"

"NO! I've reached out but he hasn't been responsive. It's like he just fucking disappeared, which isn't like him, and of course he's still active on social media."

"You mean it's not like the *old* him! That man has changed quite a bit since you first started dating."

"I guess you're right."

I met Sincere—real name, no gimmicks—two years ago back when he worked in finance. It was a random day when Reiko and I decided to deviate from our usual after work haunts and ended up at a bar in the financial district. Sincere spotted us first and went through the typical stuff. You know, buying us drinks and striking up conversation. He seemed really nice, and talking to a non-industry dude was refreshing.

I should have run when he mentioned his secret desire to become a writer. He always thought it was an unrealistic career path and never pursued anything seriously beyond his blog that he sporadically updated when he wasn't too busy with his day job as an accountant. The blog chronicled his adventures as a bachelor in New York City—cliché, I know. It was cute back then, though, especially after we exchanged phone numbers and he called me under the guise of picking my brain about the craft.

Being the overzealous altruist I could sometimes be when there was a cute face and good dick involved, I encouraged him to update his blog more, showed him ways he could strategize to pick up traffic, and even started taking him to industry events with me so that he could network. He took my advice, got hooked, and his blog took off. I let him continue blogging under the single guy persona even after we declared that we were officially a couple, especially since he publically acknowledged my presence in his life as his girlfriend, but I just wasn't prepared for him to actually start masquerading as a relationship guru and even become a certified relationship coach. He started getting TV and radio appearances and writing guest posts for major publications, and eventually he started making so much revenue from his site that he quit the Wall Street life and pimped his new found celebrity as "The Love Broker."

The charming version of Sincere that I initially began dating morphed into the industry dudes I was so sick of. He became a premium douche lord, and I started lying to myself about our relationship. I lost him to the world of instant celebrity. It was unfortunate that his minions were too stupid to realize that he was a disingenuous piece of shit.

I guess what kept me holding on was that even after he got Internet famous, he showed traces of the sweet Sincere that I fell in love with, which kept my delusion going strong. However, there was a fine line between denial and stupid, and I was teetering really close to the latter. Like I said, I haven't heard from him in almost two weeks, he hasn't replied to my attempts to reach out, and if it weren't for me lurking his social media pages, I wouldn't even know he were still alive. I knew that his communication cease and desist was all the evidence I needed to end this for good, but I wanted closure or verbal confirmation that we were done. Was real communication too much to ask?

"Ain't no guessing; we both *know* I'm right! No wonder you've been such a fun-snatcher lately," Reiko said in between bites of calamari. "You already know what to do in both situations, but I suspect you overthink your dislike for your job the least out of the two scenarios, so let's start there."

"What do you want me to do, quit my job without a backup plan?"

"Nyela, don't play with me! You're smart and valuable, *and* you underutilize your talent. Maybe this is a sign that you stop your hate crush on blogging and monetize your site. You have a decent amount of traffic already plus, you're more passionate about that TV film shit anyway so write about it for yourself." She took a sip of sangria.

"If you just start reeling in money from blogging and freelance to supplement the rest of your income, you can quit *Spark* and have more time to focus on that screenplay you're so gotdamn sometimey with."

I started my blog, Cinema Fancy, as a hobby, but the more I wrote about the TV and film world from my own perspective, and not *Spark's* sensationalist angle, the more I realized that I really needed to shift gears. I also took some screen writing classes, and published a few short scripts on my site just to test out the response. They did well with my readers. My readers also enjoyed the news and occasional interviews that I posted here and there. The screenplay that I was working on didn't have a title yet and it wasn't finished, but it was inspired by a combination of my passion for black romance flicks from the '90s, Blaxploitation-era films, and my common fantasy of running up in *Spark's* offices one day and burning the place down like Pam Grier did in movies like, *Foxy Brown* and *Coffy*. I'd been good at refraining from real life violence to that extreme because the blog and my personal writing were good escapes, but it wasn't like I had a real shot as a screenwriter. I doubted that the screenplay, even if it *were* in decent enough shape to be sent out, would ever get picked up.

"How do you know what my traffic is like? *I* don't even look at my traffic!"

"Hell-oh! There are a billion ways to get a good gage on people's traffic, which you already know, so please stop playing dumb and like you don't work in digital. Furthermore, you're so busy with your head down that rabbit hole of pessimism and misery that you fail to see the potential in your side projects. You're smart and industrious, so act like it!"

I stared at her for a few seconds in silence because she pulled my card and I didn't know what to say since she was right. I got her, but *everyone* was pimping them selves these days. *Everyone* was a brand or a character. Even more infuriating was that most of these people weren't even smart or talented, but they were winning while I was bitter and reluctant to promote myself because I was afraid to come off as obnoxious. Maybe I should get with the program because at least I had half-a-brain. Then again, what if no one understood me?

"I'm a *real* writer, remember!"

That was the best defense I had, and I knew it was lame.

"I forget how hardheaded you are," Reiko replied. "I know it takes a while for what's best for you to sink in with *you*, but I'm going to keep the faith that I have in you because once you do focus on what you need to be doing, you will catch fire. Until then, I'm just gonna let you overthink everything until you realize that sometimes you just have to play the game."

Reiko was good at playing the game. It was how she landed a spot on air at the number one radio station in the country. She built a solid reputation as the go-to girl for industry gossip, but she was surprisingly humble and low-key about it…that was, when her bad girl persona wasn't on. Although she also had a celebrity news and gossip blog, she was not an instigator in that realm, for the most part. She fact-checked and actually used discretion with what information she decided to release to the public.

She was also beautiful, with her monolid eyes and rich always clear penny-hued complexion being my favorite features of hers. I referred to her as rapper bait because they pretty much always fell in love with her looks first, and when they learned that she was also a good conversationalist, they started confiding all kinds of shit from childhood traumas to God knows what else, and thought it would somehow bring them closer. She was aware of all the above and milked the attention.

"I don't have what it takes to ham it up like you," I blurted, more to the universe than to Reiko. "I mean, I don't gossip, I don't post random rap songs, I'm not about to post pictures of myself in stylish outfits doing silly poses, and I'm clearly no relationship expert. I barely even update my Instagram."

"Who said you had to actually *be* an expert? Why do you think there's a popular saying that goes, 'Fake it til' you make it?' Also, you have like 50,000 Instagram followers without even trying. You post like, once a month."

I started to respond, but she cut me off.

"You know what, don't answer me. Like I said, I'm going to let *everything* I've mentioned to you about your career just sink in until that over-analytical brain of yours starts to map out a practical plan. At some point, you're gonna get tired of being miserable, but I'm here whenever you need me and if I hear of any opportunities in the meantime, I got you."

Reiko shoveled a forkful of chicken lo mein in her mouth and gave me a guilty look that I knew well. I remained silent for a moment, thinking she was going to say what was on her mind, but she eventually just averted eye contact and continued stuffing her face.

"Why so quiet all of a sudden? You had so much to say about my job situation, which you clearly stated we were tackling first, but what's your opinion about Sincere? Spit it out!"

"Fine, did you have reason to believe that everything between you two was on the up an up?

"For the most part, yes. It started with sporadic shady behavior, but I chalked it up to him being busy. It seemed like everything was stable-ish, no arguments, nothing. He just fell off."

"Fine, I didn't know how to tell you this, but I just saw his dumbass the other night at DJ Blackenstein's birthday party."

"And you didn't tell me!"

Reiko took another bite of her chicken lo mein.

"There really wasn't anything to tell. He was leaving as I was walking in. We made eye contact and he looked me dead in the eyes and kept walking as if he'd never seen me before in his life, so you're not the only one he apparently forgot to know."

"Fucker. What's his problem, though?"

"Nye, he's obviously a he-bitch. Consider this a blessing."

"But I can't, I want answers. I *deserve* answers."

"Sounds like you're going to have to catch him out and about, then. Felani is having a birthday/mixtape release party tonight. You should come."

"You know I hate going to events now."

I never understood how Reiko kept going to these events as if she were still a thirsty 21-year-old intern. We were both still youngish, but being in your late 20s was a different ballgame, at least for me it was. I was still experiencing the confusion of my delayed quarter-life crisis, like I said, but one thing I knew for sure was that I was over that industry party shit. It was the same functioning alcoholics at every event, the same over-salted hors d' oeuvres, the same watered down drinks, and the same disingenuous people asking you what you were doing with your life not because they cared, but because they wanted to see if they could benefit from being affiliated with you.

"Well, Felani isn't *that* industry just yet so you'd probably feel comfortable."

"She got a fucking cosign from Kanye West, and a gang of other celebrities!"

"Correction, Kanye tweeted at her that he liked her mixtape."

"Same fucking thing! Plus, she's kinda scary anyway."

"She can be a bit hood at times but—"

"A *bit* hood? She's *always* in Timbs, a wife beater and sweats and brags about carrying a razor under her tongue like this is New York City circa 1992! She was barely alive in 1992. What the entire fuck!"

"She hasn't done the razor thing in a while. That was more for show, anyway. I mean, she used to actually do it, you know who her dad is, but she's about to blow up now, and she understands that she needs to tone down a lot of the rough and rugged shit."

"But what about her name? It's fucking 'felony' for Christ's sake. That's going to follow her everywhere! Every reporter in every interview she ever does is going to ask her how many felonies she actually has, and the more popular she gets, the worse it will be!"

"God you're fucking stubborn! Stop picking the girl apart and just come with me. By the way, she's a fan of your work."

"How, and why do you know this?"

"We became friends after she stopped by my last show at the satellite station, and when she found out that you were my best friend she raved about you, especially because of the *GQ* cover story you wrote on Olu Major. She got an early copy."

I took a swig of my Lychee martini, exhaled audibly.

"I guess I could go with you. Whatever. I think I'm supposed to interview Felani soon anyway."

"Then it's settled. Let's make some moves."

#TheGreenhouseRiot

We noticed the ridiculously long line outside Greenhouse as our cab pulled up at about nine, but Reiko was the queen of walking straight in. She was cool with most of the bouncers at the most popular clubs, and all the publicists, so I knew getting in swiftly wasn't going to be an issue, not that I minded standing outside, since the tepid late-May air felt good. I watched a few people who couldn't get in right away attempt to name drop unsuccessfully, and then I saw a general bevy of people trying their hardest to affect a cool disinterested demeanor, when we all knew they were actually here to be seen and that they actually *did* care what was going on. By the looks of this line, I knew I was in for an interesting night out. This sentiment was confirmed when I spotted Sincere.

"Fuck no!" I blurted.

"Is that...SINCERE!" Reiko shouted. "Oh my God, who the fuck is that knock off Kim Kardashian that he's holding hands with?"

"Is this real life?" was all I managed to get out.

"Ooh, girrrrl, yup. See! And you almost didn't even come tonight!"

Sincere and his toy headed into the venue, as if they didn't hear Reiko calling him, but I guess she didn't react because he didn't. I basked in the calming breeze that began to blow, gently soothing my skin, in an attempt to meditate before I went inside and faced one of my problems. However, the breaths I was taking did nothing to quell my raging thoughts. I took a few more deep breaths until I felt as stable as I was going to get tonight.

Reiko, sensing my distress, gently grabbed my shoulders and faced me, making direct eye contact.

"I'd be mad too. Remember all the shit France put me through?"

France Deveaux was Reiko's asshole ex and also a legend in his own right. He has managed some of the biggest rappers in the industry and made a habit of sleeping with Instgram models and club bottle service girls often.

"This is different! He blatantly cheated on you and was very direct about his shady behavior."

"It's not that different. Look, my point is, you have every right to go off. I got your back, but please don't repeat that restraining order incident."

"I won't!" I replied, rolling my eyes.

I rarely snapped at Reiko, but I couldn't believe she would bring up that stupid situation from college that shouldn't have happened in the first place. *That* was some old shit. *This,* right now, was new and it meant war until I got my answers.

All I ever asked from any of my boyfriends was honesty. If they didn't want to be with me, fine, but don't be a jackass about it. I've *never* had a man just up and pretend I no longer existed, which made me wonder what the hell were the irony gods thinking when they decided to inspire his mother to name him Sincere!

"Are we good?" Reiko said.

She usually played it cool at parties like this, but she looked genuinely concerned.

"I'm fine."

"What's the game plan for when we get in there and you see something you don't like?"

"Girl, fuck him! Let's go inside, please. I saw what you dragged me here to see, right? I'm good so let's move on."

"You're not good, but okay."

I pushed past Reiko in a huff and stormed up to the front with her on my heels. We flashed our IDs and walked inside, but didn't get far before we started bumping into familiar faces. Surprisingly, Felani was the first person to greet us.

"WHAT UP! WHAT UP! WHAT UP!" Felani shrieked, and engulfed Reiko, now beside me, in a bear hug.

Reiko returned the excitement by screaming. She shifted her positioning after they finally came up for air, and pulled me closer to Felani.

"Yo, Fel! This is my girl, Nyela Barnes, from *Spark* magazine."

"OH SHIT! I LOVE YOUR WORK!" Felani shouted at me in one of the thickest black girl Brooklyn accents I had ever heard.

She drunkenly draped her arms around my shoulders in what became a sloppy hug, but I pulled away, hopefully without seeming stank or standoffish. I just wasn't feeling this night after what I saw.

"I LOVE THAT COVER STORY YOU DID ON OLU MAJOR. MY PUBLICIST SAID I GOT NEXT ON A *SPARK* FEATURE SO IMMA MAKE SURE THEY HOOK ME UP WITH YOU FOR THE INTERVIEW. YOU GOT A GOOD WAY WITH WORDS, MA!"

"Yes, my boss did mention that he wanted me to interview you," I replied. "Your publicist and I keep missing each other, but we'll coordinate eventually."

"SHE'S IN HERE SOMEWHERE SO YOU'LL MEET, BUT FUCK THAT BUSINESS SHIT RIGHT NOW! WE HERE TO PARTY!"

Felani and Reiko engaged in a two-step with each other for a few seconds before Felani grabbed my arm to get me in on the fun. I played along. Fuck it.

"IF REIKO IS YOUR PEOPLES THEN WE FAM NOW TOO!" she screamed. "IMMA GIVE YOU MY DIRECT CONTACT SO WE CAN BUILD BEYOND THAT INDUSTRY SHIT."

"See Nyela, I told you she was cool as hell!" Reiko said. "This is my girl right here!"

Reiko and Felani locked arms and continued dancing as they passed a bottle of vodka back and forth. I tried to feign as much excitement as I could while scanning the crowd for Sincere and *that girl.*

"YO!" Felani screamed just short of my ear while waving at a petite blonde woman, presumably her publicist, who was beckoning from across the room.

We formed a human train by holding on to each other's hips, with Felani in the lead, and headed to what I assumed was Felani's VIP station for the night. It was a plush booth situated on top of a platform so that we were visible from almost every point in the room. Felani was the only celebrity that anyone cared about here at the moment, but it was technically still too early to show up for making a scene by industry standards. I did however see some familiar journalists, bloggers and media personnel lurking nearby. They were all staring into their smartphones as opposed to actually interacting with each other, no doubt tweeting, Periscoping, Snapchatting, and Instagramming the scene instead of living it because that was how you let people know that you were important—beat it into their heads via social media that you were at an exclusive event.

"Why are you here so early compared to your peers?" I asked Felani. "Aren't you supposed to come about an hour before this ends or something like that?"

"I AIN'T WANT NOBODY WAI'N FUH ME, FUCK OUTTA HERE! FUCK ALL THAT INDUSTRY FASHIONABLY LATE SHIT! I'M GETTING A LITTLE ATTENTION AND ALL, BUT I'M STILL JUST A GIRL FROM BROWNSVILLE WHO HAD A DREAM. PLUS, I'M TURNT FOR MY BIRFDAY!"

She took a swig from a new bottle of vodka. That was when I noticed that she was dressed a little more ladylike than usual. The bodycon dress she was rocking almost made me believe that she was a prissy girl had it not been for the fact that she was toting that bottle of liquor around and taking shots to the head like there weren't any glasses and buckets of ice available.

Typically, Felani wore any combination of a white wife beater or white t-shirt a Yankees fitted cap, and jeans or sweatpants with Timbs or Jordans on her tiny feet. Tonight was one of the rare nights where she was wearing makeup—a simple black cat eye and some shimmery pink lipstick—and her hair was actually done intentionally. Her hair was usually in cornrows straight to the back of her head, or a simple Afro puff, but tonight her voluminous curly 'fro was braided on one side, which gave her a funky fro-hawk affect. Her perfectly arched eyebrows framed her golden brown heart-shaped face and overall she looked beautiful, but still gritty.

"GET YOU A DRINK, GIRL!" she said.

"No, thank you, I'm good," I replied, still marveling at how pretty she was in person.

"No you're not!" Reiko said.

She poured a glass of vodka and orange juice and shoved it in my hand. I conceded though I didn't really drink much at all because I was a lightweight. People didn't seem to understand that I didn't really enjoy alcohol, and *I* didn't get why people always seemed to need alcohol to be social.

I wouldn't have fun tonight no matter what I did because I was too preoccupied with where that cunt Sincere went with that girl. This place wasn't *that* big and while it was starting to fill up, there was no reason why I hadn't seen him inside yet.

"Get up here and dance with us!" Reiko said, pulling me on top of the couch that she and Felani claimed as their dance floor.

Couch dancing, as I liked to call it, was a common practice that I found bizarre and also pretentious yet I still found myself dancing alongside Reiko and Felani anyway, just for the fun of moving with them. I took one sip of my drink, and planned to nurse it for as long as I could. I gave up couch dancing after about 5 minutes, and found a less hectic part of the booth area to sit in.

"SHOUT OUT TO MY MAN OLU MAJOR IN THE BUILDING!" DJ Blackenstein said, followed by raucous cheering.

Olu Major and his manager appeared in our section in no less than 30 seconds after the announcement that he had arrived. I watched them make rounds in the booth greeting people, and I made the connection that Olu didn't ever seem to travel with a lot of people. When I spent a few days shadowing him a few weeks ago, it was just he and his manager, who was a longtime friend of his from college, and his publicist.

The *GQ* piece was a major accomplishment for me. My boy, who was the features editor over there, asked me to write the cover story on Olufemi Mensah, rap name, Olu Major, the next sartorially superior oft-buzzed about hip-hop genius—so people said—who was successfully transitioning from acting to music, but would definitely still have a major acting career once he started focusing on landing roles again. Typically it would have been a conflict of interest given where I worked. But I pitched Olu to *Spark* and the idea was shot down so, I decided to move forward with *GQ* since it was surprisingly my first cover story, and for an amazing brand! Plus, my boy hooked me up with a $4 per word rate for 1,200 words since there was a quick turnaround needed on the piece. That rate was hard to come by these days with all these companies bottoming out. A lot of magazines stopped hiring freelancers as much because it was cheaper to get someone to do it in-house. My boy said he chose me to write the story because Olu seemed like an artist I'd like, understand, and really capture well. He was right, so I risked my job for it.

I was actually hoping that *Spark* would fire me for it. That idea was still up in the air because the issue wasn't out yet. I knew Hot Head Tony wasn't going to take it well, despite telling me that Olu was wack and not ready for a feature when I pitched him for *Spark*. I could care less though because from a PR standpoint, a burgeoning star like Olu needed a better magazine look than *Spark* anyway.

I liked my take on the piece, especially because of Olu's unique background. He was metaphorically Prince Akeem from *Coming to America*, but replace the search for a wife with the search for fame. He was an Afro-British raptor—that's rapper/actor—who convinced his parents to let him move from London to the United States for high school. He and his immediate family visited relatives here frequently anyway, and he fell in love at a young age. His intention in coming here was to pursue an acting and a music career, but he kept that part to himself. He ended up staying with family in L.A. and got scouted by the time he had completed his junior year at a prestigious high school. He landed the role of "T.J.," the cool kid on *Lockers*, a popular teen-melodrama that aired on BBC America. His Ghanaian dad was a multi-millionaire serial entrepreneur, and owner of a private equity company, and his Nigerian mom was a high profile heart surgeon. During our interview I learned that his parents, whom he referred to as "traditional West African parents," weren't happy about his decision to pursue an entertainment career because they wanted him to be something more along the lines of a doctor, lawyer or an engineer. His aunt and uncle in L.A. weren't thrilled about him landing a role on *Lockers* either, so they basically told him he was on his own.

Olu didn't have access to his trust fund, which wouldn't have been granted until his 25th birthday, and his family cut him off. He ended up moving in with a *Lockers* executive producer and survived on those paychecks, which were good, while he finished his last year of high school under the guidance of a private tutor.

Lockers became more of an esoteric cult success than a mainstream hit, but got popular enough to run for a few seasons over the course of about three years, and eventually got picked up in syndication. He was a working actor then, but not so famous that he couldn't walk down the street without getting mobbed, so he was accessible and often spotted out and about at parties, hanging out with rappers and various other socialites. Eventually he moved to New York City and made the shift to making music. He enrolled in school where he studied music engineering, and built up a massive social media following, which lead to a few high profile festival performances, DJ gigs, and most recently, a deal with Roc Nation.

I found myself admiring how gorgeous he was, once again, particularly mesmerized by his smooth mahogany skin, but I snapped out of it after realizing that he was approaching me.

I said hello to Olu, sipped my orange juice and vodka concoction, and scanned the room more, partially so that I didn't stare at him, and also to find Sincere. I spotted more random bloggers and other popular Internet people, record label folks, publicists, wannabes, and the like, but still no prime suspect.

"You okay?" Olu said, sitting next to me.

His lips were a mere few centimeters from my ear and his tone was loud enough for me to hear him over the music, but just soft enough not to burst my eardrum. The warmth of his breath was comforting, particularly because it smelled like cinnamon, one of my favorite scents.

"I'm good," I replied, trying to appear as terse as possible.

I had to keep it ice cold, playa.

"No you're not. I know we only spent a few days together where I did most of the talking, but I can tell your energy is off."

I responded with a side eye.

"I'm *serious!* This isn't the down-to-Earth conversationalist who had me telling my life story and spilling my most personal secrets! I fucking hate interviews, mind you!"

Rappers were generally my least favorite people to interview because they tended to be cocky, vapid and devoid of good conversation. They also liked to sexually harass anything with a vagina. Not all of them, because interviewing Olu and a few others I've experienced was enjoyable, but enough to make you leery. Two of the things I liked most about Olu's personality, though, were his Zen and intelligence.

"One, it's not appropriate for me to unleash my problems on a stranger. Two, we're at someone else's victory party," I replied.

"Wow, so I'm a stranger now? I'm offended!"

His almond-shaped eyes became slits behind his high cheekbones, which rose as he laughed at his own feigned exasperation.

"Okay, you're not *that* much of a stranger. But let's just leave it at I'm having a rough night."

"I bet most of it is in your head."

Like he knew my life! I decided not to give him a flippant reply because my intuition said his heart was in the right place, and that accent was sexy as hell. I relaxed and played coy instead.

"Aw, come on with that fake ass death stare!" Olu said. "It's still kinda cute, by the way."

He looked me up and down in a way that didn't make me feel uncomfortable, but I could tell he was checking me out. It was almost as if he were seeing me for the first time as he gingerly lifted my right arm and stroked the quill pen tattoo on my forearm.

"Nice tat," he said. "Your arms were covered up the last time I saw you."

"Thanks Captain Obvious," I replied, trying not to be as turned on as I was.

Fuck. Where did these feelings come from? I was totally fine resisting his chocolatey foine force the last time I saw him. Then again, that was under professional circumstances and we were both a lot more reserved.

We had a brief moment of tense silence before I swiftly pulled my arm away.

"We should link up again soon on some chill non-business shit," he said. "Let me take you to dinner, and I'll let you beat my ass in pool again."

"I'll pass," I replied.

"Ooo-kay."

He dropped it and started replying to a few text messages. I tried to be nosey and see what he was typing, but couldn't get a good glimpse of his screen without being obvious.

"Ugh, why do I feel like you're silently judging me?" I said, and instantly regretted it.

"I'm *not* judging you."

"So then why are you sitting there with this smug silence all up in your phone all of a sudden?"

"*Smug* silence? You just shut me down, what am I supposed to say if you don't want to talk to me?"

"Well you…"

I stopped responding because he had a point and what I was about to say was most likely going to be stupid. I was always complaining about men who didn't know how to leave me alone when I wasn't being receptive and here he was, leaving me alone, which was actually kind of hot.

"I guess you're right," I replied. "Looks like a no-win situation for you no matter what."

"You're a tough lady, and I'm getting on your nerves. I get the message."

"If I'm so tough then how come you can tell that something's bothering me?"

"And she finally admits it, ha!"

"Yeah, but how do you know I'm not in a funk because I have cramps or a headache, or something small?"

"It's definitely not cramps or a headache and you're trying to play tough again, but stop frontin' because we established that you're on the struggle bus."

I laughed at being called out.

"Look, I'm very direct, and all I'm saying is, you left a major impression on me, which doesn't happen often," he said, smirking and checking me out again, probably very aware of the affect he was having on me since he was too gorgeous not to know. "I think we should keep that momentum going."

My attempt to control the smile I felt turning up the corners of my mouth was futile. Was this chocolate 6'4" specimen of a man who just so happened to be a big deal really trying to kick it to *me*? Shit. Even if he wasn't serious, I was gassed as fuck! During our interview, he was definitely a lot more reserved and low-key, like I said, but I guess he was also keeping it professional.

"There's that beautiful smile," he said. "Seriously, I think we could be good friends."

I shook my head and smiled harder. Ice melted.

He made me feel at ease. Even when I first met him that sense of comfort and familiarity was instantly present, on some maybe we've met last lifetime type shit, as cliché as that probably sounds. I relaxed, but my inner cynic still wanted to challenge him. However, I decided that I would stop being a jerk, for now.

"I'm actually not mad at that," I replied. "So, is whooping your ass in pool again still an option?"

He pulled out his phone and started tapping and scrolling.

"We can figure something out. What's your number?"

I gave up my digits and he texted me his just in time for Reiko to spill her drink on me, and before I could really process that I just exchanged numbers with Olu Major. The last time we set everything up through his publicist.

"FUCK!"

"Oh my God, Nye! I'm so sorry!"

Reiko started sloppily rubbing my breasts in an attempt to dry me off. At this point the lace from my red bra was exposed through my now wet white chiffon blouse. At least it was clear liquor with no chaser.

"You're good, Reiko. Keep doing your thing."

I was used to her drunkenness, and I was surprised this didn't happen sooner to anyone in her vicinity since she was literally dancing around all over the place.

I needed a reason to leave the booth without getting a barrage of questions, so I headed to the bathroom and saw a crowd outside the men's room laughing, cheering and banging on the door. I was going to ignore the ruckus until Sincere busted out of the bathroom, smiling as the peanut gallery started cheering louder.

"Man, y'all play too much!" he said, feigning anger as he zipped up his pants.

He nearly lost his balance as the fake Kim Kardashian-looking chick stumbled out behind him and almost tripped over him.

"SINCERE, WHAT THE FUCK!"

"Oh, shit! What are you doing here, Nye!"

He casually reached out for a hug, even as fake Kim K was basically holding onto his hips from behind.

"ARE YOU CRAZY!"

"Don't make a scene, Nyela. You knew this was bound to happen. You've been boring me lately, and that's something you have to take up with yourself."

I charged at Sincere, causing him to topple backward over Fake Kardashian who started screaming. I started shouting obscenities and tried to get in as many punches to Sincere's face as I could.

"THIS IS HOLLYWOOD, GIRL!" he shouted at me in between my punches, and tried to shield his face.

I pummeled until a bouncer hoisted me mid-air by the waist. I flailed, struggling to free myself, but I wasn't strong enough. Olu intervened just as the bouncer wrestled me toward the exit, and convinced him to let me stay inside. I still heard Sincere shouting "THIS

IS HOLLYWOOD! YOU KNOW WHAT IT IS BABY!" as Olu led me back to our booth.

"GO TO HELL! ASSHOLE!" I shouted as Reiko and Olu wrangled me into a sitting position.

I finally calmed down after a few minutes, but felt awkward as people stared at me. I purposely avoided eye contact with everyone as I sipped my now watered down drink, but it didn't stop my friends from being worried.

"You okay, girl?" Reiko said.

I nodded.

"ASSHOLE!" she shouted in Sincere's direction.

He was holding onto the Fake Kardashian who was in tears, but caught Reiko's verbal dart and threw his free hand in the air in a, "What did I do?" gesture.

"I got something for that ass!" Reiko retorted.

She fiddled with her sandal strap in an attempt to get her shoe off so that she could throw it.

"CHILL, B!" Felani said, now physically forcing Reiko take a seat next to me. "THIS IS MY PARTY! WE'LL FUCK THAT NIGGA UP LATER! LET'S DANCE!"

Felani resumed dancing, but added silly faces and gestures in an attempt to lighten the mood. I appreciated this goofy side of her and started to imagine myself, Felani and Reiko bombing Sincere with eggs after stepping out of some party, or better yet, putting out fake dating ads online with Sincere's picture, soliciting ridiculous wild sex with furries or swingers.

I took another sip from my cup, wondered why I was still here, and wished that getting drunk was actually my thing. At least that way I would have had a socially acceptable excuse for the behavior I displayed.

I watched Reiko and Felani move their drunken dance party on top of a table and noticed that Olu was back sitting next to me, staring.

"CAN I HELP YOU?!"

"I'm just wondering if you're okay."

"I'm fine! Stop asking me that!"

"I know this is none of my business, but don't let anyone steal your happiness."

"That was so cliché for such a talented wordsmith."

"And it's cliché for the jealous ex-girlfriend to spazz out in public."

Ouch, but he had a point.

Luckily, our attention was diverted from each other to Jay Z and Beyoncé's entrance, once the crowd began cheering. We watched them wade through the mob of cameras and fans attempting to get personal photos, slip their music to the royal couple and basically, all things thirst bucket certified. Jay and Bey were some of the few celebrities that I still got exited about, so I started to cheer up a bit.

I almost lost it when the Carters finally arrived in my area, but I pulled it together in time to watch Olu greet his boss, and then he introduced me as if we were old friends. I wanted to faint when Jay recognized my name and mentioned that he liked my cover story on Olu. I would have liked to die, but the issue wasn't on stands yet. I had to live so that I could add Jay Z's quote somewhere in my resume or bio, or to randomly bring it up as much as possible in future conversations with anyone who would listen. And then there was Beyoncé who came in to hug me after my exchange with Jay Z. She smelled amazing and her skin looked as if she showered in Unicorn tears. Okay, maybe I could die now.

I watched as Jay and Bey headed over to Felani and began chatting, and that was when I figured out the *real* purpose of this party. The invite mentioned special guests and a special announcement.

"Is Felani down with Roc Nation? Is that the big announcement?" I said in Olu's ear.

He smiled and just said, "No comment."

"I'll take that as a yes."

"JAY Z AND BEYONCÉ IN THE BUILDING!" DJ Blackenstein yelled in obligatory DJ shout out fashion.

I started to feel content again until Cookie Clark materialized in our section, no doubt following the Jay and Bey rush. She made her way over to me first.

"You okay?"

I wanted to go off again just because she was being nosey. I didn't know this broad from a bump on a log. Why the fuck was she pretending to care? I wanted to say, "Girl, bye!" But I kept it civil instead.

"I'm fine."

A second barely passed before Cookie went from being "concerned" about me to revealing her true motivation for being in my space. She wedged herself between Olu and I—which was ambitious considering that me and Olu were so close that it wouldn't have taken much for me to be in his lap if I wanted—and started chatting him up as if I wasn't even there. She mostly talked about her impending radio gig and other stuff that I tuned out. I felt another bout of rage rising and decided to migrate.

At this point Blackenstein started spinning '90s dancehall, so I joined Felani and Reiko next to their resident couch this time, happy that they were New York natives and understood my excitement over Shabba Ranks, Chaka Demus and Pliers, and Dawn Penn. We wound our waists as if we were on Eastern Parkway during the Labor Day Parade, and I was reminded of my childhood when my big cousins and neighborhood kids would make up dances. I almost forgot, after a while, that I tried to beat down a grown ass man in an upscale Manhattan club. However, my high crashed when I spotted Sincere headed to our area because the universe hated me.

"I'm out!" I said to Reiko, but she grabbed me before I made good progress in my exit stride.

"You can't let him win, and if you leave then that's exactly what you're doing. Have another drink and stay!"

She shoved her almost empty bottle of whatever into my chest until I agreed to take a swig. I finished the rest and started dancing again just in time to realize that Blackenstein had worked his set up to dancehall from the 2000's. I caught the wave of Sean Paul's remake of Alton Ellis' "I'm Still In Love With You," one of my favorite songs. It reminded me of my paternal grandmother, who was Jamaican. She and my American grandfather were often charged with babysitting me, and one of their favorite things to do was play music and dance around the house. It was my grandmother, who was once in a ska band, who had introduced reggae to the Barnes family, and Alton Ellis' version of "I'm Still in Love With You" was a song that was always on repeat in my grandparents' home. I loved watching them dance around the house like giddy teenagers. Perhaps the universe didn't hate me as much as I thought. I swayed to the rhythm, and eventually got lost enough to close my eyes and stop thinking, for once, but I snapped out of my trance when someone grabbed my hand and started to sway with me. I was startled when I opened my eyes and discovered it was Olu. His dancing was pretty impressive, he busted a good wine, but instead of acting like a normal person I shrieked as if I were three, dashed to the nearest seat and covered my face with my purse. Olu laughed and shook his head, but kept on dancing, seemingly unfazed. He migrated near Felani who was engaging him in dancing and singing the lyrics. I couldn't take my eyes off of him once I finally uncovered my face, and found contentment as I ogled him on the low.

"Aaaaw, I'm glad you came to sit next to me," Sincere said.

I moved so hastily to get away from Olu that I didn't realize I ran toward Satan in the process. It was the universe giving me the finger again, just a reminder that it actually did still hate me.

"You mad at me?" he persisted disingenuously.

I didn't verbalize my thoughts but my facial expression said, "Fuck you!"

"Ooooh, I know *that* face. But I also know that you can't stay mad at me."

I wanted to punch him in the face, but I got up instead and headed to the table where the drinks were, only to get intercepted by Felani before I reached my destination.

"You want that nigga outta here? It's nuffin' for me to tell security to toss him."

"Don't worry about it, Felani. I got this, but I appreciate the support."

She nodded and got back to socializing with a few bloggers who managed to get into VIP. I spied Reiko in the DJ booth with Blackenstein, who seemed to be teaching her how to DJ. I continued my mission to the drink table and bumped into Olu again.

"You're not going to run away from me again, are you?" he said, laughing. "That was cute."

No, *he* was cute, especially when he laughed. *Fuck.* I'm *not* going there. Nope.

"No, I just felt sick, that's all," I replied. "Didn't want to hurl on you."

That was the dumbest lie ever.

"Then you should probably put that drink down before we have to carry you out of here."

"There's only one person who might *really* get carried out of here."

"Who, that wanker you beat the crap out of?"

"You're so nosey."

Sincere wedged himself between us, as if on cue, before Olu could quip.

"You're Olu Major, right?" he said.

"Yeah."

I could tell that Olu was forcing himself to keep an even tone, which was great. The more people in the I Hate Sincere Club the better.

"I'm a fan, yo! I can't wait until your official album comes out."

Sincere only faced Olu the entire time. At 5'11 and with a medium build he was big enough to eclipse me at 5'4," which was most likely what he was trying to do. He was the passive-aggressive type so I knew he was trying to poke. But I took some deep breaths and decided not to give him the satisfaction of getting upset. He extended his hand for a dap and Olu obliged and replied, "Thanks, homie."

"No problem, my dude. Can I ask you for a favor, though?"

"Depends on what it is."

"Can you give me a minute to chat with the lady here?"

"Are you sure *she* wants to chat with *you*?"

Olu gave me a concerned look. My reply nod communicated that I was okay enough to be left alone, so Olu gave us space. I watched him head over to fraternize with Felani again, who was fiddling with a microphone.

"What do you want?!" I snapped.

This fool was really acting as if I didn't just try to pummel his face in 30 minutes ago, and with good reason.

"You were all up on Olu just to get me jealous, huh? You know you gotta flirt with them super-star dudes to get a reaction out of a man of my caliber."

Obviously beating him down wasn't the solution, so I improvised and threw my drink in his face.

"Ooooooh!" yelled Timmy G, a popular photographer and gossip blogger who was conveniently snapping images of us.

Several people started gathering around us, most of them were recording. Sincere appeared more amused than angry. I guess that meant it was show time in his world.

"Oh word?" he said. "So you ain't rocking with me on this Hollywood shit, huh? You don't want a threesome?"

Responding in anyway was futile, but luckily I didn't have to choose what to do next because Felani came to my rescue. She got in between us and shoved him with a surprising amount of strength for her small stature.

"A-YO, MY MAN! YOU GOTTA GET THE FUCK UP OUTTA HERE!"

"Don't be like that, Felani," he replied.

"WHAT THE FUCK DID I JUST SAY?"

Felani signaled for her bouncer to come over, but Sincere exited on his own. I was emotionally exhausted but now that he was gone, I could at least stay and enjoy myself for a little while longer after Felani made her Roc Nation announcement and got her birthday cake.

#BreakingNews

Breaking News! Magazine Editor Spazzes Out on Celebrity Relationship Blogger Boyfriend At Felani's Mixtape Release Party

Fuck. That was the first headline I saw when I went on my morning news crawl before heading to work. Actually, that same unimaginative, hyper-sensationalized headline and variants of it were the bulk of what I saw leading many of the urban entertainment sites that I followed. I knew I shouldn't have read any of those stories, but the impending stupidity and skewed facts compelled me to punish myself. That and almost everyone I knew would read it and make it a point to ask me about it the next time they saw me so, I needed to prepare myself for whatever facts were going to be untrue.

> *Roc Nation's latest signee, rapper Felani, had a release party to celebrate Money Murda Mob Chronicles Vol 2…which is out now…but also to announce that she is now down with Roc Nation and to celebrate her birthday. All in all…it was a good night with lots of celebrity sightings and Who's Who of the media (make sure to click on the photo gallery). Speaking of media…journalist Nyela Barnes was caught up in a love triangle with her boyfriend…relationship expert Mr. Sincere The Love Broker…and some Instagram model.*

You might know Nyela as the Pop Culture Editor for Spark *magazine, as she has interviewed several big name celebrities...and even occasionally gives commentary on TV, but after last night you might want to rethink her professionalism and call her Mayweather instead. My sources witnessed Nyela trying to strangle Mr. Sincere as well as punching his lady friend in the face several times to the point where she got a black eye. No one is sure what started the fight but we're not surprised that Nyela would go crazy. Word is...this isn't the first time she's had an episode like this.*

Bouncers pulled Nyela off her victims...and planned to toss her out...but it was Roc Nation rapper Olu Major who stepped in and kept her from getting the boot. Speaking of Olu Major, he was also spotted consoling her in a corner...mmm hmmm, wonder what that was all about! Nyela must move on fast. Anyway, Mr. Sincere went on about his business while his terrified jump off dashed out of the event mortified.

I don't know why Nyela was spazzing out though...because she had to have known how Mr. Sincere gets down. Didn't we all know? Seems like a lot of these modern, professional women will do anything for the sake of having a man, even one who doesn't want them. Get some self-esteem ladies.

– Chatty Abernathy, the Gossip Slayer

Why the fuck was that even considered news? I mean, if you were going to embellish a story then make it Aliya S. King good. That wasn't even hood novel from 125th Street status. I was also offended by the overuse and misuse of ellipses.

I continued trolling Feedly and saw more variations of the headline. Some people had the nerve to call it an exclusive. How was it an exclusive if all the same people were sharing badly written rewrites of the same thing? I felt my rage bubbling, but my curiosity was tragically strong, so I continued perusing where I shouldn't have. I noticed that there was a new post on Sincere's site, so I made a mental note to delete his site from my feed after I read this inevitably asinine post.

Laying Good Pipe Makes Girls Go Crazy...Literally

Many of you know that my ex-girlfriend attacked me last night in a jealous rage. I won't put her name out there, but you know she's a popular magazine editor. Let me tell you what happened, straight from the horse's mouth.

We had a good thing once, but after a while she stopped keeping my interest so I just started doing my own thing. I was kicking it at industry events, traveling and meeting some of the sexiest women I've ever seen in my life. Meanwhile, ol' girl kept blowing up my phone and emailing me on some desperate ish. I kept trying to tell her that I was doing the single thing, but my pipe game was so good that she got dickmatized and started — I don't want to say she was stalking me, but let's just say she was overzealous about my whereabouts.

I thought Miss Magazine Editor had figured out that we were no longer what was up. Plus, I hadn't seen or spoken to her in a while; I'm talking weeks. So, last night I took this bad chick I had picked up at a photo shoot to Felani's release party and guess who showed up!

I guess she felt some type of way and decided to attack me and then pour a drink on me later on when I was trying to help her make peace with the situation. My bad chick was so upset that she left, and I'm not mad at her for that because dickmatized chicks do some crazy things. Fellas, make sure you tie up your loose ends with these chicks because like I said, if you lay the pipe right then chicks will literally go crazy. I'm out for now but you know how I do. I'll be back with another tale from my wild and crazy life. Peace.

I wanted to toss my computer out the window, but I realized that was a bad idea seeing as how I'd then have to drop about $1,400 for a new one. Instead, I resolved to start working out frequently again, take a few dance classes, and dashed off to work.

—

Most mornings, I made it to my desk without anyone ever bothering to lift their heads up from their computer screens long enough to make eye contact. Today, however, was a new day. I tried to get to my desk swiftly, but the inevitable happened.

"Girrrrrl, what happened last night?"

It was Gina, *Spark's* boisterous editorial assistant.

I waved her off and continued walking. Gina, who got hired at *Spark* because of her boldness, actually followed me to my desk. She was cool and all, but it was too early for this.

"Not today, Gina."

Despite being brash and sometimes obnoxious, Gina actually had a filter and was conscience so she backed off.

"*Okay,* but I'm gonna get your side of the story at some point."

She headed back to her cubicle.

When I got close to Patrick's cube, the halfway mark between the entrance and my desk, I noticed a few people gathered around him as he packed his things. I left it alone because they were so engrossed in what he was doing that no one hounded me about what happened last night.

I finally got to my desk, settled in, took some edge off with coffee and got out of my own selfish world enough to realize that Patrick must have been preparing to leave. He definitely didn't get fired. He was too good at what he did, so I figured he got a new gig that was hopefully more promising than this hellhole. I would rather not be all up on his desk with the rest of the Peanut Gallery, so I made a mental note to check in with him later.

I prepared to start another Feedly crawl just in case anymore pressing issues came up that *Spark* should care about, but I didn't get too far before Hot Head Tony called me to his office via g-chat. This man usually came straggling into the office at about 3:00pm if we didn't have a meeting. It was 10:30. *Fuck*, this couldn't be good.

I strolled into his office and got reminded that the only good thing about this was his amazing view. My plan, as I sat down, was to tune him out as I gazed at the joggers running along the Hudson River and planned my escape to New Jersey by teleportation.

"So, what happened last night?"

"I'm pretty sure you've read about it by now, or got one-sided details and have made up your mind therefore, nothing I say will matter."

"Hell yeah! I had Gina write up a blurb about it for our site. The traffic on that shit is bananas!"

"Are you *serious*?" I replied.

I tried badly to mask my indignation. I had never *ever* been featured on a blog before, or at the center of controversy in this way.

This was truly a sign of Sincere's growing popularity, and also the fact that Olu and I were fraternizing. What. The. Fuck.

"I don't care what you do as long as it doesn't fuck with your work and as long as it gets me traffic!"

Wow. He really cared more about traffic than the fact that one of his employees got into a fight in public. I didn't know why I was surprised, though.

"You should at least know that none of the blog posts masquerading my drama as exclusives are accurate."

"I had some people there too, I *know* for a fact that you threw hands."

"I did, but I was provoked and I didn't attack his gotdamn girlfriend, like everyone keeps saying!"

"I've seen his girl on Instagram. I forgot her name, but she fine ass hell, and she has ass for a—I don't know what she is, Spanish, Arabian?"

I was *not* about to talk to this stupid ass man about some stupid ass woman's presumed ethnicity.

"So, yeah...I was provoked."

"That's why you have to explain your side of the story in an exclusive blog for our site! You haven't given any interviews yet, have you?"

"What?"

"For real. That's part of what I called you in here for. You have to write your response blog for *Spark*."

Actually, I didn't have to do shit but stay black and die, but I didn't say that out loud this time. No matter how unprofessional this place was, there were some things that I just kept to myself. I nodded instead.

"I also called you in here to let you know that you got a promotion."

"Really?"

I was surprised because I had been slacking a lot lately. I thought my non-enthusiasm for this place was obvious.

"Yup. In addition to being the pop culture editor for online and print, you will also handle lifestyles too."

"That's not a promotion! You just added another job title. Am I getting a raise too?"

"No raises right now due to budget cuts. Didn't you see Patrick packing up on your way in here?"

"I thought he quit!"

"Nah, he got laid off. This is business; we gotta do what we gotta do. You should be excited about this though. This is a good look on your resume, especially since you work for such an iconic brand."

An iconic brand that fell the fuck off.

"Adding a third job on top of the two full-time positions that I already have with no incentives is a recipe for disaster, and it's not fair."

"You either want to do this or you don't. I thought you were hungry."

I used to be hungry, but now the thought of coming in here made me want to dowse myself in lighter fluid and swan dive into a furnace, but instead I sighed and conceded defeat.

"We're cutting pages in the magazine too, so your sections won't be *that* hectic. And we got interns who can help you out. Just pimp them like they're staff. They love this shit anyway."

I should have known he was going to pull the old, treat-your-interns-like-mules method of productivity.

"So, there's only about three editors working on the entire book *and* the website, and you want us to groom inexperienced children in addition to properly executing our several other duties?"

"This isn't a Q&A session! Either you're with it or you're not, feel me?"

I glared at him.

This should have been my cue to unceremoniously quit, but I had bills to pay, and I refused to borrow money from my parents. So, I had to deal for now and get serious about planning an exit strategy.

"You just keep that traffic up on the site. All that shit you've been posting lately has been fire! Keep that celebrity drama and that Hollywood-type crossover shit going; and keep beating up your exes, and hanging out with that exotic radio friend of yours who gets all the scoops. You know, the one who looks like that singer Mila J., what's her name again, Ricky? She got a fat ass too."

"Her name is pronounced Ray-ko, and this has nothing to do with work, by the way."

"I'm just saying…I figured since you know her I might as well put it out there. I love those half-breed chicks. You think you could give her my number, or tell her to visit the office one day?"

This was exactly why Reiko didn't visit the office.

"She simply prefers black or multi-ethnic since she's technically not biracial, and to my latter point, I doubt she'd appreciate being called a half-breed."

"Multi-ethnic is still mixed, though, right? What she mixed with? I know there's some black in there, but what's the other stuff?"

"I'm not doing this with you today. Are we done talking about work stuff, though?"

"You think I'm playing. I watched her on *The Bad Girls Club*. Tell her I'm a fan. I can take care of her if she plays her cards right. She'll never have to work again a day in her life, fucking with me."

I was so used to the off-the-wall fucked up shit that came out of his mouth that I wasn't even moved enough to *really* respond in defense of Reiko and other non-basic human beings everywhere. It was that moment of my silence when I realized that my desensitization to Tony's bullshit was a serious problem.

"Are we good?" I said.

"You think I'm joking. I can show that girl some things."

I took it upon myself to walk out of his office and head back to my desk, and I heard him barking instructions behind me.

"Start with the blog post telling your version of what happened last night so we can keep the traffic momentum going off that!"

The thought of explaining my side of the story actually wasn't so bad. It was really no one's business, but I did want to clarify the fictionalized and poorly summarized accounts floating around because misinformation could easily ruin my career reputation, and I refused to let that happen.

I started a quick Feedly crawl before I began writing, just to see if I missed anything while in Tony's office vortex. I did. Olu's *GQ* cover leaked and was up on every website that mattered. Every. Single. One. I knew it would come out eventually, but my boy was supposed to warn me beforehand about the initial blast so that I could tell Tony to expect it.

"NYELA, WHAT THE FUCK!"

I looked up to find Tony storming toward me, and wondered if he was going to tip over before he got to my desk. His short legs barely supported his tubby body, and it looked like his belly was going to burst through his button down shirt.

"DO YOU REALIZE WE'VE BEEN TRYING TO GET OLU MAJOR ON OUR COVER FOR MONTHS!"

"I didn't realize that because the first time I pitched him in a meeting you said he was wack."

"I NEVER SAID THAT! WHAT FUCKING PLANET DO YOU LIVE ON?!"

"Yeah, you did say that in a meeting. There are witnesses."

Tony was notorious for backtracking statements, even if he was definitely incorrect. That man would say something clearly on camera and then adamantly deny it after the fact just to avoid admitting he was wrong.

"NO I DIDN'T! I DID NOT!"

He fell silent and glared at me, seriously waiting for a response. I wasn't afraid of him, but I also didn't want confrontation. I imagined the worst-case scenario, which would be him hitting me, thus creating more blog fodder, but also my father getting involved since he had plenty of experience working with major corporations and labor laws. That would have gotten really ugly, and as much as I didn't like Hot Head Tony, I decided to spare him the wrath of Josiah Barnes, for now.

"WHAT THE FUCK! ARE YOU JUST GONNA STARE AT ME WITH THAT DUMB LOOK ON YOUR FACE!"

I tried to keep my voice as even as possible. "I just gave you an explanation."

"ARE YOU FUCKING STUPID?"

The man who just praised me for my work, including my drama causing a traffic spike was now berating me. I was strangely calm because I was used to this sort of thing. My career was similar to an abusive relationship. The highs were so amazing that you forgot how volatile some of the people involved could be. Personalities like Hot Head Tony's were more the norm than people who actually knew how to use their words and treat people with respect. However, you always reminded yourself about the perks that you loved, or the bills you were barely able to pay, and got stuck.

Tony pulled a chair up so that he was on my level and bored a hole into my face with his angry scowl. I was trying not to laugh at the goofy prescription Cazal's magnifying his eyes, which made it hard to take him seriously, and kept enough composure to muster up another explanation, basically saying the same thing, but worded differently.

"I did the Olu Major cover story because an editor at *GQ* asked me to. I didn't think it would be a problem since our employee handbook states that we are allowed to freelance as long as it isn't a conflict of interest. This was set in motion about a month ago, shortly after I pitched Olu Major for a cover story here. Again, you told me that he wasn't hot enough, he'd never blow, and that he wasn't *Spark* material. He got signed to Roc Nation shortly after my pitch, but since you never brought it up again I figured I was good money for taking the story elsewhere."

"SO YOU'RE BLAMING THIS ON ME? FUCK THAT! THIS IS YOUR FAULT!"

He stormed away from the chair and charged around like a rhino, ranting and screaming at everyone within earshot until he eventually tired out and sat down at a vacant cubicle. He started rubbing his sweaty face and I watched his chest heave up and down, wondering if he was going to have a heart attack. After a few moments of silence and breathing like Biggie, he stood up on top of a desk—think, King Kong sans the chest beating—and began another tirade in related news.

"Y'ALL MOTHERFUCKERS THINK THIS SHIT IS A GAME! NO ONE FREELANCES WITHOUT APPROVING IT WITH ME FIRST!"

Hot Head Tony started pacing back and forth on the desk muttering obscenities, and I was surprised it held his weight. I also said a silent prayer that it would eventually give out, and started to daydream about better things. If this were a movie, I would have been the heroine charged with the duty of putting all the oppressed workers out of their misery. I would storm into Tony's office and take him out with a swift, but effective punch to the face then set the place on fire.

Back in reality, Tony finally ended his tirade, made a one-man stampede back to his office and slammed the door so hard that I was surprised the entire glass façade that made up the door didn't shatter.

Everyone else, self-included, got back to work. After I finished posting the blog I discussed with Tony, I headed to my personal blog and updated it with news that I actually cared about. I liked to blend TV and movie news with opinion based on actual facts. I was pleased to discover that one of my favorite YouTube shows was headed to cable, which gave me hope that I'd be writing for a show as awesome one day—if I took that side of myself more seriously, that is.

#MemorialDayWeekend

I made it through the rest of my workday without any further incident, but I got nervous when my phone started buzzing. It was my mom.

"Hi mom."

"Hey Dimple Doll it's your mom *and* dad. We have you on speaker, dear. Everything Okay?"

"Yes."

"You sure, what's this your father tells me about you ending up on a blog for fighting? Were you fighting? We didn't raise you like that!"

"It was nothing mom, you know those blogs lie about everything. I'm okay. Work is just getting hectic. Don't worry."

"Do I need to come see that boss of yours?" my dad said.

"Josiah! None of that shark nonsense!" my mom added.

"What? That man has some serious problems and code of conduct violations. I can get him together easily, and it's better I do it through the law than with my fists. I can bring out that Bed-Stuy boy if I have to!"

"Mom, dad, I'm okay. Intervention of any kind isn't necessary."

"Well what about that screenplay you were writing?" mom said.

"Um…it's coming along," I lied. The truth was that I was about 1,000 words in and hadn't written anything new in about two months.

"You were always writing when you were a little girl, and good stuff too. I'd love to see you come up with something now and become a professional screenwriter, or playwright, or even filmmaker one day. Haven't we discussed this already? Don't let that screenwriting boot camp you did go to waste! You hate what you're doing now, it's time to make some adjustments."

"Yes mom."

"Don't brush me off. You know I know a thing or two about the arts. I know you're busy, but if you just carve out 15 minutes a day to focus on your screenplay, that's a start. You really should quit that job of yours. I'm proud of all the work you've done there, but it's obviously stressing you out. We can help you if you need it."

"I appreciate that advice mom. I will definitely carve out the time to write and put a plan in place to leave *Spark*."

"Are you coming over on Memorial Day? Uncle Chris and C.J. are stopping by on Monday and we're going to grill in the backyard."

I forgot that it was Memorial Weekend. Sheesh! Where the hell did the time go?

"Sure, I'll stop by on Monday. Look, I have to go. I'm meeting Reiko for dinner."

"Okay baby, tell Reiko we said hello. Love you."

"Love you too."

I thought about my mom's writing advice on my way to meet Reiko and Felani. Fifteen minutes a day was pretty doable. I decided to start on Saturday and devote my Friday night, which was tonight, to whatever Reiko, Felani and I were going to get into. There weren't usually industry events on Friday nights so I might not bump into familiar faces and have to explain myself for the umpteenth time, but knowing Reiko that was probably wishful thinking. Dinner was never *just* dinner with her. She was always looking to get into something—an after the dinner party, and then an after party for the after party, and then a night cap, and probably breakfast too. It was exhausting, but as much as I wanted to go home and wallow in self-pity I knew it was probably better to apply what I learned in the one therapy session I attended a few months ago, and keep myself busy.

I was the last one to arrive at Olive Tree, a West Village eatery situated above a popular comedy club that Reiko and I loved. It was dimly lit and frequented by celebrity comedians who were able to eat in peace, but our media colleagues either didn't know or care about that spot, so it was a good place to be low-key. Obscurity was what I needed.

"What's good mama!" Felani said.

She stood up and greeted me with a hug and a kiss on the cheek.

She was wearing Timberland high heel boots, a white tank top with "Baby Phat" scrawled across the chest and some blue jeans. I was no Tracy Reese, but I had enough fashion savvy to be taken aback by Felani's outfit, which made me cringe. At least she was wearing skinny jeans this time and not baggy men's jeans like it was 1994. I noticed that she had been trying to be a little more feminine and stylish with her wardrobe choices lately, but I wished she would lose the do-it-yourself attitude and hire a real stylist. The positive here was her makeup.

"Hey girl," I replied. "What's that lip color you're rocking? I love a good red."

"Thanks boo. This some shit Reiko made me put on. You know she's been on this beauty guru kick lately."

Felani was right. Reiko has always been a girly girl who loved dressing up, but she has been a lot more intense lately. Then again, I was just glad someone was stepping up to help Felani in *some* capacity.

"Good job, Reiko," I said, settling into our booth.

"You already know how I do. You ain't hanging out with me without heels and/or at least a beat face."

"Reiko suggested the outfit I wore the other night at my party, yo!" Felani replied. "Mind you, I didn't even ask her. She straight texted me instructions out of the blue."

"Speaking of the beauty guru thing, I'm actually going to start posting my tips on Snapchat and Instagram," Reiko said.

"I don't know why you didn't start posting your tips sooner," I replied.

I chuckled because Reiko liked to dress up even to go to the supermarket and seemed to think that all women should be that way because in her world, you never knew whom you might run into. It was a philosophy she proudly credited to her paternal grandmother.

"Wow, so she got *you* to put on a dress *and* heels? I know from your previous videos and promos that you like to do the Tomboy thing," I said.

The tacky thing too.

"That's what I'm saying! I don't dress up for nobody, but I can't front, Reiko makes good points about wardrobe. This is my career we're talking about, and I guess I have to start stepping it up."

"She fights me every step of the way," Reiko replied. "Anything she wears that's remotely sexy or feminine is the result of our compromise after at least 15 minutes of bickering about it."

Felani, despite her rough and rugged appearance and hood tendencies, seemed to have a good head on her shoulders. She seemed smart and cool to talk to. I met a lot of girls like her growing up in Brooklyn.

"Don't feel bad. I go through this too," I said. "You'll learn to tune it out. Then again, I guess every crew needs the overbearing motherly one, right?"

"You mean the ratchet aunty!" Felani said.

"Okay, first of all, you ain't about to talk about me like I'm not even here!" Reiko replied.

We all laughed.

"You know it's all love, ma," Felani said.

"I'm glad I made it out tonight," I said.

"Me too. Otherwise, you would have been home on your couch eating your life away over things you can't control while your waistline suffers and the rest of us are out here living it up," Reiko replied.

"Well damn, you just read my whole life!"

"Because I know you well! Now let's get to the good stuff. What the fuck happened at the office today?"

I rehashed the day's events impressed that Reiko could tell the problem was work and not men since I only sent her a cryptic message to the tune of, "*What. The. Fuck.*"

"TONY WALKER SCREAMED ON YOU, SON! TELL HIM I SAID TO CANCEL MY INTERVIEW!" Felani yelled so loud that the people in our general vicinity heard her clearly, which was hard to do at Olive Tree.

"I appreciate it but you can't do that. *I'm* the one doing the interview! Remember? Plus, I saw the photos from the shoot and you look hot, now all you need is the words. Let it rock for your career's sake, trust me."

"Aight. I'll let it rock on the strength of my respect for you. But my pops grew up with that nigga and knows him well. It's nuffin' for me to send him a message if I have to."

"What happened to you not saying 'nigga' anymore?" Reiko said.

"I said it wasn't gonna be in my rhymes anymore, but general speech is fair game."

"You're gutter, but with a ratchet conscience. I love it," Reiko replied.

For a moment, I was hoping that Reiko and Felani would continue their conversation so that I could stuff my face with some of the delicious appetizers that started arriving, and not have to talk about any more of my troubles, but that's why they called that line of thought wishful thinking.

"You probably don't want to talk about this, but did you read the blog Disingenuous, I mean, Sincere, posted about you with all the subliminals?" Reiko said.

"I'm sorry, can you repeat that, the dickmatization is clogging my ears."

We all burst into laughter, but for me it was bittersweet because that post was actually embarrassing.

"At least you got to beat his ass," Felani said. "I saw the footage of the fight. You got some good hooks in, girl!"

"I wish I could strangle him to death and get away with it," I replied.

"I can have my pops send him a message too. Just say the word."

Felani's father, known by most people as E Money, was also her manager. His hustle was legit today, but he used to be a major drug dealer in New York back in the 1980s. There was actually a cult classic movie about his life. He used to roll with a notorious crew of dealers in Brooklyn, but eventually greed, envy and backstabbing crumbled their empire. Basically, he lived the life that most rappers fantasized about in their lyrics, but he was one of the rare truly stealthy ones who managed to never get caught. Despite being known for his goon status, he was low-key about the money he made, and didn't flash his possessions so he rarely stood out. He was also careful about the people he kept around him. He calculated every move like chess and managed to transition to legit businesses by the time Felani was in elementary school in the '90s. He opened a grocery store, a wing spot and a Laundromat in his neighborhood and employed locals. He also got into the music business in artist management and self-taught music engineering. A few local rappers, some of whom actually got successful, often used the studio set up in his basement for a fee. That was how he developed industry relationships and of course, this was what Felani grew up around. I'd never met E Money, the hood legend, but I'd heard stories. He was nice and laidback most of the time, but the goon came out when necessary.

"Girl, your dad is too busy working on major projects, primarily for you. There's no way I'd let you sick him on some lame-ass wannabe Hitch."

"True, but the option is still there," Felani replied.

She took a bite of her turkey burger and smirked as we kept our gaze locked.

"What?" I said.

"Since we're talking about boys, I know someone who likes you."

"Are you seriously doing this?"

"Yup she is. I know who it is too!" Reiko said.

"Aw, come on y'all. You can't be serious. Olu is a...*rapper*."

"SO!" Reiko shouted.

"We've all worked around enough of them to know that even the nice ones are probably not worth entertaining unless you just want a fling and I'm not about that life right now."

"You say that now, but we all have eyes and that man is foine," Reiko replied. "And he freaking adores you! I saw the way he looked at you at Felani's party. Hell, he barely spoke to anyone else."

"So, what! He was just trying to butter me up. You know how newbie artists like to try to get in good with the press."

"Um no. Your cynical theory would only make sense if you hadn't already done the interview. He was trying to butter them biscuits," Reiko replied, gyrating in her seat during that last bit.

"Nasty ass! That man ain't thinking about me."

"Actually, he is thinking about you," Felani replied.

"You guys are reading too far into this. He was probably just being friendly because he was intoxicated, and happy with the feature I wrote."

"Nope. Olu doesn't drink much. Actually, I've only seen him drunk once in my life. That was at a wedding, and he was going through a break up around that time," Felani declared. "He definitely wasn't drinking at my party, just happy to see you."

"And you know this how? And don't say something dumb like, 'He likes you because he tried to dance with you.'"

"I actually saw when he tried to dance with you and you ran. Classic Nyela," Reiko said, chuckling.

I shot Reiko the squinty-eyes.

"I know because he's literally like my brother. He used to live with me for a period sometime after he got to New York."

I raised my eyebrow.

"Don't try it," Felani said quickly. "Never ever, *ever* has there been anything romantic between me and Olu."

Felani explained that Olu stayed with she and her dad shortly after enrolling in college in New York. They met at Five Towns College where they studied music engineering and began collaborating on a lot of creative class projects. Felani eventually learned that Olu's parents were only paying for his course credits and that he was running out of funds to pay for his other basic necessities, especially his high Manhattan rent. So, she offered him the extra bedroom in her father's house as a way for him to save money.

"But you ended up having sex with him at some point, right?" I blurted.

"Hell no! I mean, I guess he's attractive, but we *never* had sex. We *never* even thought of each other that way. He really *is* like my brother, and I'm not repeating that again! At the time he moved in we were both in long-term relationships, so it was just a different dynamic for us. Always has been. Mind you, I'm still with my man, we've been together since high school."

I felt an unexpected wave of relief.

"So, who's his girlfriend?"

"I said he *was* in a relationship! And don't get me started on that bitch! It was some silly model chick. They started dating shortly before *Lockers* was cancelled. She was in L.A. a lot for gigs. She stuck around at first, even through when he started school at Five Towns and started making a name for him self in music. But when he started looking more like the starving artist, and less like the superstar people projected him to become, she bounced."

"She gets points for trying though, right?" Reiko said half-jokingly.

"Girl, bye! This bitch only stuck around with him because she thought things would pick up faster than they did, but she was cheating on him for most of their relationship, even when things were good. They then started doing the off and on thing for years, and played games with each other. Whatever it was that they were doing lasted way longer than it should have. I think Olu was just bored, but he did at least make some good music inspired by that phase, as a result," Felani said. "On the other hand, *she* definitely tried to keep things more on after he finally got access to his trust fund, but he didn't use it for balling out. He was serious about budgeting and making his own dough so she got bored, started fucking around again, and only officially broke things off with him after she got pregnant by King Tootsie."

"EW!" Reiko and I expressed our disgust in unison.

King Tootsie was the real life equivalent to an evil troll from a children's book, but the hip-hop version. He was a rapper from Atlanta who got his big break as part of a rap super group. They released an inane, but catchy song with an accompanying dance called, "Shake Them

Gumballs." The song ruled radio airways for a while, but the group didn't make it past that one single before they split and faded into one-hit-wonder oblivion. They accused King Tootsie, who was also their primary producer and writer, of embezzling money. After that lawsuit, King Tootsie embarked on a lukewarm solo career. I never paid attention to him beyond that one time I interviewed him, but the last I heard he had an independent distribution deal with a major label. He also had about 15 children with 10 different women and they were always on gossip blogs due to their shenanigans—from fighting each other to dragging him to court over child support. I was baffled about why anyone would sleep with him period, but *especially* without a condom.

My impression of him based on my one experience was that he was on a mission to impregnate the Earth's entire female population. I was forced to spend almost an entire day with him for that interview, which also doubled as a photoshoot for a *Spark* feature story. I was the only woman on set that he hadn't seen before, so in what I assumed could only be described as "Tootsie think," that meant he could try his lame pick-up moves on me. He spent most of the shoot trying to convince me to "kick it" with him in his suite at the Mondrian after our full 10 hours on set, which ended at 1 a.m. When he finally realized that his wack game wasn't working, he got crude and frankly stated that his "superstar dick" would change my life. I remained unimpressed, uninspired and reminded why it was more important to pursue my passions outside of *Spark*. That way, I could control the people I got to interview.

"I've seen all of his kids' mothers and there's only one cute one. Does that mean Olu's ex is the tall slim cinnamon-hued chick with the dreamy deep-set eyes, high forehead, and impossibly amazing bone structure, who looks like she could be Ethiopian?"

"Yup, that's her," Felani replied.

"And the baby *definitely* doesn't belong to Olu?"

"Hell no, that ain't his baby! They got that DNA test handled!"

I felt another sigh of relief. I'd hate to have to deal with a shady babymama situation. I mean, hypothetically speaking, of course.

"Olu has a good heart. He'd never father a child and not take care of it. He wanted to be sure."

That tidbit of information about Olu made me so happy that I didn't even feel the goofy smile spreading across my face.

"Ooooh, you *do* like him. I knew it!" Reiko said.

"No I don't! I was just curious. It's the journalist in me."

Shit. I was busted. I've *been* busted.

"Bitch, stop lying! Stevie Wonder saw you blushing," Felani said.

"Brown girls don't blush, thank you very much."

That was the weakest comeback ever, but it was all I could think of at the moment, and I refused to be out-sassed.

"If you gonna mess with any rapper in the world then he's the right one," Felani said.

"You are too funny," I followed up.

"And *you're* in denial," Reiko replied.

"WHATEVER!"

"Olu and Nyela sitting in the tree, K-I-S-S-I-N-G…"

"Felani, don't play with me."

She began to chortle instead of chanting, so Reiko picked up her verbal slack.

"First comes love, then comes marriage…"

She also began cracking up and couldn't continue.

"Whatever bitches! I don't have a crush."

Once again, worst lie ever.

—

"Aight, what are we doing now?" Reiko said, as we spilled out of the restaurant and headed to Felani's car.

Reiko was slightly inebriated. I didn't have anything alcoholic, and Felani wasn't drinking tonight since she was driving.

"There's a house party or some shit going down tonight in BK," Felani said, while scrolling through her phone.

"Oh shit, that's right! The Hip-Hop Slangaz are doing that birthday/housewarming/cookout thingie. They throw the best parties," Reiko added.

Hip-Hop Slangaz was one of the first blogs to blow up by posting music. They've been around for a few years and have inspired a lot of copycats, but they were one of the few sites in that genre that was actually making serious money. The three guys behind the site probably raked in at least six figures, each, a year. They also expanded their brand to include merchandise, public appearances, and endorsements. The site held weight as the number one online destination where rappers could be seen and heard by movers and shakers on an international platform. Some had even gotten deals after being discovered there. Hip-Hop Slangaz parties were always epic and I needed some fun, but there was a catch.

"I want to go, but Sincere might be there."

"Fuck him! If he's there, I'll punch him in the face for you!" Felani replied.

She was serious, but I still laughed.

"No, no, Felani, you don't do dirty work anymore," Reiko said. "The Hip Hop Slangaz are our boys, so if Sincere shows up and gets out of pocket then he's out of there. And as for you, Nyela, no more excuses, you're coming with us."

I settled into the backseat of Felani's Lexus, ready for a new adventure tonight. We locked eyes after she adjusted her rearview mirror.

"So, am I dropping you home, or nah?"

"Nah, Hip-Hop Slangaz it is."

Fuck it. I needed to have some fun.

#PartyandBullshit

We heard the music blasting as Felani turned on to the block, and we saw loads of people walking toward our destination as we rode up the street looking for the exact address, which wasn't hard to find. It was 11:30, still early by New York City party standards, but since it was a house party in the New Bed-Stuy you never knew when the police would come and break it up.

Felani luckily snagged a parking spot a few doors down from the house. As we approached the entrance, I saw the Who's Who of the bloggerati and entertainment media feigning disinterest in what was going on around them by staring intently into their phones, Instagramming, Snapchatting, and the usual.

"Nyela! Whattup chica!"

It was Morena Motor Mouth, a satellite radio host/gossip blogger whose celebrity interviews *always* went viral. She had a knack for getting people to do and say crazy shit, but unlike Reiko, she had no finesse. However, despite being loud, she actually didn't annoy me as much as most media personalities like her. She drunkenly grabbed my arm and reeled me in for a sloppy kiss on the cheek.

"When did you get here?" I asked. It was my bad attempt at small talk. I really didn't care when she got here.

"Girl, I don't even know. I'm twisteeeeed. But this party crackin!"

She laughed, took another sip from her red plastic cup and pulled her friend from another conversation to introduce us, though we had met before.

"Do you know Cynda?" she asked.

It was Cynda Bently, a publicist that I had done business with a lot over the course of my career. Most recently, she set up that King Tootsie interview I mentioned.

"Hi," Cynda said, extending her arm for a handshake.

I searched her face for recognition, but it wasn't there. It was seriously as if we didn't spend several hours together at a photo shoot where she ended up apologizing profusely for her dumbass client.

"Cynda, it's me, Nyela Barnes, from *Spark*."

"*Oooh*, okay, I know you. I think I just emailed you or something, right?"

This broad emailed me every other day, pitching her clients. And if it wasn't an email pitch, it was a blast featuring some faux motivational bullshit. Aside from being a publicist, Cynda moonlighted as a relationship blogger, life coach and I think, artist manager, astronaut, engineer, pilot, or whatever. I was pretty sure she was a Janequa of All

Trades and master of none. She had a massive following and seemed like she had it all together, but I never trusted her. She gave me fake-ass industry chick vibes, and my intuition was usually on point. I wasn't in the mood to pull cards though, so I just went along with her act.

"Yeah, it was about your new client Tut the Gut, right?"

"Tut the Great," she replied. "He's the newest signee to Grand Royale records."

I knew Tut The Great's name, but I also knew it got under a publicist's skin when popular media personnel weren't familiar with their client, especially after being sent several emails and pitches about that person.

"*Riiiiight*. Tut the Great. Oops."

Her annoyed facial expression started to shift to what appeared to be a glimmer of recognition. She must have been on to my passive aggression.

"Wait. Didn't you attack someone the other night at Greenhouse? That was you, right?"

Here we go again.

"Yes, that was me."

"Ooh, honey! I heard about that boyfriend of yours—The Love Broker, right?"

"He's my ex and yes, he has a popular blog."

"Aw, sweetie. I hate seeing women fighting over men. You need to dig deep and reclaim your crown because you are just too fabulous for the drama! Have you signed up for my workshop yet?"

The fact that Cynda was wearing a multi-colored floral blouse with puffy sleeves and a gold lamé pencil skirt—think, Sandra from *227*—to a backyard barbecue was the only thing that made this situation worth it. I wanted to crack up laughing *and* strangle her at the same time.

"Oh, that's right!" Morena said, butting her way into this useless conversation. "What the fuck happened the other night?"

"Long story. It's all up on *Spark's* website, though. Go read it," I replied.

I was sure Morena knew Sincere's side of the story since she was a religious reader and commenter on his site. He also appeared on her show multiple times to give wack-ass dating tips. I'd also wager that they've had sex. I was going on a hunch, but toward the end of our relationship, Sincere talked about her way too much for someone who was "just his homegirl," and he once dedicated an entire blog post to how "fine" he thought she was. His explanation was that he simply chose her because she was the right fit for his weekly column where he featured beautiful women, but I've never been stupid, only delusional.

"Oh shit, I didn't know you rolled with Felani!" Morena blurted, shoving me aside so that she could get to Fel, who was slightly behind me engaged in another conversation.

"Ay-yo, Felani! Girl, you are my bitch!"

She started rapping some lyrics to "Die Hard Bitches," from one of Felani's early mixtapes, released back when she was making appearances on street DVDs. Felani, still graciously humble and un-jaded, engaged Morena with a five and then started rapping along with her.

"I see you, ma," Felani said, grinning.

"You gotta come on my show, Felani."

"Just hook that up with my publicist," Felani replied. "I know you know Gina Milbourne."

Reiko, obviously annoyed, abruptly darted inside the house. She couldn't stand Morena. I never got the full story, but the gist of it was that they worked together in the past and something about Morena being a "fake cutthroat, opportunist bitch"—Reiko's exact words. I never had real beef with Morena, despite me knowing she was the type who constantly wanted to know what you were up to just in case your affiliation or status could help raise her profile. I'd rather not get sucked into more conversation with her than was necessary, though, so I grabbed Felani's arm and lead her into the party behind Reiko.

"Hit me up later, Nyela!" Morena shouted. "We gotta talk about that fight! I heard you got hands."

That was really what she wanted to talk about this whole time, but Felani's presence distracted her. Nosey beyotch.

"Yup!" I shouted back at her, still moving forward.

I felt the music vibrating as we made our way through the packed living room. I kept my gaze straight ahead as I followed Reiko toward the backyard, but I saw women looking me up and down from my peripheral vision, and I occasionally dodged random attempts by men to grab my hand and/or whisper in my ear as I passed. I was so not here for that tonight. I really just wanted to unwind with my girls, or at least try to.

"Deion, ay!" Reiko quickened her pace toward the backyard as she charged toward Deion D, the birthday boy and one third of the Hip-Hop Slangaz. He was swigging from a bottle of Moscato, which I found comical since he was such a big, tall guy.

"Heeeeeey," he lifted her off the ground into a bear hug. "I'm glad you made it *and* you got your girls too. Whattup Felani!"

"Nigga, I *know* you ain't drinking Moscato!" Felani replied, as he wrapped his long arm around her for a side-hug.

"It's my birthday! I had some cupcakes before this. Moscato's a dessert wine right?"

"Aight, you get a pass for this one."

They exchanged laughs and brief small talk about her next show before he noticed me.

"You ain't tell me you was bringing Mayweather!" he said, dancing around and playfully jabbing his fists in the air in my direction. "I heard you gave my man Sincere a black eye."

"I didn't give him a black eye. Who the fuck told you that?"

"I'm just messing with you. But I was there the other night, and you got some hooks!" he said, laughing. "That big bouncer almost couldn't pull you off."

I hadn't even been here 20 minutes and I was already getting irritated.

"This ain't no interrogation!" Reiko jumped in, wedging herself between Deion and I.

She faced him on tippy toes in an ill attempt to get to his eye level. At 6'5" and about 260 pounds, he eclipsed Reiko, who was about 5'6" in heels, even though she was right in front of him.

Big Sean's "Ass" came on and we all started dancing. Reiko and Deion started having fun with her bubble butt while Felani and I started dropping it low while holding on to each other.

I turned around to see who decided to pull up and start dancing with me when the music switched, and it turned out to be my homie, Indian Eddie.

"Yoooooo! I didn't know you were back in the United States!" I shouted over the music, leaning in for a hug.

"Yup, I got back yesterday. You know I couldn't miss this."

Indian Eddie was one of three immensely popular Eddie's in the entertainment media world. He made the "Indian" distinction himself due to his Indo-Trinidadian heritage and looks. He ran his own successful digital entertainment marketing and branding company. I met him fresh out of college when we were both interns running through industry parties hoping to finally meet that person who was the gatekeeper to our respective career dreams. Eventually we both got busy working and drifted apart. We still kept in touch here and there, especially since I interviewed his clients often.

"We gotta catch up. I want to hear about your trip to Tokyo," I said.

"Let's link for dinner or drinks soon," he replied.

"Definitely! I'll reach out next week. Have you met Felani, by the way?"

I interrupted Felani's dance reverie and pulled her closer to our conversation.

"Oh, shit, Felani! We've never met, but that last mixtape was fire!"

"Thank you, boo!" Felani replied, pulling Indian Eddie in for a hug.

She was remarkably friendly for someone who was also so tough. That trait would take her far. Now, if only she'd hire a stylist! I was going to beat that drum until it busted.

Eddie continued the conversation about how dope he thought Felani was and I found myself also amazed by her patience for this type of thing. I realized that this was the type of stuff that came with her job, but it would drive me nuts not being able to take two steps without someone fawning over me.

Reiko and Deion were still dancing, and Eddie and Felani were talking about creating an app now, so I walked over to the food and refreshments. I took in my surroundings, jealous that these guys were able to own a piece of Brooklyn real estate like this simply from blogging about music. They literally just wrote a sentence or two per post and posted a download link to new music. Meanwhile, people told me I should be excited about working for someone else because of the brand attached to the name.

I ended up at a sweets table, grabbed a box of Sour Patch Kids and plopped down on a swinging chair. Eventually Felani, Reiko, Deion D and Munch, another of the Hip-Hop Slangaz made their way to join me.

"I knew you'd find the candy first!" Reiko shouted as she grabbed a handful of Lemon Heads, two chocolate chip cookies and a lollipop.

Felani grabbed some Twizzlers and squeezed next to me on the swing chair.

Reiko handed me a cookie that I nibbled on despite not really wanting it because eating gave me something to do.

"So, what happened the other night?" Munch said.

I knew it was coming.

"Not so much as a hello your first time seeing me in a while, and all you want to know is what happened!"

"My bad, yo. You know I got love for you."

I gave him the side eye.

"*Hiiiiii Nyela*," Munch said in a sing-songy tone.

"I'm tired of talking about it, but I'm pretty sure you heard an extremely fabricated version of the story and have your mind made up about what happened."

"I know how people be talking when it comes to shit like this. That was why I asked you what was up," he replied. "My man Sincere was looking wild hurt at the party, when you was over there with Olu Major."

I started rapidly tapping my foot out of frustration.

"So you *were* at the party, huh? Then you saw what happened, right?"

"I mean, I seen the bouncer pulling you off of him and that Instagram model chick. But I had to ask because I wanted to get your side too."

"But you're cool with Sincere. Why should I tell you anything when you probably already got his deluded version of events? You're probably just asking me so you can stir the pot."

"Nah, I'm really just trying to get your side because I thought we were cool."

Deion D was the only one out of the three Hip-Hop Slangaz that I had a real rapport with. We've actually hung out and had deeper than surface level conversations. Deion was the only slanga that could actually drop facts about my personal life and me as a person.

"How on Earth are we *that* cool when most of our conversations consist of 'hi' and 'bye?'"

"Damn, you cold as hell. Sincere must have done a number on you. I'm just over here tryna get a pretty lady to open her heart up to a nigga."

I stuffed my face with another handful of Sour Patch Kids because chewing was the only way I'd keep from laughing and not having to verbally respond with an insult. Felani was facing the other way face-palming herself as her shoulders heaved up and down rapidly in a fit of silent but obvious laughter.

"You sexy as hell and I like that you not no Hollywood broad," Munch said.

He really thought this was smooth. I replied with a weak half smile, still trying not to crack up laughing. Felani composed herself and joined the conversation.

"I'm not tryna be rude but she don't want you, my dude."

I almost choked on my last bite of candy in a fit of laughter.

Much turned to Felani. "Here *you* go. So you playin' the role of the hatin' ass friend tonight, huh?"

"Nah, I'm playing the role of the bearer of truth."

"You sexy too. I like 'em kind of aggressive wit' yo cute self!" Munch said with a grin. "Keep fuckin' with me and I'll have y'all both spending the night."

Felani and I burst into raging laughter.

Munch sucked his teeth. "Stop acting like y'all ain't interested."

"Okay, we should have been cut this short," I said, grabbing Felani's arm.

Felani and I left Munch stuck on stupid. Reiko was sitting in Deion's lap and they were in their own world, so we started walking toward the other side of the backyard and I spotted Elvish-1, who I was surprised would have the audacity to show up.

Elvish-1 was another extremely popular hip-hop blogger—known for controversy more so than posting music—who happened to have beef with the Hip-Hip Slangaz. It started during a listening session for Olu Major. The Hip-Hop Slangaz made an exclusive agreement with Olu's management that they would release an audio stream of snippets from Olu's album a day after the listening session, which they sponsored. Elvish-1, whose tactics were often questionable, secretly recorded the session and released snippets of all of the songs on his blog that night. It was an unspoken rule that listening sessions were for the ears of those who were invited only. Elvish-1's stunt became a major scandal because it was a first in music blogger history, and the floodgates of hip-hop blogger beef hell were opened.

Olu and his management were so pissed that they canned the album, pushed his release date back indefinitely and started recording new music. It was months later and they still hadn't figured out what his new first single would be. Elvish-1 took the stream down and apologized, but he had already been blacklisted.

"Yoooo, ain't that the blogger who leaked Olu's music?" Felani said.

The moments following her remark were epic enough to take the heat off of *my* episode from the other night, at least for the rest of this party—I hoped.

Deion haphazardly tossed Reiko off his lap and damn near teleported across the room. "WHAT THE FUCK ARE YOU DOING HERE?!"

He was now about a centimeter away from Elvish-1. They would have been chest to chest, but Elvish-1 was barely 5'2.

"I just came to have fun, man. I got no beef," he said.

I wasn't surprised that Elvish-1 thought he could show up to this party and *not* have any problems. This sentiment was representative of a common industry mentality that fucked up behavior, no matter how dead wrong it was, would be forgotten by the victim if the offender just laid low for a while. That train of thought was also coupled with the notion that a tweeted apology, instead of picking up a phone, would make everything right with the universe. I've never seen this delusion of grandeur actually work, but people just wouldn't stop believing.

Deion D responded by grabbing him by the collar of his two sizes too big, crew neck shirt and carrying this grown-ass man toward the front of the house as if he were a kitten. Elvish-1 screamed and squirmed helplessly, pleading with Deion to put him down before getting tossed into the big garbage bin in front of the Slangaz house.

"You didn't have to do that, Deion!" Elvish-1 yelled, his voice muffled and quivering, as he made awkward attempts to climb out of the garbage can.

Elvish-1 was a bastard, but I felt bad for him because this was definitely going viral. His portly body seemed to get wedged deeper into the trashcan with every attempt he made to pull himself out. After a while, he got frustrated to tears as the rest of us snickered and gawked. Tears continued streaming down his face, even after he freed himself and started making his way down the block to the nearest train station.

"Fuck boy!" shouted Deion, in a rare moment when his Memphis twang surfaced.

I headed back to the backyard, as the rest of the peanut gallery dispersed, filled a cup with rum punch and sat on a folding chair. I was almost past my limit for the night, but I had some escaping to do, so I took a long swig. At this moment it was just me and DJ Slangatron, the other Hip-Hop Slanga, who was doing a damn good job of providing the party's music.

Ten more minutes and one less rum punch later, more people started trickling back into the backyard, some were still laughing about what they saw, others watching replays and posting the madness on social media.

I realized that my moment of solitude was fleeting once I saw Morena and Cynda headed in my direction. They grabbed the only seats next to me—one on my right and one on my left. *Fuck!*

"Ooh girl, I saw Reiko dancing with Deion. Mmhmm. What's up with that?" Morena said.

I wanted to reply with a question about why her breath was so hot, but opted against that.

"They were *just* dancing."

"I don't know, girl. Don't look like they were *just* dancing to me. They look like they're a couple."

I took the last swig left of my rum punch to give me some time to think about a response that wasn't rude.

"Reiko and Deion are grown. Perhaps, you should ask them directly," I replied, keeping my tone as even as possible.

"She might not want to go there with Deion though," Cynda said. "He's cute and has money, but he's known to chew women up and spit them out."

"Then you don't know Reiko," I replied.

Most men didn't keep Reiko's attention, with the exception of France Deveaux. He was the only man I had ever seen her go bananas for, but admittedly she did seem unusually into Deion. If what Cynda was saying was true then I hoped Reiko was ready.

"That's not what I heard," Morena chimed in. "My boy France had her whipped."

France Deveaux's success with his multi-million dollar management firm made him somewhat of a celebrity. He was especially popular online because he was fond of airing out his business on social media.

Reiko began dating him at the start of his social media experimentation. Their relationship was tumultuous, capricious and generally inconsistent over the course of a few years, and always went viral. Reiko often starred in his random vlogs. Most of the videos featured arbitrary activities like grocery shopping or most popular, Reiko lounging around his house in pajamas and sometimes lingerie and swimsuits, as they pondered the answers to trite questions like, "Why do all men cheat?" and, "Why are women crazy?"

Reiko was tough at times, but she was also an optimist, and it sometimes surfaced on rare but also inappropriate occasions. This was part of my theory about why she put up with his incessant cheating and megalomaniac behavior. I think it was France's charming moments that kept her holding on.

"It's probably because she was dickmatized," Cynda said. "That gets women all the time."

I couldn't even defend Reiko in this instance because it was true. Reiko and France were last official some time a little over a year ago. That break up, which was caught on camera, was the result of Reiko finding some pictures on his Instagram stream where he was in bed asleep next to a naked woman, who happily smiled for the photo he wasn't aware that she had taken. This was a woman who had been a problem for their relationship before and he always managed to explain her away, but not that time. The woman got a hold of his phone and uploaded the pics online to fuck with Reiko. That was Reiko's last, *last* straw, allegedly, and so she broke it off raucously at a major event. She basically cursed France out, kicked him in the nuts and cracked his phone screen after he began recording the spectacle.

Reiko luckily didn't go to jail, but France uploaded the event to YouTube. Reiko claimed that she was done with him for good, but I knew she still entertained him. She was good at ignoring him when we bumped into him out and about to keep up pretenses, but I've seen some "I miss you" texts exchanged on her phone. It was her life and I'd lectured her about him as much as I possibly could so now I said nothing. I figured she'd mention it to me if they were back on but she hadn't yet, so I was going to mind my business for now.

"I tell my clients all the time not to let their fabulousness be eclipsed by a cute man with a magic stick," Cynda said.

"Wait, you counsel people now? I thought you were a publicist." I replied, trying badly to mask my shade as a genuine question.

"In addition to doing PR, I'm a certified life coach and I have an award-winning relationship vlog and website?"

"I knew about the vlogs and the PR," I replied.

Her fake motivational video blogs were extremely popular, and she also got paid to do occasional speaking engagements. Why people followed her bullshit advice would always remain a mystery, especially since she came off as a grown-up mean girl.

"It's no secret that I have been a victim of dickmitization in the past," Cynda continued. "But I recognized my inner fabulousness and saw the error in my ways. It's actually all in my book that's coming out soon."

"Do you talk about that failed marriage in which you were allegedly abusive, too? And weren't you engaged like, three times within the last few years?"

I knew that was a bitchy thing to say, but the bewildered look on her face was worth it. Most people didn't know those details she omitted, but I got this information from Morena. I was present for at least one of Morena's rants about Cynda where she started to reveal top-secret information because she was mad. Cynda stared at me in silence for a few classic seconds, probably trying to think of what to say.

"How did you know about—"

"I don't know. Ask Morena," I interjected.

I walked away on that note, proud of my cattiness. That was what they got for lecturing me and trying to get into my business.

I made my way into the house and stumbled upon Felani finishing up a video drop for some music bloggers who accosted her for an impromptu interview. I admired her patience for this shit, once again. Then again, she was starting to live out her dream. It was understandable that she would be gracious and thankful. I hoped she'd stay that way.

Felani spotted me as I approached and yanked me by her side. *Shit!*

"Yo, yo. This is my girl Nyela! The best damn entertainment journalist out this motherfucker! Check her out online at Cinema Fancy!"

Wow, she knew about my blog! I didn't even tell her about Cinema Fancy.

"So what does Nyela have to say about that? Is she the best?" asked the random interviewer.

I froze because I'd rather be behind the camera.

"Uh..."

"She's shy," Felani said, to my rescue. "Just take it from me. She's dope and I approve!"

"Whoooooooo!" Wailed Reiko as she drunkenly wedged herself between Felani and I.

The blogger was still filming.

"These are my bitches right here! Felly Fel and Nye! Ain't nobody fucking with us! WHOOOOOOOO!"

I felt another presence hovering behind us trying to get some camera time. It was France. He grabbed Reiko by the waist, in a way that seemed intimate and I began a silent prayer in an attempt to wish him away as easily as I had thought him up.

"Tell the people who they looking at right now," the interviewer prompted.

"They *should* already know! This your girl Reiko Rodriguez a.k.a. Koko Supreme a.k.a. Radio Koko. Y'all know me already, *Bad Girls Club* and *Morning Riot* all day!

"This my baby right here!" Shouted France as he swept Reiko up into a one-arm hug and planted a kiss on her cheek.

It almost looked like he was choking her, but she didn't seem to mind. I used this moment to sneak away as Felani, France and Reiko continued hamming it up and spotted Morena, Cynda and now Cookie Clark nearby, watching us the entire time. Cynda's gaze was focused on me and she didn't look happy. Perhaps she was still mad at me for dropping that bit about her failed marriage.

By this point I was over it, so my plan was to cab it home, but I didn't get far in my sneak dash thanks to the person who yanked my hair with violent force. I tried to remember what I learned in all those years of self-defense class, which my mom forced on me to take, about how to fall properly as I tumbled backward.

"What the fuck!" I screamed, clumsily struggling to regain my footing and protect myself from the frantic pummeling.

"YOU STUPID BITCH!" shouted my attacker.

Finally, my eyes gained focus and I noticed that it was the fake Kardashian chick, and she was with at least three other girls standing around me.

One of her friends tossed a drink in my face as I managed to get back on my feet, and they all started clawing, kicking and punching. Logic told me to curl up in a protective ball, but my ego wasn't going out like that, so I started throwing as many punches as I could.

"OH HELL NO!" Reiko yelled.

She and Felani descended upon Fake Kardashian and her pack of wolves with kicks and punches. Eventually spectators who weren't busy filming the entire thing and shouting "Worldstar" started to attempt to break it up. It took me a few seconds to realize that Munch had a firm grip around me. He pinned my arms to my waist and hindered any further jab attempts.

"Calm down Mayweather," he said in my ear. He was still annoying, but I was glad he stepped in and pulled me out of the melee.

I heard Fake Kardashian and her wolves shouting obscenities at us like, "Ugly bitches!" and "Whores!" as they got pulled out of the brawl. The last dig I heard before I focused on my girls was, "That's why he dumped your ass!" obviously tailored to me.

Felani, who was being restrained by Deion D, was franticly trying to free herself from his grip. Reiko, who was being restrained by France, broke free and stunned us all by tossing an empty punch bowl at Fake Kardashian. It made a loud thud as it connected with her forehead. By this point, we were all free of our respective human restraints.

"THAT'S WHAT I'M TALKING ABOUT, BITCH!" Felani shouted.

She and Reiko, who was also screaming triumphantly, exchanged high-fives. I snapped back to reality when I saw Fake Kardashian holding on to her forehead. I didn't see any blood, but she did have a lump, and I instantly regretted not being able to sneak out of the party successfully.

#PostWeekendBlues

I made it to Tuesday with an uneventful rest of my weekend because I holed up in my apartment on Saturday and Sunday, binge watched *The Walking Dead* on DVR and ignored the barrage of nosey text messages inquiring about what happened at the party. On Monday, I spent a lovely day cooking out with my family. I didn't go online, not even for my own blog. But I knew I had to face reality eventually. That reality wasn't just about my eventful weekend, either. It was also about the shift in the mood at the *Spark* office since the layoffs. I was reminded of this as I walked to my desk and noticed how many blank stares and side eyes were actually missing. It was a relief that I didn't have to deal with scrutiny from extra bodies, but it also made me sad. I hated working here and Hot Head Tony, but I liked my co-workers.

I made it to my desk without interrogation and started trolling the web for popular stories. As I predicted, several sites called themselves getting the exclusive about the party. I cringed at the first headline that caught my eye.

Which Bird Brain Industry Chicks Were
Spotted Brawling at a Barbecue?

We were having a blast at last weekend's Hip-Hop Slangaz backyard blow out until some bird industry broads ruined the fun.

You all remember Nyela Barnes from Spark *magazine, right? Well, she was in the center of drama, once again. She and her birdbrain friends, Reiko Rodriquez from the Morning Riot and that terrible rapper who just got signed...child I can't even remember her name...oh, it's Felani or something stupid, got involved in a brawl with some* Shah's of Sunset *looking chicks at the party. Apparently Nyela and some wannabe video hoe were fighting over Sincere McDonald, the so-called relationship expert. Nyela musta been salty that she got dumped but what took the cake was when Reiko Rodriguez threw a punch bowl at the video hoe, I think her name is Nazareth of Bethlehem or something like that. Anyway, the bish ended up with a purple bruise on her forehead, and got escorted out of the party after being holed up in the bathroom trying to make the swelling go down. Them wild banshees — that is — Nyela, Felani and Reiko are lucky they didn't get arrested or slapped with a lawsuit. And in case y'all didn't remember, Reiko got her brief 15 minutes of fame on* The Bad Girls Club. *I guess her current radio gig just isn't enough but you know how attention whores do. Speaking of attention whores, how desperate is it that Nyela would act like that over a man? She's a pretty girl with a seemingly good job — even though I heard they were laying people off left and right at Filliblue Publications, but I'm just saying, it's never that serious over a man.*

Story developing...

--Chatty Abernathy, the Gossip Slayer

I knew that most gossip blogging trolls couldn't write for shit, but that was especially cringe inducing. I usually didn't read the comments section of anything online because they made me sad for humanity. However, I decided to play myself this time:

"SOUNDS LIKE A BUNCH OF DESPERATE WHORES! PATHETIC. NONE OF THEM ARE EVEN RELEVANT ANYWAY. NEXT!"

I ended my comment trolling a few scrolls after that first one. Most of the comments went something to the tune of how irrelevant we were, how desperate we were, and in some cases there were random rants about how we made every black woman on the planet look bad. It must have felt good for people to lambast strangers as if they actually knew them while remaining anonymous online since so many people did it. I never understood that phenomenon, but I also didn't have an IQ of 20 coupled with the comprehension and critical thinking skills of a toddler, like many of the left behind children who were so adamant about posting hateful comments and arguing with people online. What pissed me off even more was the fact that these dumb-ass websites made it seem as if *I* was the aggressor in the situation when the truth was that *I* was attacked. The fight was on camera, but of course, no one's video clip seemed to start recording until *after* it started.

I kept scrolling for more stories as if they weren't all going to be the same.

EXCLUSIVE! Mr. Sincere speaks on Hip-Hop Slangaz
Fight Between the Ex and the Next

Nyela Barnes of Spark *magazine was involved in yet another brawl over the weekend over her ex-boyfriend according to Chatty Abernathy. Sources say she went ham on popular relationship blogger Mr. Sincere's girlfriend and her friends radio host Reiko Rodriguez and Roc Nation signee Felani jumped into what became a massive brawl. For those who don't know, Nyela and Mr. Sincere were a couple for a couple of years before he finally broke it off, citing neediness as one of many reasons. Obviously, Nyela didn't take it well. If you recall we posted footage of Nyela spazzing out on Mr. Sincere and his new chick at Felani's last mixtape release party and it got ugly. She has a mean right hook though!*

As usual, GRYND TYME HIP-HOP was on the scene at the Hip-Hop Slangaz party where this most recent fight went down but surprisingly Mr. Sincere wasn't in attendance but we caught up with him anyway...since that's our boy...to get his take on the situation.

"You already know what it is when you get a girl and that thang is so good to her that she don't know how to act. If you read my blog daily then you know Nyela is what I like to call dickmatized. She still thinking about me. It's cool, that's what happens with chicks sometimes. I just

124

didn't think she would get all combative and shit. Hopefully she don't start stalking me."

As far as Mr. Sincere's new chick, you may have seen her in Crowne *magazine as the exotic banger of the month. Her name is Nasreen Javadi, and we must say, she looks good. Nyela is cute too but Nasreen got that exotic Persian thing about her that we love. We don't blame you, Sincere. Anyway hopefully Nyela can calm it down and not end up in jail for knocking females out.*

It was only 10 a.m. and my brain was already broken from dumb shit posted online. The grammar and punctuation, or lack thereof, in that piece was enough to make my head implode, but I took a few deep breaths. The only thing useful that came out of that for me was information about Sincere's new girlfriend. I was eventually going to Google her so I could feel worse about myself, but first I had to check out one more site that I was pretty sure had posted video from the party by now. They didn't post much of a description beyond, "Felani and crew Pacquiaos model chick and her friends," followed by footage that started from the moment my girls and I, plus France, were doing drunken drops for the camera, but it didn't clear my name. *Shit!* The cameraperson wasn't at an angle where they could catch the fight from the beginning because I snuck away while Felani and Reiko were still carrying on, so the focus was still on them. From what they caught we were already scrapping and either one of us could have started the fight.

Fuck it, on to Miss Nasdaq, or whatever the fuck her name was. I discovered, after about 15 minutes of Googling and searching, that Nyquil was a spoiled brat who lived off her parents' money while trying to pursue a modeling and acting career. She was every bit of cliché that I expected based on the gratuitous duck faces, selfies and #ThirstTrap shots all over her various social media networks. She also had a sex tape out that didn't seem to give her career much of a boost. If Sincere wanted trash like her, then whatever!

I shifted focus to researching stories for my site and discovered that a legitimately exclusive news item made its way to my inbox directly from the publicist. It was about an actress I once interviewed for my blog, who landed a major role in an upcoming period drama. Her name was Quita Ravenell and I had been following her work as a playwright, before she landed roles on screen, for years before I finally reached out to her publicist for an interview. I initially tried to set her up with *Spark*, but Tony didn't like her. He said no black woman named Quita and with homely looks would ever make it in Hollywood. She wasn't homely by the way, but realizing that I was dealing with Hot Head Tony, I featured her on my site instead and it got so popular that Hollywood Newzer, one of the biggest entertainment media websites ever, linked to my piece. Since then, Quita's career as an actress, writer and producer in TV and film has flourished and she and her publicist have kept in touch. I was elated that she had finally landed what would definitely be her most pivotal role thus far. The role was also historic because it was that of Cleopatra. I repeat, an actual black woman playing Cleopatra. She will definitely be an Oscar contender for this, and her publicist wanted *me* to break the news first, so I planned to oblige. I couldn't wait to see where Quita's career would go.

I got back to *Spark* duty and assigned a few news items to interns to write for the site so that I could get back to focusing on what *I really* wanted to do—work on my screenplay. It wasn't the great American film or anything like that, but I decided to take my mom's advice and work on a little bit every day, which made me happy. It was a romantic comedy about research scientist exes who had seemingly moved on but not really. One got married and the other one decided to move in with his longtime girlfriend but unfortunately, the respective couples ended up coincidentally moving in next door to each other after years of being broken up, and hijinks ensued. As the exes attempted to make each other jealous and one up each other in life, they started to ponder why they actually broke up in the first place. Things got even more complicated after they decided to pick back up some shelved research on engineering body parts to regenerate lost limbs. They had conducted their research secretly, so they thought, and were close to a break through just as they were realizing that they were still in love with each other. However, they also discovered that their respective significant others were corporate assassins hired to murder them and steal their research. I was used to writing highbrow theatrical pieces, but I decided to go the b-movie Blaxploitation-style route with this one. It was a vision that came to me when I started to write, so I let it flow. I was about ¾ of the way done and I was pleased with what I had written thus far. Would I have the guts enough to actually shop my script? I wasn't so sure, but I had made enough contacts as a journalist to get something going if I tried hard enough, even though part of me would rather just keep my art to myself and protect it from hypercritical eyes.

"NYELA! GET IN HERE!" Hot Head Tony yelled from his office, interrupting my screenplay reverie.

Shit! I didn't even realize he was here. I made my way to his office and didn't bother trying to figure out what I was about to get scolded for now.

"Have a seat!" he commanded as I got to the doorway.

His computer screen was positioned at an angle so that we could both see it. My site was open to the Quita Ravenell piece I just posted, which was already starting to get traction elsewhere.

"WHY THE FUCK WOULD YOU GET AN EXCLUSIVE NEWS ITEM AND NOT POST IT ON *SPARK's* WEBSITE?"

His face was turning red and I wanted to laugh because he tried desperately to intimidate me, but that just wasn't the case. He was so over-the-top, ridiculous and obviously feeling out of control of the situation.

"I didn't think it would be a problem since you said you weren't interested in Quita Ravenell when I pitched her for the 'Next in Hollywood' issue."

It was beyond me that he didn't even remember the fucked up things he said about her now that she had landed a game-changing role. I had this problem way too much in my field—people, who were allegedly tastemakers, that couldn't see someone's potential unless they already had a famous cosign, or unless they already had major accolades, talking smack, and then getting amnesia about all the terrible things they said.

"Are you trying to undermine me?"

"No, I'm just explaining why I didn't post a news item about an actress you previously shot down for *Spark*. You also mentioned that the movie stuff we post generates the lowest traffic, so I just didn't think it would be a problem."

"GET OUT OF HERE YOU IDIOT!"

"How am *I* an idiot?"

"WHO THE FUCK DO YOU THINK YOU'RE TALKING TO?"

"I'm talking to a man who is being unreasonable."

"GET THE FUCK OUT!"

I guess he didn't call me a bitch due to that sexism lawsuit filed against him a few years ago by a former *Spark* editor, but apparently calling me an idiot and using "fuck" in every other sentence to deflect from the fact that *he* was in the wrong here, was okay.

I wanted to quit on the spot, but admittedly I couldn't fucking shake the fear I had about becoming a fulltime freelancer, so I just stormed back to my desk instead.

Now I *really* wasn't going to do any work. Fuck him!

#Pleasantries

The rest of my day went by without incident and I was glad that I hadn't heard from Reiko or Felani, which meant that I went straight home and caught up on some TV after work. I ate my takeout Thai as I watched back episodes of *American Horror Story,* and didn't realize that I dozed off until Olu's call at about 9:30 startled me awake.

"Hello?" I answered, still trying to figure out what year it was.

"What's good, love?"

I was never going to get over how sexy his accent was and I loved that his vibe was London, but with a New York edge.

"*Love?* What's with you calling me love? I feel like you're trying to butter me up or something."

He laughed. "There are so many directions I could go with that last statement, but I'll keep it clean for now."

"Ew, someone is feeling himself."

"A little bit. But for real though, I'm just calling to check up on you."

I paused.

"You still there?"

"Yes. Check up on me, why?"

"Well, there was that nasty fight you had with that wanker at Felani's party. And we did mention that we were going to be friends, right? I'm a man of my word."

"When did we ever talk about being friends?"

I knew damn well I was playing myself.

"So, you don't want to be my friend?"

I lost my cool and laughed until I snorted. I didn't know why that was so funny but it was, and I definitely needed a laugh even if it was from an unlikely source.

"You're laughing. My job is done," he said right before the call dropped.

I called back. "Was that a dropped call or did you actually just hang up on me?"

I was trying to be ice cold again but my amusement was palpable.

"I told you, I just wanted to check on you. I got you to laugh so my job is done."

"Wait, don't hang up! You still there?"

"Yup."

"But what if I was really on a ledge and trying to front like I'm okay? Hanging up on me would have hardly been the solution."

There was a short pause as I heard someone in the background saying something to him that I couldn't quite make out. "Nyela, I'm actually on a break from recording and I have to go. But are you free on Saturday?"

"Saturday? Um, what time?"

"Probably late afternoon/early evening. I'll get back to you with details. Later."

He hung up abruptly again, and I wondered what I was getting myself into, yet felt excited at the same time. I technically didn't say yes or no, but I also kind of said yes because I didn't object, right? I definitely wanted to hang out with Olu, but would it be a date? Also, I knew how industry dudes were. He was probably just interested in keeping in touch for now until the next intriguing thing snagged his most likely short attention. Then again, I also knew that I was playing myself with all this overthinking.

—

"I can't believe no one got footage of them bitches attacking you first!" Felani said, while rummaging through Reiko's trunk.

It was the Thursday before my meet up, or whatever, with Olu, and Reiko convinced me to stop by her house to pick out some dresses that I could possibly wear. She recently did a photo shoot for a magazine spread on radio it girls and the stylist let her keep some clothes and accessories.

"That's the age we live in now. Everyone is a half-ass detective, so even when it comes to getting shit on video, you still often only get part of the story in some cases," I replied. "Unfortunately for me, there was no reason for cameras to be on me when *you* guys were interviewing, so these ass-hat media people are making shit up and sensationalizing as usual."

"You say that like it's the worst thing in the world," Reiko said. "Sensationalism can work to your advantage, you know! Think of all the people who are winning because of wild press, whether good or bad."

"She has a point," Felani replied as she examined an Ankara print dress.

"First of all, that dress is cute, Felani, and I'm salty that I didn't spot it first," I said. "Second of all, I'm not into attention whoring, *especially* when it comes to negativity."

"You just reminded me—my publicist wants me to do an interview with Hip-Hop Slangaz radio about our fight and I want y'all to roll with me," Felani said.

"Wait, why are *you* being asked to do interviews about *my* fight?"

"One, don't forget I did jump in. Two, they don't *really* give a fuck about the fight. They're just using me for ratings," Felani replied. "I'm going to milk that shit and promote my upcoming shows. So, there goes that press for negative behavior working out for good."

"See? Felani has the right idea. This is attention for negativity, but she might as well move forward with the interview and use it for her own benefit."

"There has been a spike in my mixtape sales ever since that fight became news, so I'm gonna rock with it and see where it goes. I might talk more shit just to keep everyone interested. Now, are you two rolling with me to the interview or nah?"

"I'm in!" Reiko replied.

They stared at me, telepathically communicating that I better not decline because it was more like me to say no to this sort of thing, but I actually wanted to do it.

"I'll do it, when is it?"

"YAY!" Felani and Reiko shouted in unison.

"It's Monday night at 8. I'll keep you both posted! Now how about this dress?"

Felani held the dress closer to her figure for further inspection.

"If you don't want it, I'll take it!" I said.

"You like it, *really*?" Felani replied.

"That dress is bad!" Reiko said. "Plus, you got the body for it and it beats you hiding under those baggy ass jeans and frumpy wife beaters you always like to wear."

"And let the church say, Amen," I chimed in.

"So, you bitches *really* don't like my style, huh?"

"It's not that we don't like your style, but…"

I couldn't figure out how to break it to her diplomatically so I waited for Reiko to chime in.

"Yes it's true. We don't like your style, chica!" Reiko added.

"Damn! Am I really *that* bad? My pops is always getting on me too. I just figured he didn't know any better because he's a man."

"Did you just say your dad, Mr. Smooth American Gangster himself, doesn't know anything about style? You're crazy!" I replied.

She looked at me with a blank expression on her face. This was probably the first time since I'd known Felani that she actually didn't have anything to say.

"Here's the thing," I started. "You're beautiful but…"

"It's hard to tell that you're such a baddie because you dress so hood and frumpy," Reiko chimed in. "Your wardrobe would be what's up if you were Da Brat and this were say, the early to mid '90s. But we need you in the new millennium, and we need people to know that you're a grown ass woman with a banging-ass body."

"I've been getting that from a lot of people around me lately, but I like style from the '90s. I'm a tomboy, and I like dressing the part," Felani replied.

"Yeah but not even your music matches your look," I said. "What *I* like about your sound is that I can sense your golden era hip-hop sensibilities and appreciation, but at the same time you're aware that we've stepped into the twenty-first century, and that you actually *are* a millennial. Now it's time to get your wardrobe together."

"Right! We understand that you don't like being hyper-sexual, but girl, your body, that smooth golden brown skin and those cheekbones give me life," Reiko said.

"Really?"

"YES!" Reiko and I shouted in unison.

"Put on that dress," Reiko commanded.

Felani obliged and we were in awe of how stunning she looked.

"AEOW!" I said. "Girl, what are you a 32D? And you were hiding them!"

"And that ass, yaaaaaaaassss honey!" Reiko added as she and I began dancing around Felani, cat calling like some degenerates on the 2 train.

"Ew, *stop*?" Felani replied.

Reiko grabbed Felani's arm and dragged her toward the full body mirror in her bedroom, with me in tow.

"Look at yourself! You are fly, girl!" Reiko said.

"Hel-lo!" I added as I started undoing Felani's cornrows.

"What are you doing to my hair?"

"You have the most luscious, beautiful fro' in the world and do nothing with it!"

I started taking bobby pins from Reiko's desk and twisted Felani's hair into a funky French roll with a pompadour in front.

"*Now* look at you!"

"Yaaaasssss!" Reiko said.

"Damn, so you're serious about me changing it up, huh?"

"YES!" Reiko and I said in unison.

"Seriously, you gotta start making better and bolder statements with your wardrobe," Reiko said.

"Okay, I'll think about this."

"You got that video shoot coming up in a couple of weeks. Don't think. Make it happen!" I said.

"Like I said, I'll give it some thought, but enough about me. What's good with you and my brother?"

"Olu?"

"*No, Olu!* You know who the fuck I'm talking about!"

I was pretty sure I looked like a dear in headlights because I wasn't expecting the Olu talk tonight, and now I had to give them an update.

"Aw, she's hiding something," Reiko said.

"I'm not! And since Olu is your brother, you probably know all you need to know, right, nosey!"

"I do know all I need to know, including where he's taking you!"

"WHAT!" Reiko shouted. "WHY DIDN'T HE..."

Reiko fell into what could only be a guilty silence.

"Why didn't he what, Reiko?"

"Uh, well, so, remember, he stopped by my radio show yesterday? Well, he pulled me aside after the interview and started picking my brain about things that you like—"

"And you snitched?"

"I mean, I...yeah, I told him what he wanted to know. I didn't get too specific, but I gave him enough detail about the types of things you like, and placed emphasis on the fact that the less over-the-top the better."

"Blasphemy!"

We all laughed.

"I think it's sweet," Reiko said. "Plus, you need to get out and live. See what he's all about and at the very least get some dick!"

"Reiko, you freak! Let's not even go there yet. But since we're talking about this, we are supposed to hang out on Saturday."

"Whaaaaaat?" Reiko said.

"Wanna fill her in, Felani, since your *brother* told you what's up already?"

"Do you really think I'm going to tell either of you? I'm under strict orders not to say anything, and I can keep a secret."

"Bitch!" I grabbed a Beanie Baby from Reiko's dresser and chucked it at Felani.

She laughed.

"Don't be salty! I promised I wouldn't tell, but if Reiko's snitching checks out, Nyela, you'll enjoy yourself."

"So, I guess this could be classified as a date then, huh?"

"You big dummy! Of course!" Reiko snapped.

"I don't know about this, ladies," I said.

"I know you're scared to rock with Olu, but he's a good guy, better than any you have or ever will meet. Trust me on that," Felani replied.

"Sincere started out as a good guy too, though. I put nothing past anyone!"

"But don't you think Olu would already show signs of being a dick by now? He actually has shit to be cocky about," Reiko said. "Also, as someone who doesn't like clichés, you're starting to sound like a fucking broken record with this misanthropy shit."

Those were all excellent points, but I just couldn't shake my cynicism, so I glared at them with a stank look on my face for lack of not knowing what else to do.

"Trust me on this, Nyela," Felani jumped in. "Like I said, I haven't seen Olu *this* interested in a woman since that ex I told you about, but *you're* obviously worthy of his time. I still don't know what he saw in her beyond looks."

"Exactly! You and Olu will be spectacular, end of story!" Reiko said. "Now, try this dress on! You got a date with yo' future babyfawvuh on Saturday, remember?"

She tossed a beautiful fuchsia Catherine Malandrino maxi dress at me and I instantly fell in love with how light and airy the summery fabric felt against my skin. The color also looked nice against my warm brown complexion.

"Girl, you got it going on too! Look at that tiny little waist!" Felani said, patting my butt.

"Right! All that ass back there," Reiko added.

I smiled and admired the dress in the mirror.

"You should wear that on Saturday," Reiko said. "It's supposed to be hot that day."

I looked at Felani, who was definitely reading my mind.

"Don't look at me like that! I'm still not telling you where you're going, but I *can* say the dress is appropriate."

"Then this is it."

#BrooklynNights

It was a quarter to seven when Olu texted me that he was downstairs. I did one final check of my dress, hair and makeup just to make sure I looked yummy enough for him to be impressed, but not so much that I looked like I was trying too hard. My hair was usually in twists, but I decided to wear Bantu knots this time since that was a style that I got the most compliments on.

I stepped off my building's stoop and spotted Olu standing in front of the backseat portion of a luxury town car with tinted windows. There was a sort of Billy Dee Williams circa *Mahogany* kind of cool about him, but with millennial sensibilities. He was tall, lean, delicious, and looked fly wearing a black t-shirt that read, "iRep The Diaspora" in funky red, gold, and green bubble letters that were trimmed in white, dark blue jeans that fit just right—thank goodness they weren't skinny jeans—and some throwback Nike Heineken Dunks, which indicated that he was a sneaker head because those kicks were definitely rare. I was impressed and decided not to try to front like I was too cool, for once.

"Bruh, are you wearing the Heineken Dunks?" I said.

He smiled, and pulled me in for a hug. "What do *you* know about Heineken Dunks?"

"Don't let these sandals fool you. I have had quite the sneaker habit since I was little. The Heineken Dunks have been on my list for a while, but I can't find my size."

He looked me up and down, but lingered for a moment on my feet.

"5 in boys, huh?"

"Yup!"

"Yeah, my sister has that same struggle, but now I just get her customs."

"How's your sister doing anyway? I loved how you gushed about her during our interview."

I slid into the plush backseat as Olu opened the door for me.

"Yup. That's my baby. She's good. She's moving to Cali in August to start her freshman year at USC."

"She got in! That's so dope!"

"Yeah. How about you? Got any siblings."

"Nah, I'm an only child. I have cousins my age though, so I wasn't always totally lonely."

He smelled like Issey Miyake's L'Eau D'Issey Pour Homme, my favorite scent on a man.

I noticed him still sizing me up from my peripheral vision as the driver pulled off. He was intense. I didn't mind, but I still had to summon a little bit of tough girl, even if it wasn't genuine.

"Well!"

"You look stunning. That purple dress might get you in trouble."

"In trouble with whom? Furthermore, this dress is *fuchsia*." I couldn't resist being a smart ass that time.

"I'm a guy. The shit looks purple to me, but that doesn't change the fact that you're wearing the hell out of it."

He gingerly tugged at the strap on my left shoulder and it turned me on, but I ruined the moment, of course.

"Well, fuchsia is an interesting color. Like, it's fuchsia, but it's kind of a pinky-purple, so calling it either pink or purple is technically not wrong, I guess."

He didn't reply verbally. He chuckled and then just studied my face silently for a moment, probably wondering what the hell my problem was, and then started lightly tracing the top of the left side of my neck to my collarbone with his fingers so deftly that I closed my eyes briefly, and inhaled as a quick shiver shot through my body. I at least managed to keep the shiver from being visible, but he probably felt it.

"Nice necklace," he said, referring to my Melody Ehsani lion head choker.

I actually liked that he was so comfortable being in my space, but I still had an ounce of tough girl dignity left.

"Thank you, but you're laying it on thick with the compliments, aren't you!"

He smirked and shook his head.

"So, where are we going?" I added.

His smirk turned into a mischievous grin. "Patience, love."

"I can't take you seriously with that accent."

"You're riffing on my accent now? So you want me to tawlk like dis, hah?"

He started feigning his version of a New York accent, and he was actually good at it, but I still gave him a playful side eye.

"I forget that you're actually an actor," I replied, and then I started trying to fake an English accent. "By the way, that New York accent is actually kind of good."

"But that English one you've got needs a lot of work!"

We laughed and talked about a lot in the 20 minutes it took us to get to our final destination. He told me about the birthday trip he was planning for himself at the end of the year to celebrate turning 27, more about his little sister, his impending t-shirt line, a new investment in a street wear store opening in Brooklyn, his long time fascination with Black American culture, history, and Pan-Africanism, and I told him about my passion for arts and culture, how I hated *Spark*, and eventually began to let my guard down enough to *really* enjoy him. He had always been cool in my encounters with him thus far, but here he was definitely more relaxed and open than the first time we met. I could get used to being acquainted with him on a personal level.

Eventually, we pulled up in front of Lucali and I almost died. It was a quaint old school pizza joint—my favorite type of pizza place. One of many highlights of those field trips that I took with my dad was visiting New York City's best pizza spots. Pizza was our favorite non-vegan food to sneak away and indulge in, and I wanted to surprise him at some point with a visit here but hadn't had the time lately to check it out, though I had long heard the pizza was amazing.

"You good?" Olu said.

"I'm fine, it's just that – did Reiko tell you to bring me here?"

"I did my research, but Reiko was a tough nut to crack. She didn't tell me to bring you here verbatim, but I figured you might like this place based on my chat with her. She's a good friend," he replied.

"I'm flattered that you thought enough about me to even chat with her."

"Yeah, I'm thorough."

I smiled, assured that he was thoughtful. I followed him inside and watched him greet an older man with a thick Italian-New York accent who I guessed was the owner. Olu introduced us briefly, and the man told us to get whatever we wanted before disappearing into a back room.

The restaurant had a grandma's kitchen kind of feel to it. It was dimly lit, surprisingly not crowded for a Saturday, and there were only a few tables and chairs set up. You could also watch the cooks preparing the pizza.

We grabbed a seat at a two-seater nestled against the wall in a corner.

"I love this place. Hov put me on shortly after I signed with Roc Nation," Olu said.

He smiled, obviously pleased with himself.

"Stick with me, love!" he replied, placing a bottle of red wine that he had been holding on to in the center of the table.

I wasn't one for being called names like "honey," "sweetie," or "love," by anyone other than my parents, but there was something about the way Olu called me "Love" that I could get used to.

"I've had this bottle from my uncle's vineyard for years, so I figured I might as well just bring it tonight," Olu said.

"Your uncle *owns a wine vineyard*?"

"Yeah, out in Cali."

"Sheeeeit, people in my family *might* own *one* home, but that's about it!" I replied.

We laughed.

"Yeah, I don't bring it up too much, you know? I'd rather people see *me* first for who I genuinely am and not the privilege. I have trouble with that a lot."

"I'm starting to see you, Olu."

I broke down and told him about the Barnes daddy-daughter dates, and he found it hilarious.

"You mean to tell me your mother doesn't know that you and your dad have been cheating on her vegan diet all these years?" he replied, laughing.

"Unless my dad told her, which I doubt, she still doesn't know. But she's smart, practically psychic, and obviously knows us well, so I'm sure she has an idea what we've been up to, but just lets us slide," I said. "She went vegan shortly after they met and my dad wasn't with it. She can be a bit of a drama queen though, so she kept preaching that she was scared for his health. Eventually, he caved and allowed her to establish a vegan home by the time I came along, but he'd still sneak away and eat what he wanted, and I adopted his habit after he let me taste non-vegan pizza for the first time. Soon, indulging in non-vegan food became our fun secret past time."

"Wow, and I thought *my* parents were out there!" Olu said.

He rehashed some of his story about growing up in London, his travels around the world, his fascination with the United States, and how overbearing his parents were, especially when it came to his education and social status.

"I know you were thrilled when they let you move to the U.S. for high school."

"Hell yeah! See, my mum is more rigid than my dad. He used to do music before he became a stuffy businessman. That musician's spirit never left him, though he has toned it down considerably. That's how he and I did a lot of bonding. He taught me how to play the djembe, and about Fela Kuti, and Ghanaian high-life, but he and my mum were horrified when I expressed interest in music as a career, especially when

I started getting into hip-hop after visiting my cousins in L.A. It's like they forgot that they met at one of my dad's concerts back when he was in a band, but I think the fact that it was hip-hop was extra horrifying for them."

"I think it's so dope that you decided to follow your intuition, and at a young age."

"Yeah, and I'm happy it paid off. My parents and I still have some things to work out when it comes to our relationship, but they're at least speaking to me again now that I'm making my own money and proving them wrong."

"So I guess we're both just born rebels, huh?" I said.

"Yup, we're outliers."

"Hold up, what do you know about Malcolm Gladwell?"

"I've read a book of his or two," Olu replied. "Reading is my next favorite thing to do aside from music."

"I like that about you," I said. "You're smart and you aren't afraid to show it, but you're not haughty about it."

By this point, I didn't even realize that he had grabbed my hands from across the table and started caressing them. His hands were big, but smooth.

"I like a lot of things about you."

"Oh, really? Tell me more."

"Something about you just fucking inspires me. And I mean, those dimples, damn, girl!"

I smiled.

"See, there they are! And that smile too! Seriously, though, I'm not a fan of doing interviews, so I was prepared to be closed off the whole time and not really answering your questions, but you felt familiar," he said. "Not to sound corny, but my brain went into some movie montage type shit like, Ghostface's 'Camay' started playing in the background—"

"And then I started moving in slow motion with my hair blowing in the wind, right?" I offered, cutting him off.

We laughed.

"Yoooo, on some realness, something like that! I brushed it off at first since I see beautiful women all the time, and I was expecting you to ask me the same silly questions they always ask," Olu replied. "But you came prepared, you weren't trying to be buddy-buddy with me too soon, your questions were thoughtful and made me think, and you didn't let me off easy. The energy you brought to our conversation made that cosmic sense of familiarity I felt when I first saw you, feel more real."

"Boy, stop! You gassing me up," I said, delivering my best New York City hoodrat accent.

We laughed.

"I was tight that I didn't ask you for your number then, but I did ask the universe to allow me to run into you again under more casual circumstances."

He winked.

"I appreciate you for keeping it professional. You were definitely one of my favorite interviews ever. And I can't front, I may have had a montage going on in my head too," I replied, still surprised by how open I was being. "But you're used to chicks drooling over you, so you ain't hearing nothing new. I'm surprised I didn't do something goofy like trip over a coffee table or something, though."

He smiled. "See, I like that quirkiness about you. I mean, I would have laughed if you tripped over a coffee table, but I don't doubt that you'd still make it look cute."

"I wouldn't have made that shit look cute. I would have done something dumb like try to play it off by pretending I was doing yoga or some shit, like a cat-cow pose."

"With *that* body you can do whatever you want! Arching your back in a cat-cow pose? Shit, now you got my mind wandering, and I'm trying not to be a savage!"

"Oh, so you're saying you like my bum, huh!" I said, once again feigning an awful English accent.

I cracked up laughing at my own corniness.

"You Americans find English colloquialisms so funny! You got jokes, but saying bum is a lot more subtle than saying ass, donk, or cakes, right?"

We both laughed, and I admired his face again. I loved his full lips, and when his chiseled cheekbones rose every time he guffawed or smiled. He had one deep dimple on his left cheek. I wanted to climb inside of it and stay there forever, cushioned by its surrounding soft flesh.

"I can see how you became the resident heartthrob on *Lockers*," I blurted.

Shit. I was starting to fall for him. Like, for real, for real. I didn't want to give in, but his mahogany gravitational pull was too strong, and I knew I was a goner.

"Thanks, but my inner-caveman wants to get back to how gorgeous *you* are, and how amazing you look in that dress tonight! I'm over here writing rhymes about you in my head."

"Spit something right now!" I demanded.

"Nah. My mum told me if I don't have anything PG-13 to say, then don't say anything at all."

He took a long sip of wine purposely in a way that reminded me of the Kermit the Frog sipping tea meme, and I shook my head playfully. We laughed more, and kept indulging in wine while waiting for the Margherita pie we ordered.

"So, that's why you hired a driver, you wanted to get drunk and talk shit," I said, for lack of anything else more smartass to say.

"Spoken like a true lightweight," he quipped. "I don't drink much, but you buggin' if you think I'm getting lit off this one bottle we're sharing."

"Whatever!" I replied.

"But you didn't say you weren't a lightweight, though," he said.

I rolled my eyes playfully.

"You'll never see me sloppy," he added.

"Duly noted," I replied. "You're a living paradox, but that's not a bad thing."

"Everyone else gives me grief for it, especially my publicist."

"Shouldn't she be happy about that? You're a nice chill client with a good head on your shoulders, and you don't roll with a massive entourage that's always getting you in trouble. No fires to put out, so what's the big deal?"

"I wish you could convince her that! She has been on my case lately about making more of a spectacle of my life. She wants me to be more active on YouTube, making studio and travel vlogs and shit, and she wants me to feed her information about my life so that she can leak it to bloggers. Like this date, for example, if I had mentioned it to her she'd try to have paparazzi waiting for us outside."

"I'm glad you didn't ell her about this, but I get it. She's just trying to do her job. Unfortunately, we're in an age where it's not so much about talent as it is how many people are gawking at you, whether good or bad."

"Yeah, she's good at what she does, but I'm not with the over-sharing, especially when it comes to my personal life, unless I put it in a song. I want the focus on my music and artistry."

"I see that you're active on Instagram, which means you enjoy it. Perhaps the compromise could be that you post more video content there, and occasionally on Snapchat. When you get closer to releasing your album, *that's* when you start posting longer vlog content on YouTube or wherever."

"My thing now is, once the album comes out and once I start acting again, I may never again have the type of privacy that I like again, so I'm enjoying it now, you know?"

"You didn't even have to explain. I totally get it."

"I do like your compromise, though. That's a good work around."

I noticed an elderly couple at a table positioned at an adjacent table and appreciated the fact that Olu didn't try to get cute by buying the place out so we could be alone. I couldn't get over how humble and down-to-Earth he was.

I enjoyed his presence as we continued bantering over pizza and wine for the next two hours. After dinner we went to the Brooklyn Ice Cream Factory for dessert, but it was closed, so we strolled the nearby promenade, and before I knew it, we were at my place for a nightcap at 3 a.m. I was tempted to invite him upstairs since neither one of us wanted the night to end, but I knew what would happen if I did, and I wasn't sure I was ready. Instead, I brought down what was left of a pint of Ample Hills Ice cream that I had, and we chilled on my stoop.

It was cooler outside, but not cold just comfortably breezy. We sat next to each other close enough that our thighs touched.

"I can't believe you've been in New York this long and have never had Ample Hills! This stuff is crack! Try it. There's only a little left, so we can finish it."

I fed him a spoonful of milk chocolate cookies and cream, and watched his eyes roll back with delight.

"Fuck yeah, that's delicious!" he replied.

"You can't be making faces like that around me, yo," I said.

"Why not?"

"I'm vulnerable right now and *you're* liable to get in trouble."

"I don't believe I'm inviting anything I'm not prepared to handle."

He looked me dead in the eyes, and it made me nervous, good nervous. I stuffed my face with the last bit of ice cream to hopefully shift the mood away from the sexual tension we both felt, and he laughed.

"You have this adorable way of trying to redirect energy that's really endearing," he said, draping his long arm around my shoulders and pulling me closer to his side.

"Damn, is it *that* obvious?"

"Probably only to people who study you," he said, staring at me with even more intensity. "Speaking of studying you, let me ask you a more serious question since we're trying to shift focus away from the sexual tension we're *both* feeling right now."

I laughed. I loved how direct, but not in a douchie kind of way, he was.

"Shoot."

I felt slightly more relaxed because questions meant we could get away from the tension for a moment.

"You mentioned a lot tonight that you're not happy at *Spark* anymore, so what's next?"

"I guess I'm still searching for that next thing, you know? I just wish I had the zest for life that I used to have and unfortunately, a lot of that is tied into me being able to make a living by doing what I love."

"I know this might sound cliché, but the only thing stopping you is you," he said, his hand gently gliding up and down my shoulder, making me feel calmer. "What about that screenplay you mentioned? You tried to downplay it, but it's a big deal to write something like that."

"I mean, I guess there's something there. I started working on it again, but—"

"Why don't you complete it and shop it around? You never know what could happen."

"I just don't know."

"Let me put it in better perspective for you. Who are the people and/or things in life that you still have passion for? What lights your soul on fire?"

"Since you put it that way," I replied, sitting up straighter and making eye contact. "The thought of becoming a screenwriter really does make me happy. I guess I just got so used to being frustrated about my life that I suppressed the idea that I deserve happiness."

"Just mentioning that screenplay created a noticeable shift in you. You're glowing now just thinking about it. You did the same thing when you mentioned it at dinner, which means it's something you *need* to make happen."

We locked eyes again.

"Living out your dreams *is* nice, huh?" I said.

"Absolutely. You had a dream to become an entertainment journalist once and you made it happen. Now you're on to the next thing. You're a go-getter, Nyela. I *know* you can make it happen. It's not going to come without struggle, even *I* know that."

"Your passion for your life and work really inspires me. That's why the story I wrote turned out so well. There's something about how you live what you love, and how you want other people to be great, that's just very provocative to me."

My arousal intensified. How is it that in trying to shift the mood we only made the tension between us worse?

"I have a new passion you forgot to mention," he replied.

He brought his face closer to mine before I could respond, and we kissed. It was fervent, and what I didn't even know I needed, but I was sure by now that I wanted it. I wanted *him*. I wanted whatever *this* was happening between us. The more we kissed the more intense we got. I ended up straddling him. My dress was hiked up and I didn't even care. There was no one on the street at this time of night, so we had the block to ourselves.

He started kissing my neck, the top of my breasts, exploring my body with his hands and tongue, and I started fiddling with his belt buckle, but struggling to get it open is what snapped me out of my trance.

"Wait, not here," I said.

"Are you sure you want to do this?"

"Yes. Come upstairs."

When we got up to my apartment, I pulled him inside and slipped my dress off. He took his shirt off and revealed a chiseled arms and torso. I pushed him back onto the couch and straddled him again. He unsnapped my bra, and *that* was another sobering moment. I definitely wanted this, but not yet. I wasn't on some righteous quest to prove my purity or anything like that. I just felt that it was best to get through this date without letting my lust get the best of me.

"Hold up," I said, out of breath.

"You good?" he replied, still cupping my breasts."

"Yes, but—"

"Don't worry about it," he added, gently stroking my cheek.

He got up, put his shirt back on and headed to the door. I followed him.

"I'll call you tomorrow," he said before kissing me one more time, and exiting my apartment.

Did I blow it? *FUCK.*

Part II

#FuchsiaGirl

I found myself back in the midst of routine *Spark* life, nearly a week after my date with Olu, but I didn't even notice the wackness of the last two shitty days of my work week because I was still high from last weekend. I guess I didn't blow it after all because we kept in touch via text messages, phone calls, and even emails—but avoided talking too much on social media other than Snapchat, for now. I liked where this seemed to be going, and I was actually starting to give in to the idea that Felani was right about him.

As far as work shit, we finished closing our annual "Next to Blow" issue for the magazine, which meant no more 16-hour days at least for another three weeks. I was back focusing more on web duty, but I was also in constant brainstorm mode for the print side of things too. I couldn't ever turn my brain off in this line of work. I turned on the radio to catch Reiko's morning show.

"Welcome back to the Mega 109 Morning Riot! This is DJ Blackenstein and I got your girls Cookie Clark and Reiko Rodriguez with me. If you're just tuning in now, you just missed Lady Blaq Widow, who came through to promote her newest mixtape."

"Ooh, yes, there was a little tension in the room too," Cookie said. "Reiko, please tell us what that was all about."

"First of all, y'all know the footage of that wack interview is going to start circulating soon, so everyone will soon be able to see it. The short story is, she's just mad because I blogged that I didn't like her mixtape," Reiko replied. "She subtweeted me about it instead of acting like a big girl and bringing it to my attention offline, as if she can't get in touch with me. I wrote that review two weeks ago, but she decided to wait until the day before she came here to go off on me on Twitter, and then tried to show off here, in my house, for her audience of like, three people."

"Yoooooooo! Reiko, you wildin," DJ Blackenstein said.

"No she's not," Cookie replied. "Homegirl had the ill attitude from jump. She was nice to you, but she was coming at me crazy too and I have no history with her at all."

"Maybe it's a female thing," DJ Blackenstein replied. "Anyway, we gotta get into this new joint sent over from the Olu Major camp, shout out to his manager Fish for sending this exclusive!"

"Hold up, he got a new single?" Reiko said.

"Yup. I'm sure you all recall that whole incident where the blogger who shall remain nameless leaked Olu's original album *material, and then there was all that controversy about Olu's camp changing the album around,"* DJ Blackenstein said. *"Welp, my man Fish hit me this morning with a new joint. He said Olu recorded it in an hour earlier this week straight off the dome. This one is definitely gonna get the ladies. It's called 'Fuchsia Girl,' featuring Big Rick on the hook."*

My heart started beating faster as the beat came in with heavy synths. I also heard some light djembes in the background and saxophone riffs. It was gritty boom bap, but also jazzy and sexy with a hint of Afrobeat, and it made me want to two-step. It had an "Excuse Me Miss" vibe to it. Olu lead in with a laugh and then started speaking over the music.

"There's not enough love in hip-hop so fuck it. You ever met a girl so bad that your heart belongs to her and she don't even know it? You know how you go through the motions plotting about how you're gonna make her yours, and then you finally get that chance to talk to her? But you gotta be ice cold too, so you try to fight it, but then she does some shit like rock a sexy dress that complements her complexion and hugs her curves just right, and your heart just goes dead on arrival. Yeah, she got me like that, but I'm not too proud to be a goner. Ha! Let's go, Big Rick!"

"Fuchsia, hey fuchsia, can you be my future/fuchsia girl, hey fuchsia girl, stick with me and it's all your world."

Big Rick assisted Olu's hook by adding beautiful tenor riffs to the background. I liked this song so much that I unwittingly started to sway to the music and then it hit me. *Oh. My. God. This is about me!*

"Sexy brown girl her heart is guarded/Enters my world and got me started/It began with pool and she beat me at my game/ I tried being cool but my heart's not the same/ Shorty bad got beauty, brains and body/ I'm still dreaming of my fuchsia dress goddess."

I was stunned, but also overwhelmed by a sense of gratitude. I didn't know what my next course of action should have been. Should I call him, FaceTime or text him? No, I should FaceTime. But Felani called me first and interrupted my overthinking.

"Sup, Fel?" I answered, trying to play it cool.

"ARE YOU HEARING WHAT THE FUCK IS ON THE RADIO RIGHT NOW? GIIIIIIIIRL! WHAT DID YOU DO TO HIM?"

"Felani, I didn't *do* anything. Why would he write a song about me?"

"Bitch, are you slow! This ain't some left field shit! You inspired this song! Now own it and stop fucking fronting!"

"I take it you haven't talked to him about our date yet, then."

"He sent me a quick text about how you were a winner, but he didn't give me any details. We've both been busy and as you know, he left for London today."

He had a few UK shows coming up.

"Damn, can't y'all FaceTime or something?" I said. "I'd like to know what's up, and you're the only one who can get the inside scoop!"

"Girl, you acting like *you* can't chat with him directly and get the inside scoop. That's your man, right?"

"Oh my god, Felani, you're so dramatic! No, he's not my man. I mean we've established that we like each other, but we didn't have *that* talk! I gotta get back to work, but we need to link up, me you and Reiko, three the hard way. You're not touring anytime soon are you?"

"Nah, I'm local for now. Gotta work on this album."

"Okay, I'll hit you up."

I hung up just in time to catch the end of the song.

"Whooooooo, that was sexy," Cookie said. *"All that heart and soul he put into it. He had to have been talking about a woman who is or was actually in his life."*

"Why you got that look on your face, Reiko?" DJ Blackenstein said.

Shit. Reiko was good at verbally keeping a secret, but her poker face rendered her a terrible liar. I prayed that she didn't blow my spot up.

"What look on my face? I'm just chillin."

"Ooooh, you're right, Black! She does look shady right now," Cookie said. *"Lemme find out you're Fuchsia girl?"*

"No! HELL NO!"

"Oh that's right your man France ain't having that shit."

Wait, did I miss something? Was she back with France and didn't tell me? We definitely needed a girlfriends powwow.

"You're up to something," Cookie said.

"Um, but, I'm not up to anything. I promise."

"Whatever girl, Imma get it out of you."

"Chill out, Cookie, she's not talking for now. But speaking of, shouts to the homie France Deveaux," Blackenstein said. *"We gotta get into this next commercial break. Mega 109 Morning Riot, keep it locked."*

I've always been intuitive, so I knew this sudden fluttery feeling in my gut was the cosmic workings of fuckery brewing in the universe, hopefully in a good way.

#TheShadyBrunch

I preferred to be at home stretched out on my couch, eating my frustrations away on Saturdays, especially today, but I promised Felani and Reiko that we'd play catch up this weekend.

They were already seated by the time I got to Bedford Hall slightly late. Reiko and Felani insisted on coming here since Felani was also considering the place for her next video shoot and wanted to scout. I *really* didn't feel like dealing with people after what happened to me at work on the same day "Fuchsia Girl" came out, so I had to brace myself because brunch in Bed-Stuy on a Saturday was asking to run into everyone you knew and probably didn't want to see, but at the same time I needed to vent to my girls. This might be my last brunch out for a while anyway, so fuck it.

"Heeeeey boo!" Reiko sang as I greeted them and slid into a chair.

"You aight? You haven't been very responsive to any of my attempts to get the scoop on 'Fuchsia Girl!'" Reiko said.

"I got laid off."

"WHAT!" they shouted in unison.

"But you've been ride or die with *Spark* since you were an intern. How could they do this to you?" Reiko replied.

"Apparently, it's just business, not personal. Budget cuts, yatta, yatta."

"Well, they just lost one of the best editors *and* writers they've had in years. Fuck them! At least you went out on a high note, that Felani feature story for the 'Next To Blow' issue is going to be fire."

"Yeah, print journalism has gone to digital hell, anyway," I replied. "It's time for me to transition."

"Now that you're out of there, which is what you wanted anyway, what's your game plan?" Reiko said. "How's that screenplay been going for you?"

"There's nothing to say about the screenplay. I started working on it again, but not as much as I would I have liked to because of that stupid job. However, I don't even know if I like it enough to actually do anything with it."

"Bullshit! You're so ill with words, whether fiction or non-fiction," Reiko said. "It's time to get over yourself and start pushing your own brand and talents as a business."

"You sound like Olu, and my mom! Geez!" I replied. "That's cool and all, but I'm going to have to freelance for now so I can keep making money. Once that's secure, then I'll worry about pushing my brand more."

"My site just got put on the Queen Nation blog network, so I'm about to start pulling in enough money to hire contributors," Reiko said. "I know you're not into the celebrity gossip thing, but I'm going to need help managing and I want you on my team."

"Thanks for the offer, but no thanks."

"Fine. I could always just put in a good word for you too. Your site has good numbers and I think they'd take you on their network for their TV/film niche as long as you're consistent with posting content."

"I'll think about that, thanks boo."

"I can hook you up with some stuff too," Felani said. "I could hire you to update my site more consistently, and for social media management, which would help my publicist tremendously. She needs to get a fucking clue."

"But I thought you had one of the best publicists in the game," I replied.

"I mean, my father swears by her because of the weight her name carries, but I think she's just okay. She's too Hollywood—you know, one of those people who works behind-the-scenes and pretends to love their job as is, but actually wants to be famous them selves, and she calls everyone her best friend, which gets on my nerves."

"But isn't your goal to reach a wider audience?"

"I guess it is, but she's talking all this stuff about how I need to start informing her of my whereabouts so she can have paparazzi show up. I ain't with that shit."

"Well, she is a socialite, so that comes with the territory," I replied. "But to answer your solicitation about your site and social media management, I'll think about that too. I may actually have a new gig coming up. I got an e-mail today about a possible opening at *Regality* magazine. They're looking to step their website up and thought I might be good, so I meet with them next week."

"Those bitches stay putting me on their worst dressed list," Felani said.

"Aren't we supposed to be working on that, though?" Reiko replied.

"Yeah, but don't rush me. I'm working some things out. I need to make a shift that's going to get some *real* attention."

"What are you planning?"

"You'll see."

"Aight, she's not talking," I replied. "Anyway, Reiko, when the fuck were you gonna tell me that you're back with France?"

Reiko took a swig of water and gazed at a table across the room, most likely willing herself to disappear.

"I…I know you don't like him and I honestly just didn't know how to tell you."

"I don't know your situation with France that well, but I do know that that dude is a dick and I'm also concerned," Felani said.

"Everyone says that, but they just don't know what we have. I *know* we're good together—"

"If he'd stop fucking cheating on you, then maybe," I interrupted.

"What do you know about relationships? You still held on to hope when Sincere started acting like you didn't exist anymore."

"Yooo, you ain't have to go there!" Felani jumped in.

We all got silent momentarily, and I took a sip of my iced tea to keep myself from responding because that low blow hurt.

"Shit. That was a fucked up thing to say," Reiko said. "I'm really sorry. I just—"

"Forget it. I should have known better than to question anything about you and France."

The waitress interrupted our awkward moment by asking if everything was okay. The interruption was brief, but it helped to soften the mood, and Felani took advantage of it to switch the topic to Olu and I.

"So, Miss Fuchsia Girl…"

I looked down and started massaging my forehead.

"Nothing to say, all of a sudden?"

"What do you *want* me to say?"

"You can start by telling us how your date went. Did you have fun at Lucali?"

"Aaaaw, it's so dope that he took you there!" Reiko said.

"Right! That spot was at the top of my hit list!"

"Did you like it?" Felani said.

"I did. I'm *definitely* going to take my father there, now."

"So, how was the date? How do you feel about Olu now? Still think he might be shady?" Felani replied.

"The date was amazing. We ate and then pretty much chilled the entire night at the Brooklyn promenade, and then on my stoop just talking. We have a lot more in common than I thought. It's surreal how thoughtful he is, and his attention to detail is superb. He is actually a good guy, dare I say it!"

"I told you! When he's into a woman it's a wrap," Felani said. "He doesn't fall often, but when he does, he goes *all the way in*. You got yourself a good one."

"Well, I can't say that I *got* him."

"But he wrote you a fucking love song!" Felani said. "You *know* he's into you. Why are you being so gotdamn difficult! I'm calling it right now. Olu is your boyfriend and soon you'll be at paparazzi's favorite couple status."

I sighed.

"Whatever. Look, again, we didn't have any discussions about getting involved, so I don't want to get too ahead of myself," I replied. "You already know how creatives are. They take inspiration in some muse, run with it real quick, and end up with a hot product, nothing more or nothing less, before getting bored."

"Nah, definitely something more," Felani added. "It's a wrap for him, and probably you too if you'd stop fronting!"

"I'm with Felani on this one," Reiko said. "But stop trying to act all demure! What happened *after* you *talked* on your stoop? You know, during that span of time that you inspired this song."

"Word!" Felani added.

"Damn, you chicks are nosey!"

I started stuffing my face with home fries. I couldn't talk if my mouth was full.

"Look at her trying to avoid this part of the conversation," Reiko said. "I know you can be secretive, but spit it out! Did you get some Olu peen?"

They high-fived each other, and I almost choked on my last mouthful of potatoes.

"No! Well…I mean, almost."

"ALMOST! AAAAAW!" they chorused in unison.

"We started making out on my stoop. It got really hot and heavy so we took it to my apartment, but then he unsnapped my bra and that was enough for me to snap out of it. I stopped it before it could go any further."

"WHY!" Reiko yelled.

"I don't know. It was just a feeling, I mean, hell yeah I want him, he's yummy, but I also just decided not to do it then. It is what it is."

"What is this high school?" Reiko said.

"But it was our first date!"

"SO!" they chorused.

"I mean, I felt comfortable enough with him, but something just told me to leave it alone in that moment. Sex can complicated things sometimes, you know?"

"You just like to front, but you're definitely no goody-two-shoes," Reiko said. "Olu is *not* Sincere. Get into him please, and let him literally get into you! You could use a bit of loosening up!"

"I *am* into him, but Sincere started out as a nice guy too."

"You making me repeat myself again!" Felani said, starting to clap in between each syllable. "Olu has *been* friends with some of the most influential people in the world, he comes from well established money; he has *been* around power and glitz his entire life! He'd already be a megalomaniac by now if that were going to happen!"

"Right! He's a *real* celebrity, remember?" Reiko said. "*Why* do we keep having to repeat this? God, you're fucking stubborn!"

I scrunched up my face like a petulant child.

"Have some faith! He's not going flip it on you *and* he's like, *the* bluntest man on the planet," Felani said. "And if I have to repeat any of this again, I'm going to knock you out!"

"Bye Felicia," I said. It was all I could think of.

Felani cringed at the sound of her real name as well as the now common colloquialism, #ByeFelicia, both of which she hated.

"You lucky I like you," she replied.

"You love me, by the way, but I guess you might be right."

"I *know* I'm right, you just hardheaded, beyotch!"

177

Felani stuck her tongue out at me and we laughed. Our moment was interrupted when Cookie appeared at our table.

"Heeeeeey, girls," she said, bending down and kissing Reiko on the cheek.

"Hey boo," Reiko replied. "What you doing here?"

"Girl, I got dragged to some Women of Power brunch that Cynda does. She's my manager now."

"But I thought you didn't trust her," Reiko said.

"I didn't used to really rock with her like that, but I'm about my business. I'm trying to raise my profile, and to be honest she gets the job done. Plus, we went to college together. I didn't know her that well then, but I'm going to show a little Tiger love, for now."

"But I thought she was a publicist," Felani said.

"She is. You know she's one of them chicks with a million slashes in her name and no one really knows what she does. I don't know how she keeps it together but she has a good business track record, so here I am," Cookie replied.

"She keeps it together because she's a publicist with a publicist and a team of assistant minions that she probably emotionally abuses," I quipped.

"Girl, you are hilarious," Cookie replied. "You're right though, but I'm trying to get my current book sales up, which would help to convince my publishers to give me a new deal. Any networking I can do is crucial, even if it's with people I only half-like."

"Thanks for the clarity," Reiko replied.

Cookie wedged a chair between Reiko and Felani, who were sitting opposite me at a rectangular wooden table. I smiled half-heartedly, wondering when Reiko and Cookie got so cool.

"I'm the first one here from our group, but the others say they're nearby so I'll sit with you for now," Cookie said. "By the way, Felani, you did your thing at Webster Hall the other night. I can't wait until your album drops. When's the release date?"

"The label is still figuring things out, but most likely I'm out a month after Olu. They're trying to do this summer/fall takeover thing, but it's not set in stone."

"That would be dope," Cookie replied. "Speaking of sexy ass Olu, how fly is that new song? I wonder who he's talking about."

Felani sipped some water and Reiko and I exchanged quick glances because we knew she was fishing. Cookie didn't seem to notice our reactions, but thankfully the conversation got cut short by Cynda's arrival, along with Morena and two other women in tow.

They headed to our table once they spotted Cookie.

"HEY GIRLS!" Morena shouted.

She headed in my direction first and I barely spoke a greeting before she kissed me on the cheek, like I had forgotten about that bitchy ambush at the Hip-Hop Slangaz party. I tried to feign excitement, but I was pretty sure my fake smile and uncomfortable demeanor gave me away.

Morena made the rest of her rounds, skipping Reiko, while Cynda headed over to me.

"You ladies should join us at this table, it's big enough, plus there aren't any other tables available at the moment" Cookie said.

I gave Cookie the side eye, but got a group text from Felani sent to Reiko and I saying, *"Let's play along, please. I know this isn't ideal company, but I see that fashion blogger who keeps ignoring my publicist."*

We complied.

"Hi, I'm Cynda," she said sticking her hand out.

Was this broad serious?

"Cynda, we've met before. I just saw you at the Hip-Hop Slangaz party."

"Really?"

"Yes, it's me – Nyela."

There was no hint of recognition on her simple ass face.

"It's *Nyela Barnes*, from *Spark* magazine. We spent the day together at the King Tootsie shoot, you pitch me other clients every other day, and you randomly gave me some relationship advice the last time I saw you at the Hip-Hop Slangaz party."

"Oooh girl, that was you! You look different. I didn't recognize you with your twists out."

I was pretty sure I looked the same whether my hair was twisted or pulled back into an Afro puff. I suspected that this was more about trying to make me feel insignificant than it was a genuine issue of recognition.

"Yeah, well, you know, people tend to change clothes and take their twists out," I replied.

We shared a moment of fake laughter. She *had* to have known that I was being sarcastic—but I wasn't too sure, because then she handed me a book with her picture on the front cover.

Do Your Thang Girl: Cynda's Surefire Tips For Love, Life and Success. I read the title out loud and miraculously managed to keep a straight face.

"Because you know I do it all," Cynda said. "I just figured I might as well make a book out of my excellent advice since everyone is always asking me to lend my wisdom."

I felt a smile creeping across my face yet managed to successfully keep myself from falling apart.

"How nice," was all I mustered back.

I made eye contact with Reiko and Felani, but we averted our gazes swiftly to keep from cracking up. Cynda made her rounds to the other ladies, and she was dressed just as ridiculously as her behavior. She was wearing a green sequined maxi dress and 6-inch Louboutins covered in silver rhinestones, and she was passing out copies of her book to everyone who didn't have one.

"Ladies, this book isn't even out yet, so you got the exclusive. Aren't we excited? Yaaaay!"

Cynda and her cronies, except for Cookie, clapped for her and finally, the introductions of the other anonymous women began, though I did recognize their faces from social media and being on the scene. The first woman who stood up to greet us, at Cynda's suggestion, was also from the Cynda School of Ridiculous Wardrobe Choices. It wasn't artsy ridiculous, though. She was simply trying too hard to serve eccentric chic.

Her weave was black with pink and blonde ombré tips, and it was styled in barrel curls that flowed down to her waist. She was wearing a white tank top with a high-waisted purple mini tutu—a first dance recital kind of tutu, not a chic tutu—leopard print Jeffrey Campbell Litas with knee high socks and a yellow blazer with pointy shoulders.

"Hi, I'm Princess Jones and I run the number one urban fashion site in the world," she said, followed by a twirl. "Follow me on Instagram, Snapchat, and Pinterest for a daily dose of what to wear when you need chic the most."

No thanks.

The next girl who stood up was really fucking pretty. I hadn't been able to keep my eyes off her since she arrived with the hyena pack. She was tall and slender with a smoky cinnamon brown complexion. She was wearing a black and white striped shirt-dress, one of the more minimalist wardrobe choices of women in that crew today, and her curly hair was piled on top of her head in a messy bun.

"Hello, everyone," she said, in a way that came across as more demure, and not as obnoxiously sycophantic about herself as the other women, but still with a slight twinge of self-importance.

"I'm Miriam Ghirmai, and I'm a model."

"Hold up," Felani interrupted. "You were in Olu Major's video for 'Lady Gamers,' right?"

"Yeah, I've been in a few videos since then, but Olu and I go way back."

Felani and I made eye contact and I realized from the look on her face that she only asked the question so that *I* could know that this was the woman responsible for Olu's previous epic heartbreak.

"You guys go back, alright, *mmm hmm,*" Morena said.

"What?" Miriam replied, followed by a feigned coy laugh.

"Child, that man was sprung over her," Morena explained.

"Until she got knocked up by King Tootsie," Felani replied.

"That's his side of the story, " Miriam said. "And I'm sorry, you are?"

"Bitch, you know who I am!"

"This isn't how brunch with wonderfully fabulous women is supposed to happen," Cynda chimed in. "Let us settle down and remember that we're classy ladies."

This was the first time I actually appreciated Cynda's existence.

"We're all introduced now, so what's everyone working on? Felani, I hear your album is coming along well," Cynda said.

"Yeah, it's coming along," Felani replied, taking a swig of her newly replaced cranberry juice while glaring at Miriam.

"Well, you know Reiko and I have our radio show already slaying in ratings," said Cookie. "We just found out yesterday that the Morning Riot is already the number one syndicated morning show in the country."

We all cheered, which helped ease some of the tension, even though some of the clapping was definitely disingenuous.

"You guys dropped that new Olu Major song," Princess said. "Oh my god, how much do we love it?"

A few women at the table, myself included, shot her a glance. Why did she think it was appropriate to bring the song up after what almost just happened between Felani and Miriam? I wished I had a seat ejection button with her name on it.

"'Fuchsia Girl' is bananas!" Morena said. "Miriam, you my girl, but you played yourself."

"Whatever," Miriam replied, "I'm good with my new boo."

"That's what gold diggers like you tell themselves so they can sleep at night," Felani said.

"Anyway!" Miriam snapped, rolling her eyes.

"Try me!" Felani replied.

Miriam let Felani's last quip slide after Cynda told her to settle down.

"Personally, I'd be kind of salty if it were me, Olu really came up in the world," Morena said. "And once again, he's fucking gorgeous."

Miriam gave her a side eye.

"So you like being part of King Tootsie's babymama army?" Felani said.

The rest of us remained silent, mortified and not sure which way to look. The only salvation here was that Miriam and Felani were on opposite sides of the table, but there was no telling what an angry Brownsville girl was capable of. Felani might fuck around and teleport to the other side of the table to beat Miriam's ass if she got mad enough. I was secretly here for it.

"So, we can all agree that 'Fucshia Girl' was an amazing song," Cynda said. "Now can we please move on to another topic? Ladies don't behave this way. I'm getting embarrassed."

"I got this, Cynda," Miriam replied, screwing her face up in a way that you'd imagine a gold-digging-mean-girl-model-bitch preparing for battle would, while still looking freakishly beautiful in the process. "Olu's nice guy shit got boring, so I bounced. It is what it is. By the way,

I'm King Tootsie's number one. And I should note that my man just bought me an Audi and a house in New Jersey. I'm good."

King Tootsie lived in Miami most of the time, and at least two of his babymamas lived with him there. I was going to keep that thought inside my head, though.

"Uh…speaking of 'Fuchsia Girl,'" it's projected to hit number one as early as next week," Reiko jumped in.

She was definitely trying to poke.

"That's dope! Classic songs live forever," replied Morena. "Material things depreciate in value over time. I'd take the song any day."

"Whose fucking friend are you!" Miriam snapped.

Morena shrugged and mouthed, "Sorry."

"Morena has a point. When someone makes art about you it means you've made a phenomenal impact," Cookie said. "And I did hear that the song was inspired by actual events, even down to the woman actually wearing this bad-ass fuchsia dress."

How the fuck did she know that?

I glanced at Reiko, who swiftly averted her eyes and looked down at her plate. I wished I had telekinesis so I could yank her chair from underneath her.

"Whoever she is, she's a lucky girl. We've already established my next point, but I can't stress enough how foine he is!" Princess said. "You know how much ass probably gets thrown at him on a regular basis? He *has* to be smitten to write something like that. But I hope that girl is smart. I mean, if *I* were Olu's girl, I'd use it to help further my brand. She could probably launch a line of cosmetics, or open up a fashion boutique or something. I sure would!"

I shifted in my seat, wishing I could disappear.

"Oh, Please! Olu is a sucker for a pretty face," Miriam replied. "It don't take much for him to go gaga, but you got the right idea about branding, Princess. That's why I played my position and got what I could out of the situation."

Felani teleported to the other side of the table and we all watched, stunned for a brief second, trying to make sense of when she got super powers. I snapped out of my shock, sprang out of my seat and grabbed Felani right as she swung, causing her Brownsville Fist of Fury to lightly graze Miriam's face versus making its intended impact.

"Chill! *We* know he moved on. Let it go," I said, happy that *I* wasn't involved in the brawl.

Reiko joined me to help wrangle a belligerent Felani back into her chair as Cynda and Morena worked in Miriam's corner to get her to calm down too. Felani returned to her seat, but Miriam decided it was best to leave, which actually eased some of the awkward tension. Luckily we didn't get kicked out of the restaurant.

"So what's going on with you and Sincere, Miss Nyela?" Cynda said.

This bitch went from allegedly not knowing who I was, to all up in my business in zero to sixty.

"There's nothing going on between me and Sincere, and didn't you just meet me for the first time today, or something like that?"

It was all the shade I could summon for now, but it seemed to work for a moment. Cynda gave me a diffident smile and shifted focus back to stuffing her face.

"But if nothing is going on with you and Sincere then what was all the fighting with Nasreen about at Felani's party, and at the Hip-Hop Slangaz shindig?" Morena said.

I took a deep breath to keep myself from chucking my fork between Morena's too thickly drawn in eyebrows. I was starting to see what Reiko was talking about.

"Sincere is a douche who doesn't know how to break up like a big boy," Reiko said, sensing my annoyance.

I glanced at her, telepathically communicating my appreciation, but the moment was fleeting.

"That's not what *I* heard," Morena replied. "He said that you'd cry and threaten to hurt yourself every time he would try to break up with you, so he'd stick around for your safety."

"WHAT?" Felani, Reiko and I chorused in unison.

"And you believed that lie?" I replied.

"That's my best friend," Morena said. "He usually keeps it one hundred."

I wanted to question exactly when she and Sincere became "best friends," but Morena was another one of those industry types who claimed to be best friends with everyone, so it was a moot point.

"I'm pretty sure I know Sincere better than you do. *I'm* the one who introduced him to this world," I replied. "The version you know is a downgrade from the man *I* met, so you and basics everywhere can hang on to his every word if y'all want to."

"Oh, come on! You know he's good at what he does! Girls are jocking him because he's talented and *foine*!" Morena replied.

She had a point; he did look good, but I would not surrender to her madness about him being talented.

"That's great, Morena. This conversation is over."

Cynda's end of the table stared at me as if I had a penis growing out of my forehead.

"I cosign Nyela on this one. I know how Sincere gets down and he is an asshole," Cookie said. "Speaking of…Nyela, girl, he has been writing a lot of blogs lately about how to deal with desperate and psycho ex-girlfriends and the general assumption is that he's talking about you."

"I know about the dickmatized joint, but there's more?"

Cookie pulled up his latest post on her phone and handed it to me.

The Crazy Ex-Girlfriend Diaries

"Sometimes you move on, but your ex is still stuck in the past. She's so stuck in the past that she doesn't want to see you happy to the extent that she'll terrorize you and your new girl. I'm not gonna lie, I know my pipe game is crazy, I'm making money and basically, I'm a good catch. So, of course it's hard to let go of a fine specimen such as myself. But at some point, she gotta give it up.

First it was the party where I was unceremoniously attacked. Now she got my bad chick scared out here in these streets…"

"I'm done reading this bullshit!" I snapped, shoving Cookie's phone back in her hands.

Everyone at the table was staring at me.

"Here's the thing. He's getting away with what you put up with in the relationship," Cynda said.

"Say what?" Reiko replied, while looking at Cynda with a raised eyebrow.

"I'm serious, my girlfriends. Nyela allowed him to deny her of her Queenly Essence and now he's still putting that negative energy out there even though they're no longer together."

I made eye contact with Felani and almost choked on my sip of water because I wanted to laugh so hard at the look on her face. We telepathically communicated the ridiculousness of this entire situation. In fact, this ambush brunch was so fantastically absurd that we *had* to let it continue just to see how far it went. Perhaps we'd all share this story with our grandkids one day.

"So, tell me more about this Queenly Essence theory," I replied, briefly catching a glimpse of Reiko trying to stifle her laughter.

"When it comes to your divine Queenly Essence, you have to learn how to meditate and pray so that you can always remain on your game and become an alluring woman. I explain it all in my book," Cynda said. "You have a free copy now so consider yourselves blessed. It officially comes out in July, so you should read it as soon as you can and thank me later."

"Girl, you are so amazing!" Princess said, genuinely in awe. "I'm always trying to share your sage wisdom with other women but sadly, not all of them are ready to receive such brilliance."

Felani glanced at Princess, who was oblivious, with her mouth agape and eyes widened in disbelief. It was the funniest facial expression I had ever seen her make. Cookie was staring into her phone probably doing whatever she could to tune out the madness around her.

"I can't!" Reiko said, palming her face and finally breaking down in a fit of laughter.

I started cracking up too and so did Felani. Even Cookie had a smirk on her face and appeared to be trying really hard to keep from cracking up. Princess, Morena, and Cynda weren't amused.

"You ladies are laughing now but read my book, then come to some of my life coaching workshops. You'll gain a goldmine of wisdom," Cynda said. "You can also check out my blog. There's tons of free advice that I provide there too, and the real testimonials speak volumes. You won't be laughing at me for long."

"*Riiiight*," I replied, just as my phone vibrated. It was a text message from Olu.

Hey Fuchsia Girl, Miss u.

I stared at my iPhone screen longer than I should have and cracked a smile.

"Oooooh, what you smiling about?" Reiko said.

I snapped out of my trance and put my phone away.

"Nothing, just a funny text from…my dad."

"Whatever, b!" Felani said. "Imma leave it alone though."

"So, you got a new boo?" Princess said.

"Something like that."

#RegalityMagazine

Regality was a fashion, pop culture, and lifestyles magazine geared toward women of color that was started in the '60s. They'd recently been acquired by Kingsly Placid, one of the biggest publishing houses in the magazine world, and had been expanding their brand in the digital department. Their digital portion was relatively new, and late, which was unfortunately the case for a lot of magazines that once used to be the shit back when print was a thing. However, despite my understanding that this was the 21st century, I still preferred print to digital. I still had actual copies of some of my favorite magazines and often reminisced about when my mom would get *Regality* in the mail when I was a little girl. The photo shoots were always fresh and unique. I loved staring at the pages for hours and being inspired by the images of women who looked like me, and reminded me of what I wanted to become one day, as well as the solid writing. There was a nice balance of intelligent progressive feminism with fluff entertainment, and I devoured every word.

Today it seemed that they were struggling to stay relevant, and the Kingsly Placid merger only added more pressure to be more active in the digital space and keep their numbers high across the board. Unfortunately, the latter manifested in the form of most stories on the

195

site being sensationalized and egregious gossip with questionable sources, just like the rest of them, even though that wasn't *Regality's* overall brand. As far as the print magazine, they rotated the same five women who were proven to sell on the cover every other month.

The *Regality* magazine headquarters looked exactly as I imagined—like a pink frilly nightmare. I noticed when I got off the elevator that the walls were baby pink. There was a hot pink rug in front of the receptionist's desk and to my right I saw cream armchairs in front of a glass coffee table, covered in *Regality* magazines from various decades.

I greeted the receptionist and headed to the armchair swathed in pink leopard print pillows, to wait until the website's deputy editor was ready for my interview.

I did what I do best: pulled out my phone and started trolling the web as if it ever really changed. Eventually, I found something on Morena's site that piqued my interest. It was only noon, but somewhere between yesterday and today I missed more drama between Reiko and Lady Blaq Widow. The item was on Morena's site, but she picked it up from Chatty Abernathy who seemed to be the originating source, so I headed to that site for the scoop.

> *First it's popular writer Nyela Barnes*
> *fighting every damn body in the world over her*

celebrity blogger ex-boyfriend. Now, her bestie Reiko Rodriguez is Twitter beefing with some rapper on the come up. Apparently Reiko posted a blog linking to Lady Blaq Widow's mixtape but she added her own two cents about the project, saying that it wasn't Lady Blaq Widow's strongest material and all hell broke loose.

Last week, Lady Blaq Widow paid a visit to the Morning Riot to do a promotional interview for her upcoming promo tour and confronted Reiko about what she said.

Reiko, like the hoodrat that she is, took the bait and the interview got tense. Both angry birds continuously shaded each other throughout the 40-minute interview despite DJ Blackenstein and Cookie Clark trying to diffuse the situation, and Lady Blaq Widow did not leave a happy camper. She took to Twitter again and started venting her frustrations. See the tweets below:

People who know wassup r diggin Webbed 101 *but it's 2 bad there's more fake ass tastemakers like @RadioKoKo in positions of power.*

Funny thing is, when I called u out in ur face u ain't have much to say @RadioKoKo.

First of all, I ain't never fake. My track record speaks for itself and ur mixtape just ain't poppin   @LadyBlaqWidow_.   #OwnIt #SorryNotSorry

We'll see how wack I am when I come see u after work so-called bad girl. Won't be no cameras rolling @RadioKoKo.

SMDH. It gets worse. Lady Blaq Widow actually did show up to the radio station with some of her cronies, carrying bags full of candy — like the kind you give out at a kid's birthday party — with "Trick or treat Reiko" written all over them. But according to Reiko, Lady Blaq Widow was all talk and no action. More from her Twitter:

So, @LadyBlaqWidow_ and her squad of donkeys couldn't get upstairs because my place of business has security.

When I came downstairs after wrapping up the show, I walked right past those broads and they ain't say nothing to me LOL @LadyBlaqWidow_.

Stop lyin' u didn't come downstairs but I guess thumb thuggin' ain't easy! @RadioKoKo

#GirlBye @LadyBlaqWidow_.

I'll catch yo ass next time when you can't hide behind security @RadioKoko.

And on that note, I'm blocking you. I'm tired of giving you attention and followers @LadyBlaqWidow_.

Welp, we'll see what happens next time these two end up in a room together. You know the beef is never over with birds of this variety. How much y'all want to bet these broads get to brawling at the next event? Seriously, though, they all need to grow up. Lady Blaq Widow needs to toughen up as an artist because there will certainly be more critiques of her music to face,

and Reiko and her little writer friend Nyela both
need anger management.
            -Chatty Abernathy, the Gossip Slayer

A few things: I wanted to know how the fuck my name got involved in this nonsense when I wasn't even involved. *Why* did this Chatty Abernathy person feel the need to *keep* bringing *me* up? And *who* the fuck *was* Chatty Abernathy anyway? I knew most of the popular bloggers running the gamut of topics by face, faux personas included, but this bitch was still anonymous yet he or she seemed to have all the industry insider information. Someone I knew, or at the very least someone with access to this world must have been feeding him or her information. Chatty Abernathy is way too fucking accurate despite his or her penchant for exaggeration. I needed to start paying closer attention to the people in the room at the next event. I refused to believe that anyone close to me would sell me out like that.

"Nyela?"

Tina Jones, the managing editor for *Regality* magazine in print and deputy editor for the website, interrupted my thoughts.

She was gorgeous and dressed impeccably. I enjoyed fashion, but I was no label whore. However, I browsed enough knowledgeable fashion sites and magazines to know that I spied at least three major designers across her boobs, ass and feet. She was wearing an Yves St.

Laurent blazer, slouchy sequined Tete by Odette pants and Isabel Marant wedge sneakers.

I had heard stories that the women at this place were big on having a polished image, which was a huge difference from the urban world. I thought I had a nice sense of style, or at least that's what I'd been told, but I hoped they didn't expect me to dress as if I was walking a runway every day I showed up to the office if I got the gig.

She gave me a quick handshake and looked me up down. The imperceptible expression on her face gave me no inclination of how she felt about my appearance, which made me nervous, but I breathed and tried to remain calm as I followed her down the pink corridor to her office.

"Get comfy," Tina said, gesturing to the chair in front of her desk.

I obliged.

"That is a lovely dress you're wearing," she said, intensely eyeing me. "Diane Von Furstenburg?'

"Yes," I replied.

I put no thought into what designer made this pastel shift dress when I yanked it out of my closet this morning. I didn't know whether I should have been impressed or concerned that homegirl just called out my label off the top of her head like a human *US Weekly*.

She explained that she used to work strictly for *Regality's* print side, but the company thought it was cute to also place her in charge of the website after a round of layoffs. It was the old two jobs, one salary okie doke, once again.

Tina initially had no support online because the big wigs didn't see the point in hiring a multi-person staff for a website, but she convinced them to get some bodies working after realizing that running a website wasn't as easy as the suits often thought, and also because she was hospitalized for nearly two days due to exhaustion and dehydration as a result of overworking. They now had three other permalance girls—permalance was basically a freelancer that worked full time hours, but with no benefits and more flexibility to work from home—in addition to a few freelance columnists working on everything from music, to fashion, to beauty, but they needed someone who could give them the goods on TV/Film. That was where I was necessary.

"Bottom line. I like your blog, I've seen you're clips—good story on Olu Major in *GQ*, by the way," Tina said.

"Thank you."

"How was that?"

"How was what, the writing process for that piece?"

I knew damn well what she was *really* asking me about.

"Spending the day with Olu, duh! He's a hit with our online crowd, especially since that 'Fuchsia Girl' song came out."

She was still hard to read, but I felt a tinge of jealousy as I started to wonder if she also had a crush on Olu and I hoped my fidgety hands weren't making me look guilty.

"*Hello?* What's that look on your face about?"

Shit! My polka face failed.

She seemed like the type who would try to formulate opinions and spread gossip based off of body language and assumptions. I sat up straighter in my chair and did my best to keep my hands still and my face blank.

"Oh, I was just making this face because of how much success he's having with his female fans. I got to see more of his goofy side that day, so it's funny to hear women gush over him because he's actually very normal," I replied. "Almost too normal, a little awkward even."

Olu was far from awkward, but it was the best deterrent I could come up with.

"The finest ones are always the goofiest," she said.

"Ain't that the truth?"

We shared a quick laugh, and it was the first time I saw her shed some of her iciness.

"Anyway, I like you. Think you can handle this gig? It's simple. Eight updates a day, maybe more or less depending on news flow, five days a week, occasional weekend pieces if there's breaking news, and celebrity interviews," she said. "I'd need you in the office at least once a week and on our weekly content meeting call. But for the most part you can work from home and I won't bother you as long as you stay in your lane."

"What's the rate?"

"$2,500 a month. You invoice every two weeks."

$2,500 a month for a gig that was really just a full-time job, and without insurance! It was always companies that actually had money that were the cheapest.

"Can we bump that to $4,500 a month?"

"Nice try. You're lucky they're giving me *this* budget. So do you want it or not?"

Shit! I needed to bring in at least *some* money, and no one was really hiring at the moment. I refused to dip into my savings or ask my parents for money. Plus, my mom would be so excited about me working here, and I could hopefully get more cover stories. I also had other freelance offers on the table so I guess this couldn't hurt.

"I'll take it."

"Great, I'll take you to Sheena in HR and she'll get your paperwork started. Online content meetings are every Tuesday at noon."

She swiftly left her desk and exited the room without warning me to follow her, but I got it. I trailed behind her as she walked briskly ahead of me, leading the way to HR, and rattling off information. She talked straight ahead as I followed closely trying to keep up with her pace.

"My assistant will send you the dial-in number for the editorial meetings and I need for you to get back to me by end of day tomorrow about what day you'll be available to come into the office so we can have a desk set up for you. Cool?"

"Got it!"

I didn't know what I was walking into with *Regality,* but I was glad it was a slight deviation from what I was used to. Perhaps this environment would be more civilized, and I wouldn't have to prepare to be cursed out on a daily basis simply for breathing.

I stepped out of the Kingsly Placid building onto chaotic Midtown streets. The mid-June air felt good, and I was unusually optimistic. I took advantage of this surge of good energy flowing through me and decided to walk 36 blocks to my favorite Barnes & Noble in Union Square, instead of going home right away. I hadn't worked out in a while so fuck it, walking would be good! I changed into my flats and first headed to Duane Reade to get some water. Olu texted me as I pondered life's important quandaries like, Fiji or Smart Water. It had been at almost two weeks since our first date and I missed him. We had often FaceTime'd, texted and Snapchatted since we last saw each other, but nothing beat seeing him in the flesh.

Hey Fuchsia, I'm back in town and would love to see you. You free this weekend?

Sure, what did you have in mind?

I got something in mind, but I need you to block out your entire Saturday afternoon.

You're not plotting to kidnap me, are you? Why so cryptic?

You worry too much. I'll pick you up at your crib at noon.

Sounds good.

I was less surprised at myself this time for being so excited about another date, and a lot more cooperative. Fuck it! I liked him a lot. There was no future in my frontin,' but I still couldn't help but hope that this man was genuine.

#SomethingMajor

Olu still wouldn't tell me what we were doing today, but I couldn't wait to see him. I also couldn't figure out what the heck to wear. I mean, I would love to just show up in sweats, but I was definitely not going out like that. If the last dress inspired a song then I had to look just as yummy so, standing on top of a pile of clothes, wearing only a towel, I did the only thing I could think of–FaceTime Reiko.

I got a text message notification just as I picked up my phone, and it was from Sincere. I couldn't imagine what he'd have to say to me so I paid it no mind and proceeded to hit up Reiko, praying she was available.

"Heeeeey girl…ooh, are you, naked?" she said.

"Technically no. I'm wrapped in a towel, which counts as coverage."

I saw a tan round, bearded face appear in Reiko's screen. It was France.

"Whaddup Nyela!"

Ew.

"Hi France," I said flatly.

"Where are your clothes, young lady?"

"Oh my god, Reiko! Get him outta there!"

"It ain't nothing he never seen before."

"Reiko, I'm serious. What I have to talk to you about is *classified* information! France, you gotta go somewhere!"

"*Oh word*, it's like that?" he replied.

"Babe, give me a few minutes."

"Aight, yo," he replied, heading out of her bedroom. "Imma go see what snacks you got poppin' off in the kitchen since you don't cook."

"So what's up, chica?"

"Why are you doing this with him again?"

"We're talking about *you* right now, right?"

She was right and she was grown, so whatever. "I'll let this go for now because I need your help. I don't know what to wear!"

"Eeeeeeee!"

"Oh my God Reiko, you're such a girl. You damn near busted my eardrum."

"And you're always too cool for school. *You* know you're excited. And can you please get some this time!"

"Reiko, shut up! I'm freaking out over here. You see what the last dress did. I *have* to look just as fly this time, if not better!"

"Don't act like you don't have a closet full of fly gear—some of which with the tags still on! What happened to that fly red-orange mini-dress that you got from ASOS?"

"Oh shit, you're right!"

I rescanned my closet and found it tucked it away in a plastic bin. I bought it back when it was cold and forgot about it. My closet tended to become a black hole in that sense.

The flirty A-line mini-dress had spaghetti straps, and was revealing enough, but not too raunchy.

I slipped it on and pinned my twists into an abstract updo. I accessorized it with my gold lion's head necklace, and made a mental note that I wanted to get a nameplate necklace at some point. I piled a couple of gold rings on various fingers, added a stack of chunky cheetah print bracelets and some gold Chanel logo button earrings that I scored from a vintage store years ago. I finished the look with some nude mid-heel height strappy sandals, and Olu called me to let me know that he was downstairs just as I buckled my last shoe.

I did one final check of my dress, hair and makeup just to make sure I liked how I looked, and tossed some last minute just in case essentials—an extra pair of panties, a travel toothbrush, and my cosmetics bag in my purse. I stepped outside my building and saw Olu standing in front of a black Mini Cooper this time, still with that cool demeanor I was falling for.

"How is it possible that *you* drive a Mini Coop? You're like eight feet tall," I said as I approached the car.

"Perhaps you'd feel more comfortable if it was a tricked out Maybach?" he quipped as he drew me in for a peck on the lips.

"You look amazing," he said, opening the car door for me.

"Thanks. You're not so bad yourself. Hold up, are you wearing the De La Soul's?" I replied, admiring his Nike Dunks. "I haven't seen those in years."

"Let me find out! You really *do* know your sneakers like that!"

"We already went through this, Olu, you know I love a good pair of Dunks, especially obsolete limited editions!"

"You and me both."

I climbed inside the car, giddy.

"So, where we going?"

He glanced at me briefly with a mischievous grin spreading across his face, turned back to the road and then laughed.

"We're going to a good place for inspiration."

"Thank you, but that was so fucking vague. Come on, yo! Where are we going?"

He smirked.

"Patience, Nye."

We drove for about an hour, listening to and talking about various types of music before we pulled up to a Georgian-style estate. Based on the signs I saw, my guess was that we were in Greenwich, Connecticut or nearby. I noticed a short white man with short, wild dark hair organized in random spikes atop his head. He was wearing thick, black-rimmed wayfarers, a black t-shirt that read "Fangoria" across the chest, and blue jeans with floral house slippers. After taking in his quirky appearance I realized that I knew *exactly* who he was and unwittingly placed my hand over my mouth to stop myself from screaming. Okay, I wasn't *really* going to scream, but I did have to stifle a gasp. I was usually good at keeping my cool in these types of situations, but *this* was fucking fantastic if this man was who I thought he was.

"Is that…Nero Benvenuti?"

I barely got the words out above a whisper, but I knew Olu heard me based on the cocky expression on his face. We finally got close enough for me to see that it *was* actually Nero Benvenuti, one of my favorite current movie directors, and I almost passed out. I repeatedly told myself to play it cool, but I was definitely not leaving this place without at least one usie with the famed director.

"OLU! MY MAN!" Nero said energetically.

They slapped five and pulled each other into a hug. Then Nero turned his gaze to me. He was intense, but I wasn't uncomfortable because he was known for being passionate, which I liked. He had won every film award known to man for various classics like *Cult Fantasy*, *Kiki Fox*, *River Cats* and more. Most of his most popular films drew inspiration from the Blaxploitation era as well as other types of b-movies that I loved. He was still a great screenwriter despite the fact that a lot of his movies were inspired by films that weren't typically known for good dialogue or plots. His screenplays were always thoughtful and intelligent.

"So *you're* Nyela! The guest of honor."

He grabbed my hand and kissed it. He was surprisingly smooth.

"You're even more stunning in person."

His urbane demeanor didn't match his heavy Italian-Brooklyn accent, which amused me. I was still perplexed about this entire situation. This had to be kismet, but my tendency toward cynicism wished that the little person dressed in an elf costume who would eventually dash out and announce that this had all been one cruel joke would pop out and get it over with already.

"Guest of honor?" I replied, glancing at Olu who still had that sexy cocky smirk on his face.

He shrugged and didn't say a word, but Nero filled me in.

"Of course you're the guest of honor! Olu told me what a wonderful time you had the day you shadowed him. Usually, those things are just business and you grin and bear it for a day, reveal as much as you need to and go about your life, but Olu said you guys had a real connection. I've been there. The best writers that I've ever encountered during the course of my career are still my friends today."

"So you just go around talking about me to folks," I said to Olu.

"Something like that," Olu replied. "But Nero isn't just folks. We go back."

"I was already curious about you after having read how you crafted your words in Olu's feature story," Nero said. "But then Olu told me about your movie mania and I knew I had to meet you. You're an impressive young lady! The piece you wrote about the evolution of women in action films was spectacular."

My heart started bitch-slapping my chest.

"But that wasn't even published professionally."

"It was on your site, which is just as good as any publication. You certainly know your stuff."

"I…I do?"

Stammering wasn't becoming, but I was useless at the moment.

"Good job, Nero. You got the witty writer to struggle with her words," Olu said.

"I may need to pick your brain, my dear. I started my own blog and I'm going to need some help with all that tech and SEO stuff."

I wasn't sure whether my gasp was audible or if I managed to keep it inside my head. I was actually not sure about much of anything at the moment. The fact that one of my artistic crushes complimented me assured me that this was a hoax or that I was dreaming.

"Um…yeah…of course," I replied, appalled by how stupid I probably sounded.

We followed Nero to the patio. It was an expansive area behind his home that looked more like a chic outdoor café. There were several tables and benches spread out, cabanas, well-manicured flowers and shrubbery trimming the parameter, a bar, and a massive pool with a grotto. We parked at a table that was situated somewhere in between the bar and the pool, and there was a grill fired up not too far away from us. Nero headed over to check on some vegetable and chicken skewers.

"Wait, *you're* cooking for us?" I asked.

"Of course! I love cooking. I've always said that I'm going to have a cooking show at some point in my life. It will happen when the timing is right."

"I don't think you understand. This dude throws down!" Olu said. "I'm trying to get him to start selling his barbecue sauce."

Here I was, thinking I knew all there was to know about Nero Benvenuti.

"Wow, I'm surprised you're such a cooking enthusiast. That's not something that has ever been put out there about you."

"This is why we fall in love with writers like you," Nero replied. "You know how to pull seemingly small details out of people."

If I were lighter, I'd blush. But since my almond brown cheeks didn't visibly flush red without actual blush, I offered a goofy smile instead.

"And there's the real sunshine," Nero said. "Why haven't you brought her around sooner, Lu?"

"*Lu?* Ha! That's so cute."

"Thanks a lot, Nero, you blew my cover," Olu replied.

We laughed.

"You need any help?" Olu said.

"No. Everything's fine. You two just relax."

I took in the perfect sunny day and silently thanked the newscasters for getting the weather right this time. It was about 85 degrees with no humidity. I admired my surroundings in silence. My cynicism didn't allow me to be inspired or impressed by much, but I was definitely impressed, amazed, and grateful that I was actually here, and that no hidden cameras had been revealed just yet. This was freaking real!

"This is dope, right?" Olu said, sensing my awe.

He placed his hand on my thigh, and I didn't mind, but I had to take a breath because I didn't forget how hot and heavy we got the last time we saw each other.

"Hell yeah!"

Nero joined us at our table underneath a large umbrella staked in the center. There was a mixed vegetable, hummus, and pita chips spread, in addition to several pitchers of cucumber, lemon and herb infused water and various other kinds of mixers and chasers placed for our comfort.

"So, how did you guys meet?" I asked, reaching for a pita chip.

Olu and Nero exchanged glances and laughed. Nero explained that Olu auditioned for his last film, the award-winning, *Cult Fantasy,* which premiered two years ago. It was about two assassins who went rogue after their boss' daughter, with whom they were charged with protecting, mysteriously died in their charge, and needed to clear their names.

"His audition was great, but he wasn't right for the part," Nero said. "He was too young, too attractive and too polished for what I was looking for. But he was just so talented and such a cool guy that I kept in touch because I knew at some point I would write the perfect role for him."

"He took me to dinner to soften the blow of not getting the role," Olu said, laughing. "And we've been friends ever since."

We continued chatting about music, pop culture and the controversy and criticism surrounding Nero's forthcoming flick, *Harriet's Big Payback*, which was a B-movie style reimagining of how a shotgun-toting Harriet Tubman helped slaves get to freedom, over the Mediterranean-themed lunch that Nero prepared. In addition to the chicken and vegetable skewers, we enjoyed couscous salad, labneh cheese and wine.

A few hours later, we headed inside the house because Nero had a new plan for our night of fun despite the fact that he had to catch a chartered flight in a few hours. As we followed him through the first floor, I noticed that the house, contrary to the elegant Georgian theme on the outside, was adorned with pop culture memorabilia—the way you'd expect a nerd to decorate. I saw movie posters from various decades and action figures everywhere—on walls, in corners, on top of coffee tables.

I even spotted a Talking Tina Doll from the eponymous classic episode of *The Twilight Zone*, one of my favorite TV shows. I was still too in awe to ask him about it, but I made a mental note to do so when he and I became friends, for real, for real. This was the best date I had ever been on even though there was a third party involved. I loved the thought and details behind this, and suddenly got the urge to kiss Olu for being so amazing. I refrained for the sake of being cool, but I couldn't front, Olu was the shit. Fuck that ice cold too cool for school shit! We ended up in Nero's home studio and he began setting up his equipment after handing Olu and I scripts.

"Okay, page 30. Nyela, you read for Chickie."

"You want me to read what?"

"I'm working on a new script and I've got some ideas for it that aren't quite right yet. You just became another muse so I think you reading this can help me perfect the role of Chickie. She's beautiful and capricious. I like those qualities, but there's still something missing."

"But I've never *really* acted be—"

"Don't worry about that. Just read."

Olu stood next to Nero, pulled out his phone and started taping my impromptu read. Chickie was a corporate assassin who had a change of heart about her profession after discovering she was pregnant by her secret lover whom she didn't realize was really a foe assassin charged with killing her. There was a scene where she was talking to herself in the mirror about her situation, trying to figure out how to tell her lover that she was pregnant, and also conflicted about her desire to keep the child. In this scene, she was pondering whether she should just disappear and raise her child under a different identity or have an abortion and continue the dangerous job she hated. I guess I could kind of relate. I had never been pregnant and didn't plan on it anytime soon, but I have had friends who had been in situations like this sans the corporate assassin thing.

I stopped overthinking, channeled that energy while hearing my mom's stage production voice in my head, and read.

A few moments later, Olu, no longer filming, and Nero stared at me with huge grins on their faces.

"That was pretty good!" Nero exclaimed.

"Aw, come on!"

"He's right. You were brilliant," Olu replied. "Almost as good as me."

I gave him a side eye and he winked.

"Do you have an idea who could play Chickie?" Nero said. "I want some fresh blood, someone on the come up."

"Huh? Are you asking me for casting help?"

"Why not? You study the industry as a writer, so your opinion would be valid."

"Um. You should probably look at Quita Ravenell, but with all due respect, I'm no casting director."

"I didn't even think about Quita Ravenell, and yet you're right! See, like I said, your opinion is valid."

"Um, okay."

"The script isn't complete yet so you're off the hook for now, but I'm going to revisit this conversation with you," Nero said.

"Uh, sure."

"You know, Nyela is working on a script of her own, too," Olu said. "She told me the concept and it sounds pretty good."

"OLU!" I snapped, mortified.

"What's it about?" Nero replied.

"I'm almost done, but it's a romantic comedy with b-movie elements," I said, explaining the concept.

There were only a handful of people that I actually went into detail with about my screenplay's concept, but I couldn't pass up this chance, even though I hadn't planned on bringing it up at all.

"I'm sure she'd love to pick your brain," Olu said.

"Shit, I want to read it," Nero replied.

"What? You. Want. To. Read. My. Screenplay."

"I do. I love investing in young talent. How far away from completing it are you?"

"It's almost done."

"So, call me when it's done and I will check it out."

I caught eyes with Olu, who was silently cracking up at my facial expression. My eyes were wide and mouth agape. There was no keeping my cool here. Millions of screenwriters in the world fought every day for years, in some cases, to get the chance for someone who could actually make a difference to read their work, and here I was getting the hook up by association. I didn't take this moment lightly.

"I will. Wow."

It was 10 p.m. before we knew it, and it was almost time for Nero to catch his flight to L.A. By this point, we were sitting in his home movie theater chatting about film again. I wasn't surprised to learn that Nero was a movie Wikipedia, even with regard to Black classics like *Cabin in the Sky*, and *Stormy Weather*, and Olu was impressively knowledgeable too for a non-American, but my time meeting with Nero was cut short when he realized that he needed to catch his red-eye.

"I gotta get going, but Nyela, it was such a pleasure," Nero said, kissing my hand.

"Mine too!" I replied, still not getting used to the fact that I was now acquainted with one of the biggest directors in the world.

Like, we had *actually* exchanged information, and planned on using it.

"You two are welcome to stay the night. Olu knows his way around this place and my house sitter, Magda, will be here in the morning, but she's on call just in case anything urgent arises."

"Sounds like a plan I like, what say you, Nyela, wanna stay the night?" Olu replied.

"Hell yeah!"

"Then it's settled. Call it a night when you want, and finish that screenplay, Nyela!" Nero said before disappearing.

"I will!"

I glanced at Olu with a huge grin on my face.

"You're so cute," he said.

"And *you're* amazing! Thank you so much for this."

"Of course. It was amazing to see you so happy. I'm glad I could be the one to make that happen."

"So what now?" I snuggled up next to him.

"Want to raid the kitchen for dessert?"

"Absolutely!"

My phone buzzed again, reminding me that I never checked Sincere's text earlier, so despite my common sense, intuition and the angels sitting on each of my shoulders telling me not to, I looked at it anyway.

Hey u, I know it's been a while and all but I'm just reaching out to make sure ur okay. Hopefully there are no hard feelings on ur end. I know I'm straight, even though u gave me a swollen eye lol. But seriously, love, light, peace and only the best to u.

I huffed and shoved my phone back into my purse as we got up and headed to the kitchen. Surprisingly, I wasn't perturbed by Sincere's passive aggression this time, just annoyed, but definitely not annoyed enough to mess up this lovely night I was having. I felt a wave of relief as I realized this was a pivotal moment of growth in The Nyela Saga. The old me would have taken the bait and returned the text or even called. I could care less at the moment, though. I just wanted to focus on Olu, and what was happening between us. Fighting it was futile, and giving in would be amazing.

"You sure know how to pick them, huh?" said Olu.

"What?"

"That text from Sincere. He aight?"

"How did you figure it was from Sincere?"

"I don't know of anyone else besides maybe Cynda who could get such an exasperated reaction out of you, and *I know* you and Cynda don't talk like that so, educated guess."

"Yeah, it was. He's on some bullshit again, but whatever. And I *know* you don't have jokes about knowing how to pick 'em."

"True." He laughed.

"Speaking of Cynda, I know Felani told you about that ratchet-ass brunch we had where she almost beat the shit out of that bird brain you actually once called a girlfriend."

"She did, sounded like loads of fun." he replied, rolling his eyes.

We raided Nero's kitchen, and discovered an impressive pantry, but I was particularly drawn to the fact that Nero kept a stockpile of ice cream in his freezer.

"Oh my God, it's Ample Hills! What are the fucking chances! See, I knew I liked Nero! We fucking go together!"

I pulled out a pint of bananamon ice cream from the freezer and transferred some to a bowl.

"I've never seen someone so excited about ice cream. It's endearing."

"Next to pizza, *real* ice cream is king in my non-vegan foodie handbook. Here, let me show you what I'm talking about."

I fed Olu a spoonful and watched him close his eyes as he savored his first taste of this odd flavor.

"Wow, that *really is* banana and cinnamon. I wouldn't have thought that would make such a good combination."

"Yup," I replied, taking a spoonful for myself before feeding him again.

"Man, I can't get over how good this stuff is," he offered mid-taste, still in bananamon reverie.

He and I relished a few more spoonfuls before taking a turn toward the obvious.

"You got a little bit still on your lip," Olu said.

He smirked, leaned in and dabbed the bit of ice cream off the corner of my lip with his tongue.

"Did you get it all?"

"No, there's still a little bit right here..." he said, before going all the way in for a kiss.

The feeling of his full lips against mine was even more intense, and more meaningful than before. Instead of overthinking things and getting in my own head, I just let go and gave into him.

In one swift move, Olu wrapped his arms around my legs and lifted me up on to the countertop so that I was sitting, as he stood in between my legs. All the while our lips never parted. I felt boneless as he went from kissing my lips to my neck and back again. I began breathing heavily and writhing with excitement as his skilled hands glazed over various parts of my body. His touch electrified my senses.

I pulled his body as close to me as possible as he continued tracing my flesh with his tongue. He made his way downward, slowly sliding the straps of my dress past my shoulders and exposing more of me. Olu tattooed my breasts and stomach with more kisses. It wasn't long before he hiked up my dress so it orbited my waist, parted my legs and began licking in between my thighs. Before I could manage to eek out a sigh of approval, he was expertly shifting my panties to the side with his mouth and devouring me whole like a warm piece of mango.

I dropped my head back, closed my eyes, and placed my hand on the top of his head. Gently I stroked his Caesar cut as his tongue explored every millimeter of my pudenda.

"Come here," I said, barely able to get the words out between moans. I wanted to pull him up for another kiss, but he was stubborn.

"Nah," he said, before burying his face deeper into me and making even more intense motions with his tongue.

I squirmed more intensely until I just blurted out, "FUCK!"

I was starting to lose control and Olu knew it. Pausing for a moment, he looked up at me to get a glimpse of my face twisted in delight, and smirked before diving right back in.

Olu tasted me one more time before gently pulling me off the countertop, allowing my dress to drop to the floor in the process and began leading the way out of the kitchen. I followed him to a giant bedroom that looked as if it belonged to Goldie from *The Mack*. It was covered in plush burgundy carpet and the walls were adorned with Blaxploitation movie posters from flicks like *The Big Doll House*, *TNT Jackson*, *Coonskin* and possibly every movie from that genre ever made. I also saw life-sized cutouts of Pam Grier from her role in *Coffy*, and Fred Williamson from *Black Caesar*.

I recalled my first ever conversation with Olu where I revealed parts of myself and mentioned my B-movie fetish in passing. I remembered that he kept asking me questions about my favorite titles and I just assumed he was making small talk, but I guess he really wanted to know. The fact that out of all the rooms in this house, he brought me to this one specifically, made me fall for him a little bit more as another wave of wetness rushed through my body and coated my flesh in the area where my thighs met.

By this point, I was completely naked. I didn't remember when my bra and panties came off—not that it mattered—but I helped Olu take his shirt and pants off and marveled at his body, once again. His skin, which was the smoothest and deepest rich brown I had ever seen, was flawlessly perfect—no tattoos, birthmarks or scars.

Now that he was standing in front of me in all his glory, I couldn't wait to return the favor of pleasure he had bestowed upon me in the kitchen. Wasting no time I dropped to my knees and willingly took him into my mouth. He moaned as I worked my tongue around the head and shaft of his fully erect penis, which I familiarized myself with quickly. He responded more when my motions were slow and steady, so I kept that pace, as I was eager to please him. Perhaps too eager.

Gently tugging my hair, he exhaled deeply and whispered, "You gotta chill, babe. Damn."

It felt like I was drifting backward as Olu gingerly nudged me on to the opulent bed. The sheets felt cool and comforting as I landed.

"You're so fucking sexy," he purred into my ear. "Are you ready?"

I nodded in the affirmative. Olu reached into his pants pocket on the floor and I watched him skillfully place a condom on. He parted my legs and eased his way inside of me, letting out a low grunt as our bodies fully merged as one. Each stroke was calculated and rhythmic. His motion was somewhere in between rough and gentle. It was everything that had imagined and all that I needed.

Instinctually I wrapped my legs around his back and pushed my pelvis up to allow him as much access as possible. It had been a while since I last had sex, but *this* was an experience unlike anything I had experienced before. I felt more relaxed and vulnerable than I had ever been with anyone, and he was just so fucking dexterous and smooth.

Without missing a stroke, Olu twisted my legs into a scissor-like position and I felt a strange but delightful feeling that I couldn't quite explain. It was almost as if I had this uncontrollable urge to pee but not quite. I didn't say a word but somehow he sensed it as I let out another yelp.

"I gotcha," he whispered, making me arch my back a little more before extending my legs out so that they fell back toward my ears. He took full advantage of the flexibility I had developed from years of dance, but even that couldn't stop my legs from trembling.

"You still tryna fight me?" he said.

"OLU...I FEEL..."

"You feel what?"

My shivering got faster as he continued stroking my body. He maintained that same rhythmic pace, just now with more aggression.

"You heard me talking to you," Olu barked, looking me square in the eyes.

His confidence and cockiness turned me on to the point where my body couldn't be as still as I willed it to be. My shivering turned into violent convulsions as he pushed deeper, harder and faster. I could feel my body getting ready to explode, so I wrapped my arms around his pelvis as tight as I could as a way to brace myself.

"You tryna make me cum with all that shaking," he smirked. "But you first."

The sound of his voice only amplified the sensations I was feeling. That's when I *really* lost control of myself.

I liked that Olu was talking to me, and that strange but amazing sensation that I was feeling intensified as he pushed my legs back even more. He stroked harder and with more purpose, but I could tell that he was also starting lose control. I could see it in his face and felt it in his movements. I bit my lip and gave into the force inside of me until finally, I squirted. I had never experienced that kind of ecstasy before. There was just a rush of warmth escaping my body and enveloping Olu, who drowned in my fluids until he exploded as well with a guttural grunt of pleasure.

Olu collapsed on top of me, letting the full weight of his body lay on mine for a moment before rolling over on to the bed, pulling me close so that I could rest my head on his chest.

"I never squirted before!" I said, laughing.

"I want to be many firsts for you, Nyela," he replied, smiling. "I like this."

"I like this, too."

#LikeForLike

Olu and I ended up at his apartment in DUMBO on Sunday, after staying the night at Nero's place, and we got sucked into a vortex of bliss—watching TV, listening to music, talking about everything, and having more banging sex.

Now that I was back home, a couple of days since I left my place for Nero's house, it was time to emerge from the rabbit hole and see what was going on in the world, so I started making my morning rounds online. The first headline I stumbled upon was, "Bad Girl Radio Host Throat Chops France Deveaux."

I sighed and braced myself.

> *So you all know that Reiko Rodriguez chick right? How could you not? She and her birdbrain girlfriends, a group that also includes that rapper chick Felani and writer Nyela Barnes, are always getting caught up in some kind of drama. I swear some broads will do anything for attention. But whatevs. My inside sources say that mega industry manager France Deveaux — he manages the career of rap super star Fredrick Thuglass — and Reiko showed up at gossip blogger Tiffany Truth's bloggiversary bash and acted the whole entire fool. They didn't even make it inside because they were arguing so bad, and then that Reiko Broad went all WWE. Watch the video!*

I knew I shouldn't have watched the accompanying video, but when did I ever listen to my better judgment in situations like this? I pressed play and got reminded why I hated the fact that Reiko was back with that loser. I couldn't make out much of what was being said, but it sounded like an argument about the contents of his phone. From what I could make out, Reiko found incriminating text messages some chick, as usual, a factor in all of their previous break ups. She was screaming at him while France, also a hot head, got right back in her face, yelling his innocence, and Reiko's subsequent insanity for "believing every rumor she heard."

Reiko finally calmed down after a while and seemingly listened to his condescending rant about her being a jealous lunatic. However, her eyes were glazed over because she was in the beginning stages of an impending spazz out. I watched with glee, but also horror as she punched him in the throat, and continued to read the rest of the story.

I told ya'll it was bad. Birdy Reiko hopped into a cab and left but France Deveaux went into the party and acted like nothing happened. My sources say he was getting lap dances from another crew of industry bird chicks who have often been seen hanging out with Nasreen and her golddigger crew. You know word travels fast so I wouldn't be surprised if we get wind of Koko's flying fists of fury connecting with France's face again. That's why they've been off and on so much throughout the years anyway.

232

Not only was I seething about Reiko getting involved in drama she knew was inevitable with this dude, but I was also still proverbially annoyed by this Chatty Abernathy person. At some point, he or she had to be held accountable for his or her actions.

I took a deep breath and continued scrolling for more news. It was typical stuff like, new music, celebrity baby bump watches, celebrities doing mundane things like grocery shopping without makeup, and then I got to another gossip site that also had a Reiko and France Deveaux-related post, but it was an update from what I had been reading thus far.

Exclusive: Radio Personality Reiko Rodriguez and
France Deveaux Address their Haters

You probably saw the now infamous video of radio personality Reiko Rodriquez Hulk smashing her on-again, off-again boyfriend in front of a club last night, but the couple has sent us an exclusive rebuttal. As you all know, France Deveaux is a friend to the site so we got first dibs. Watch the video below:

Pressing play meant there was no turning back. Even when it got progressively worse I was probably not going to stop it, so I accepted my fate due to being nosey. I watched the video and it was bad, but surprisingly not as bad as I thought. It was a vlog featuring Reiko and France trying to convince everyone who saw their fight that they weren't fighting anymore and that they were in love and that some "hater" leaked the footage to try to break them up because, "that's what haters did."

Reiko always got basic like this whenever France was around, but there was nothing I could do but lend my shoulder and some chocolate ice cream when they broke up again. We were past the "I told you so stage."

Feeling my head about to explode, I continued my Feedly scroll and noticed a YouTube video from Cynda promoting her upcoming book. She was trying to convince masses of pea brain women to drink her arsenic and enroll in her course about how to be a so-called "alluring woman."

I chuckled, continued scrolling and noticed that Olu actually updated his blog, which was surprising because he rarely blogged. I smiled, thinking about the lovely couple of days we spent together and started to really miss him.

The headline read, **"Dear Fuchsia Girl, I Forgot To Ask You…"**

Was I ready for this? I took another deep breath, and continued reading.

> *Hey Fuchsia, hey Fuchsia, can you be my future? Stop looking at your computer screen like that! I know that was corny, but I bet you're smiling now, or frontin' like you don't want to. We both know how you do. Anyway, you can now credit yourself with inspiring this post too. I told you you're a muse! There's one thing I forgot to ask you so I decided to make a spectacle [winky face]. Will you be my lady? Let me be more specific, because I know you. Let's make us official. Like this post if yes, dislike it if no. I'm going to sift through all the subsequent likes and dislikes until I find your answer later, and if you don't reply, don't forget, I know where you live, work, and I have your phone number lol.*

I laughed at the absurdity of Olu's post, but I was also flattered. It reminded me of the digital version of what we did in kindergarten, passing boyfriend/girlfriend letters complete with yes and no boxes. Olu's post already had 500 likes on it, probably from thirsty chicks who commented things like, "I'll be your girlfriend," and "Yes, boo!" and then his fans who liked it just because he posted it. I broke my no reading comments rule and discovered more comedy or tragedy, depending on how you looked at it.

"Sucka 4 luv ass nigga!"

"Fuk these bitches yo. Olu, she gon tek all ur money like the gold digging bird she probably is. Make music my dude. Money over byches!"

"ALL Y'ALL THAT DON'T LIKE IT IS SOME FUCKIN HATAZ! DO YOU OLU! KEEP WINNING WITH THEM BAD BITCHES! I CAN'T WAIT TO COP YOUR ALBUM."

"Hopefully it's a black woman. We know how y'all black men do when y'all get famous."

The typically egregious misspellings, misogyny, and Internet thuggery oft apparent in the comments section didn't bother me as much today as they usually did. I guess happiness could do that to a cynic like me. The gravity of this turning point hit me after I clicked the like button, hoping I didn't regret this decision.

#NotSoRegal

I wanted to cringe as I walked through *Regality* magazine's lobby. I didn't really have a good feeling about this place, but I reminded myself to deal with it by remembering that this gig was going to help keep me out of my parents' pockets, and that it was an iconic place that would look good on my *résumé*. How bad could it be, right? Never mind, I knew what industry I was in. The biggest lesson I have learned in my career thus far was that perception was a motherfucker. I'd already experienced one of the most iconic publications in pop culture history, but I'd also seen and heard enough from friends to know that when it came to the companies that we all worshipped as kids and that seemed to have everything all together, how they *really* operated vs. how they *appeared* to operate were two different concepts. I often questioned my sanity for moving forward with this industry for as long as I had.

I would love to be my own boss full time one day, but one of the frustrating things about being an entrepreneur was, you just didn't make ends meet fast enough in the beginning so you'd still get caught up in working for others to make a living. I was lucky that my blog was starting to bring in some decent chunks of money enough to at least cover my cable, electric, and cellphone bill, but it was my script that I *really* needed to focus on, and I've been scheduling my time better since meeting with Nero so that I could finally get it ready.

I was a pretty determined person. I got that trait from both of my entrepreneurial parents. I'd watched them manage and operate their respective businesses my entire life. They were both lucky enough to still be in business for decades, and now it was my turn. Honestly, I was afraid to work on changing my situation, and also of subjecting myself to the kind of scrutiny that came with artistry and entrepreneurship, but it was time to stop with fear and excuses and be more positive, so I decided to end the self-doubt and deprecation session for now. In the meantime, I'd fantasize about Olu and pretend that the stories I'd heard about this place being a mean girl sorority house weren't true.

"Nyela, follow me please."

Tina's curt greeting snapped me out of my thoughts.

I stood up and extended my hand for a shake. "Hi, Tina."

She grabbed the tip of my four fingers and gave me a limp shake as if she could care less, and it made me want to slap her. I hated shaking hands too, but at least I pretended to be into it for the sake of business pretenses, and at the very least simply being cordial. She looked me up and down and cracked a slight smile.

"Nice dress," she said, seemingly through gritted teeth. "Demestiks NYC?"

It looked like it hurt her to at least pretend to be remotely friendly, but I was still impressed with and also disturbed by her ability to call out labels so easily. I don't think that fact would ever get old to me! I've had this dress for so long that even *I* forgot that it was Demestiks NYC.

"Yeah," I replied, trying to keep up with her rapid pace as we headed to my workspace.

She was so type A.

She led me to a cubicle big enough for two people, with one side already occupied. I assumed the empty space was mine and put my bag down. Based on the fact that the other girl didn't even turn around to greet me, I started to get the vibe that this place was going to be déjà vu, but with a bunch of passive aggressive women in fly clothes, instead of petulant man-children.

"Nyela, meet Kimmie. She's our online fashionista and celebrity gossip girl," Tina said.

Kimmie finally spun her chair toward me and extended her hand. "Hi," she said, also looking me up and down.

Her handshake at least had some effort behind it.

"Looks like we picked the same in-office day," I said, realizing how pointless my comment was when her facial expression changed from apathy to judgment.

"Is that Demestiks NYC?" she said.

What the fuck!

"Yes," I replied, forcing a smile.

Tina was too busy with whatever was going on in her phone to be concerned with our exchange.

I started getting settled at my desk and when Tina finished with her phone, she handed me my building ID.

"So, I gotta run to a meeting but I forgot to tell you, you don't just cover film anymore. Given your background at *Spark*, we've decided to make music your beat too," she said before dashing off.

"But what happened to the music girl you were going to hire?" I yelled after her, as she got halfway down the hall.

"Budget cuts!"

She disappeared around a corner.

"Budget cuts?" I repeated out loud rhetorically.

"That's how they do it around here," Kimmie said. "Prepare for the grind, but if this is what you really want then you'll do it and be happy. I mean this *is Regality*. Tons of women would love to be in your shoes, but they chose you, so work it out."

I imagined myself asking her who the fuck asked for her unsolicited sanctimonious mini speech. I'm not a 22-year-old naïve fucking assistant! However, instead of being rude, I kept my face neutral and eeked out the only reply I could think of that didn't involve the words: nobody, asked and you.

"True."

I noticed she was on TMZ right before I decided to mind my own business and get my desk area together. It made no sense to decorate, but I could at least know where my office supplies were, especially my trusty Post-its, so I started searching the drawers.

"HOLD UP!" Kimmie shouted.

I turned around to see what the drama was about just in time to see her yanking her headphones out of the jack and swiveling her chair around to face me.

"Did you know about this?"

Confused, I pulled my chair up to her desk and noticed she was now on a popular gossip and entertainment site that wasn't Chatty Abernathy, for once.

***Nero Benvenuti Launches Blog With Acting
Video of Brawling Writer Muse…***

You all remember the scrappy writer chick Nyela Barnes who just got fired from Spark *magazine, right? Well, looks like she's been keeping busy. Apparently, she's good friends with Olu Major, who we all know has a bromance with iconic director Nero Benvenuti. Well, looks like Nyela got involved in the friendship mix and somehow inspired Nero to join social media. He not only opened a Twitter account, but he also just launched his new blog. It's a movie industry news blog geared toward directors, and his own production company, but his first post is about his "new muse." Here's a snippet followed by video:*

"I had the pleasure of meeting a new muse a few weeks ago. Her name is Nyela Barnes. She and my boy Olu stopped by one lovely Saturday for food and merriment. She's stunning, smart, magnetic, and she inspired me not to give up on a script that I had been struggling with. I filmed her doing a cold reading just for fun, and she doesn't even know how fucking talented she is. As a director, I couldn't keep this to myself. Watch and enjoy."

And there I was, acting out the scene that Nero shot. He posted about five minutes of it. Most of it was just me reading my lines, but there were playful moments between takes where Olu video bombed me, and our interactions could have been seen as us flirting. *FUCK!* I mean…I knew people would find out about Olu, but I was hoping it wouldn't be this soon. Then again, maybe I was just being paranoid. It's not like we were kissing in the video, or being super blatant. We could always just cop to the whole, "we're just close friends" plea if asked. The last thing I needed was more exaggerated and fabricated speculation about who I was and what I was doing. However, as I continued reading the text under the video, I realized it was probably too late.

> *Olu and Nyela just so happened to stop by Nero's house? Y'all already know Nyela has a tendency toward the scandalous, and she is out of a job so...just sayin...she could have picked up a new career in snagging ballers. Mmhmm...peep this photo...*

It was one of a few photos of Olu and I from our fist date, taken while we were goofing off with his phone on my stoop. He posted it the day after our date with a caption that read, "With the dope ass @NyelaBHurston, pick up that GQ on stands now!" You could clearly see the top of the fuchsia dress I wore that day, but other than that there was nothing suspect about the photo.

That didn't change the fact that the post annoyed me, though.

I was good at not blurting my raging thoughts out loud so I shifted my focus to forcing my facial expression to remain neutral as well. The positive in this was that no one, even in the comments section, seemed to make the connection between "Fuchsia Girl" and the fuchsia dress I was wearing in that photo. I got out of my head in time to catch

Kimmie staring at me with a quizzical expression on her face, and hoped I hadn't thought I was in the clear too soon.

"Why did they even make that news!" was all I said while still trying to keep my face locked on stoic.

"Are you shitting me? *You* know Olu *and* Nero Benvenuti? But...*how*?" Kimmie replied.

She spoke in a tone that suggested that I was some kind of bum bitch who could never possibly know anyone of note.

"I mean, well, Olu and I got cool when I did that cover story on him. He invited me to Nero's house because we're friends and he knew that Nero was one of my favorite directors. I've been writing my own screenplay, so who better to talk to than an Academy Award-winning director, right?"

Kimmie was silent for a moment. She was still sizing me up, but the look on her face was different this time. Apparently, I was now worthy of her interest.

"You are crazy! Why are you trying to downplay those relationships, *especially* with Olu? If *I* knew him, we wouldn't be *just friends*. That man is foine."

I still struggled with the neutral face situation, but I thought I was doing a good enough job as I carefully plotted my reply. What I really waned to say was, "He's my man and he's just as great as you think he is," but instead I gave a struggling smile accompanied by a sound that resembled a low-pitch incredulous whimper.

"Girl, I'm serious. You think you could get him to come to the office or give him my number or something?"

The thirst was real, and this was only the beginning.

"Uh, well, I don't know about an office visit because his schedule right now is…"

A deliveryman interrupted. He was holding a giant bouquet of fuchsia orchids—it was the biggest bouquet of flowers for any one person that I had ever seen—in addition to a medium sized box wrapped in fuchsia paper.

"You Nyela?" he said.

I figured the other women must have directed him to my desk and contemplated saying no anyway, but that would have just been dumb at this point.

"Um…yes," I replied, not even believing myself.

He placed the bouquet and the box on my desk and I found the envelope that came along with them.

"WHOA! Is it your birthday?" Kimmie said.

"No."

"OOH, you're getting married!" declared another random *Regality* staffer who, just a few hours ago, quickly averted her eyes without uttering so much as a "hi" when I attempted to greet her since we happened to make eye contact and, you know, work at the same company.

I placed the envelope back on top of the box, and decided that it was best to open my gift later, but it was too late. There was a small crowd gathered around me, gawking. Even busy-ass Tina found her way to my desk.

"We love it when *Regality* ladies get personal gifts here," she said. "You gotta open it now! Ooh and read the card too."

Are these bitches on crack? I didn't even know these women. No one made an effort to talk to or even look at me beyond the once over to see what I was wearing, since I stepped into this place, and now they wanted the run down about this gift?

"No. I'm going to open this stuff at home," I replied.

"AAAAAWWWWWW," screeched the chorus.

"You can't! You absolutely can't!" Tina said. "It's an office tradition to open fancy packages from bae in front of all of us! "

"Right! I know that's from your boo," said another woman. "We gotta see if he's *Regality* approved."

If I shut them down I wouldn't look like a team player and that could create serious tension, but I didn't know what was inside the box or how the card was worded and I really didn't want to risk blowing up my spot. Ain't office politics some shit!

"Uh…" was all I could muster.

I opened the card that was taped to the box and read to myself silently, as if the odds were actually in my favor.

"Uh uh, hunty! You gotta read that out loud," Kimmie said.

I accepted my fate, took a breath and read.

> *Dear Nyela,*
> *LA's weather is great, but I'm not enjoying it as much as I'd like to because you're not here. I know that's corny and I should be more original. Don't make that face at me, either, even though I secretly, but not so secretly think it's cute! Anyway, I can't stop thinking about you, so I figured I'd send you a token of my appreciation for you being you. The flowers are in your best color and to lift your spirits because I know you can be hard on yourself, but the content of the box is something I know you will use well. Hopefully it'll get you motivated to finish that script, and do some video blogs on your journey to becoming a full time screenwriter and filmmaker! Keep me on your mind until I see you again soon."*
> *Love…*

I paused because it said, "Love Olu."

I needed a fake name, but I wasn't thinking fast enough. I was a terrible on-the-spot liar.

"What's the silence for?" Kimmie blurted as she snuck up behind me swiftly and glanced at it before I could hide it. I didn't even realize she was that close to me before.

"Oh. My. God. It says, Olu," she replied, staring at me intensely, eyes widened in disbelief. "This isn't…you mean, as in…*Olu Major?*"

I was trapped. Once again, lying would just make me look stupid. Like I said, I knew the secret was going to get out eventually, but I didn't want it to happen like this. Damn you universe!

"Yes," I replied, defeated.

Tina's intensity shifted to shock, and Kimmie now looked mortified. The other women were examining me, most likely wondering what Olu saw in me or how it happened. Don't get it twisted, I was cute and all but I wasn't a model, and he did have a history of dating more model/actress types, so even *I* wasn't sure how I ended up starring in this episode of *The Twilight Zone.*

"Ooooh girrrrrl! You snagged one of the hottest men of the twenty-first century! Eeeeeeek! Teach us!" screeched one of the peanut gallery girls as she raised a hand toward me for a high five.

I half-smiled and delivered a weak return five.

"What's going on ladies?" shouted a cheerful voice from down the hall.

The sound of her jingling keys amplified, as she got closer to the group.

"Aren't you supposed to be hard at work here?"

FUUUUCK! It was Cynda.

"BOOSKI!" Tina squealed, nearly toppling her over with a bear hug.

All of the other women followed Tina's lead and rushed over to greet her.

I stayed in my original spot and watched the sycophants grovel. Tina focused her attention on me after the obsequious salutations started waning.

"You two know each other?" Tina said.

Cynda showed no recognition on her face. She was going to play this stupid game again, so I cut her off at the pass.

"Yes, we've met. I got to experience one of Cynda's power brunches a couple of weeks ago," I replied.

"Ooooh, yeah. Girl, I remember you," she came closer and drew me in for a kiss on the cheek. "You look different with your hair like that."

I took a deep breath to keep from rolling my eyes at her. My face hurt from all the fake smiling I had been doing, but I hoped my forced friendliness would make things easier for me with the women around here.

"So what's all this fuss about?" Cynda asked me.

"Nyela is dating Olu Major!" Tina interjected before I could reply.

"*Oh, really?* How long has this been going on?"

She made a face that looked as if she had discovered a new island or something, and I figured I knew why. She was trying to see if we were together at the time of that stupid ass bum rush empowerment brunch, so I kept my response as vague as possible.

"Uh, it's fairly new."

"Hold up!"

I turned back toward my desk and saw Tina inspecting my flowers and my gift, which I hadn't unwrapped yet.

"Fuchsia flowers, fuchsia box. OH MY GOD! OH MY GOD! *YOU'RE FUCHSIA GIRL! EEEEEEEEE! HE WROTE THAT SONG ABOUT YOU!*"

All the women, except for Cynda and Kimmie erupted into another shrill screeching chorus, and I cringed. They went from couldn't be bothered with me to all up in my business—and my ears—within a matter of a couple of hours, and I actually missed the stank indifference that I had already gotten used to.

I couldn't think of anything else to do with my anxious energy but open the gift. As embarrassed as I was on one hand, I also kind of liked the idea of gloating since they had been so bitchy toward me earlier. Fuck it.

"Girl, he wrote a song about you and bought you a DSLR!" shouted one of the banshees as I pulled it out of the box. "You must have *really* put it on him!"

The DSLR she was referring to was the Canon digital camera that I had been coveting for months. I mentioned it at Nero's place when I was ogling his equipment. Who did Olu think he was, Superman? Actually, nah, he probably thought he was Gambit. Gambit was cuter and had more edge than Superman.

I smiled momentarily, forgetting that I was surrounded by the witches from *American Horror Story: Coven*.

"So, *you're* Fuchsia Girl, huh?" Cynda said.

It sounded like a simple question, but given the circumstances and the way she placed emphasis on the word, "you're," I was sure it was a loaded question. She probably couldn't wait to report back to her minions, especially Miriam.

I just nodded. Fuck it.

"So, tell us the story of how you got together. How long has it been? Has he said, 'I love you,' yet?" Kimmie said.

"Sorry ladies, the circus is closed."

"Aaaaaaw!" replied the peanut gallery.

"After all that, you're not going to tell us how it happened? What's his sex game like?"

"I *said. I'm. Done,*" I replied, trying to sound as stern as possible. I've already allowed enough from them. They weren't going to get the drop on me any more.

"Settle down, Kimmie! We've pushed her enough! Let's leave her alone for now," Tina said, turning her attention toward Cynda. "There's a new woman of the hour here, and her book release is coming up soon. Aren't we excited? Yaaasssss!"

Tina and Cynda grabbed each other's hands and began shrieking.

"It's an honor for me to have built such a major following on my own," Cynda said. "I want to thank you ladies for selecting me as this month's *Regality* Book Club Pick of the Pile."

"Girl, it was nothing. You've taught me so much about being a take charge, alluring woman, and I love how you share your important message of female empowerment via social media," Tina replied, tearing up. "You are truly gifted, inspiring, and fabulous, so sharing that gift is the least I can do."

"Sometimes it's hard to be fabulous, but I think I've finally figured out how to maintain all the time," Cynda said. "All I ever wanted to do is share my gift and help other women recognize their own light. It is possible, as long as you understand that the universe will provide for you if you just believe in all things faithful. It's not easy being a publicist, manager, life coach, and an author but I make it work because I believe in myself and I ask the universe for all that I believe in."

I was the only one in the room not crying. Actually, I was trying not to laugh. I couldn't believe these chicks couldn't see how disingenuous Cynda was. They were allegedly smart writers and editors who actually thought that little speech made sense.

Our girl-bonding circle finally started to dissipate and I started to relax again. I sat back at my desk, swooned over my new gift and Olu thinking enough of me to send me something, but I sobered up as I prepared to become blog fodder, once again. These chicks were going to tell as many people who would listen about this.

There was nothing I could do about that now, so I started trolling the web for stories I could snag and rewrite for the sake of my lame ass paycheck. The first thing in my feed that grabbed my attention was a picture of Felani looking absolutely crazy—crazier than usual. The headline read: *Are You Feeling This Get Up?*

I was horrified. I never liked Felani's style, but *this?* She was wearing a gold lamé spandex halter-top shorts jumpsuit that gave her a camel-toe, with purple cornrowed extensions braided into her dark brown hair, and purple moon boots. I read the caption in spite of my intuition:

> *Rapper Felani was spotted leaving the Highline Ballroom last night after a Shawt Yung Yungin show. The Brooklyn rapper, usually known for rocking hoodrat gear, took it to another level for her impromptu guest spot. We're told the crowd loved her verse, but what we wanna know is, when did she decide to start dressing like a Ratchet Space Alien?*

I knew that Felani was starting to be more receptive to our conversations with her about switching up her style, and I knew that she mentioned that she had plans to *really* make waves with her new, uh, style, but *this* was criminal and admittedly kind of funny. I made a note to call her and continued trolling until I saw an item that I might be able to use on Miss Morena's site: *Vh1 Picks Up New Reality Show About Hip-Hop Couples.*

Just what the world needs, another reality show about hip-hop couples...

> *It's official! They rounded up some of the craziest people they could find for a new reality show titled,* Hip-Hop Love Affairs. *The show is said to follow It-couples like King Tootsie and his long time model girlfriend/babymama Miriam Ghirmai, relationship expert Sincere McDonald and IG model/sex tape star Nasreen Javadi, and France Deveaux and radio personality Reiko Rodriguez, who have a tumultuous on-again, off-again relationship. The show will take an in-depth look into their lives and how they balance love with busy careers.*
>
> *These couples are going to be ratchet as hell. Between King Tootsie's one million babymama's and the fact that France can't keep his Groupon penis to himself, this is going to be a wild ride. Taping is said to be starting soon so we can all gear up for a fall premiere.*
>
> *Will you watch?*

My best friend was starring in a fucking reality TV show and didn't tell me. Great. Reiko could be shady when it came to France, but why wouldn't she tell me something like this? I was beyond judging her antics. I mean...I didn't hate on her when she did *The Bad Girls Club* despite everyone's better judgment. My phone buzzed. Normally I would have ignored it, but I checked right way because I hoped it was a text from Olu.

I know you're still hurt and you think you're paying me back by ignoring my messages, but can we be adults about this? I've been reaching out just to see how you've been doing and you can't even respond to a nigga?

Nigga? Since when did Sincere *ever* in his affluent, son of a councilman and an app developer, suburb-raised Ivy League-educated life say "nigga?" I chalked it up to his usual babble and ignored it, once again. If this were me just a month ago I would have been all over it, but I was not, so thank goodness for growth.

My phone started ringing just as I was about to bury it in the nether regions of my purse. This time it was Reiko. I mad dashed to the kitchen, not wanting to get spied on. At this time of day, it was probably empty.

"Reiko, what the hell!" was my choice greeting.

"So, you know about the reality show," she replied.

"You're so casual about the fact that you kept this from me."

"Well, we were kind of under a gag order. France hooked it up for us and the producers made us sign all this stuff about not talking about the show, and I know I usually tell you everything, but having done reality TV before I just couldn't risk any slipups. I mean, you mighta went and told Olu, and then he woulda told Felani and she woulda told who knows, for all I know. That's all it takes, and I'm not trying to get sued or kicked off the show before it even starts."

"You told me about *Bad Girls Club*, though," I replied.

"I know, but this is different. It happened so fast and they made us sign some crazy legal agreements, worse than I've ever seen. It's not that I don't trust you, Nye. I'm sorry. Can we catch up tonight? I can apologize in person. Meet me for dinner. Puhlease!"

"Okay, Reiko. I get it, you're forgiven and we actually are overdue for a powwow anyway. I need to vent."

"What happened?"

"My spot got blown at work over this Olu stuff."

"*What?* How? Is it that Chatty Abernathy again?"

"No. He sent flowers and a gift to the office, long story. Look, I'm still here so let's talk about this later."

"Okay, cool. By the way, I invited Cookie."

"*Why?*"

"She's not so bad. I've gotten to know her a little bit. Give her a chance. And I guess I should tell you this now that it really doesn't matter anymore, but I told her about you and Olu."

"REIKO, WHAT THE FUCK! I knew it! You've never been this loose-lipped. What's happening to you?"

"Hear me out. I never would have told her, but she figured it out. She picked up on the fuchsia dress in the IG photo Olu posted and asked me about it. At that time I just told her that I couldn't reveal your identity, but that I knew the song was inspired by actual events. Then she saw today's blog post featuring the video with you at Nero's house and asked me again. I couldn't deny it without looking crazy, and you know my poker face is terrible, so I figured there was no point in lying, especially if she was sharp enough to pick up on the dress that early on. Think about it, she asked me about it almost immediately after Olu posted it. Of all the sites that *just* picked it up, *no one* made that observation but *she* did, and she didn't leak the info, right? Give her a chance, please."

"*Maybe* I'll give her a chance, but I'm not making any promises. What time tonight?"

"8 P.M. I'll text you the restaurant. See you later."

I headed back to my desk and got back to work.

—

I walked into Sazon and found that Reiko was the first one to have arrived. I immediately started in about my day once we got the greeting stuff out of the way. My goal was to get as much out as I could before Cookie arrived. Reiko knew the gist of the story so I explained all the technical stuff, and managed to get all the important stuff out of the way just before Cookie sauntered in about 20 minutes later.

"Hi ladies," she said, settling into her chair.

For the first time ever, I *really* noticed how pretty Cookie was. She kind of resembled Chanel Iman in the face, and would have been perfect as a high fashion model if she weren't a 5'1" pixie. She had smooth, naturally dewy, honey-coated skin, and her short curly Caesar cut emphasized the perfectly constructed angles of her face. Despite being petite, she was curvy, but not exaggerated like the stereotypical video girl physique. However, I still suspected that she had breast implants, not that it mattered, because they looked good either way. Today, she was wearing a multi-colored floral pencil skirt, and a white tank top with Frida Kahlo's face on it set off by a classic red lip.

"Sorry I'm late. I got caught up in a meeting with Cynda and my agent. We're negotiating the details of my second book and it seems like none of us are on the same page," she said.

"Wait, you're not gonna do another tell-all, are you?" Reiko said.

"I have enough material to do another tell-all, but I'm over that shit. The first book was a memoir based on a journal I had been keeping. I just got lucky in that I was able to monetize it. But that part of my life is over," Cookie replied. "I do realize that blowing the whistle is now a part of my rep, but I think I can move past this if given the right chance. I want my next book to be more of an inspirational book—something comedic but enlightening, like the it-girl's guide to breaking into and surviving entertainment media, or something like that."

She went on in explicit detail about what some of her tips would be and I was disturbed that she was so open.

"You give up too much information way too easily," I replied. "I'd *never* go into that much detail about anything I'm working on unless the project is ready to go. People have no qualms about stealing your idea and passing it off as theirs, you know."

"I trust you guys. I mean, Reiko and I are friends now, and I get good vibes from you so I don't mind."

"About that book though, you mentioned earlier that no one saw your vision," Reiko said. "What's up with that? Is Cynda at least fighting for the direction you want to take?"

"Don't get me started on Cynda!" Cookie replied.

"But you hired her," I chimed in.

"I know she can be funny-style, but she's about her business and good at what she does," Cookie replied. "Look at what she did for King Tootsie!"

Reiko and I simultaneously furled our brows.

"I know I sound crazy, but I also know how to play the game. As long as she can deliver the type of exposure I'm looking for, she stays on board with me. But to your question, she and my publisher think I should write a part two to my first book. But they'll see my vision eventually. I'm finishing up some chapters in a couple of days and I promise you, by my 30th birthday bash in August, I'll have that new book deal for the book that *I* want."

Reiko held up her mojito for a toast, but paused as another familiar face approached our table. It was Mandy Jones, executive producer of several hip-hop-related reality shows, including Reiko's upcoming show.

"Hi ladies," Mandy said.

"HEEEEEEY Mandy," Reiko replied, standing up to give Mandy a kiss on the cheek.

"I'm not sure if Reiko mentioned it, but we planned to start shooting tonight," Mandy said. "When she told me she was meeting up with you ladies for dinner, I just had to get some cameras here."

"Nope," I replied, gathering my belongings.

"Aw, Nyela come on! Don't be like that. *Please,*" Reiko replied. "The restaurant already approved the shoot. You *have* to appear on camera with us!"

How could this chick be so fucking secretive and selfish?

"Come on, stay!" Cookie said.

"It'll be simple," Mandy chimed in. "I'll plant my camera guys at various angles, and you ladies just have a conversation like we're not even here. What were you talking about anyway? If it was good we can have you repeat it on camera?"

"We were trying to get Nyela to join us next week for Cynda's book release party. I think Cynda is a phony bitch and I just want all my girls there with me so we can laugh at her together," Reiko said.

I let out an exasperated sigh knowing that I was now dealing with Camera Reiko, or Koko, as she sometimes liked to refer to her on-air persona.

"Ooh, tell me more," Mandy replied.

"That's just Koko's deal," Cookie said. "*I* was just telling them that Cynda manages me, but I'm not so sure about how our business relationship is going to turn out because she's not seeing my vision on a future project. Actually, she's been more focused on her own projects lately than paying proper attention to her clients."

Cookie was no better than Reiko. Fuck.

"Then we can shoot this conversation on camera. You're going to have to rehash it, but make sure you're dynamic and animated."

"You're Nyela Barnes, right?" she said, making intense eye contact with me.

"Yeah."

"I'm familiar with your work. You know Nero Benvenuti, right?"

Ugh, did everyone see that fucking video?

"Yes."

"We need you to tape this segment."

Her tone suggested that she wasn't asking. There was one time in my life, back when I first started fantasizing about becoming an entertainment writer, where meeting and interacting with Mandy Jones would have been considered a career highlight. She was at the helm of one of biggest urban record labels in hip-hop history from the early 90s to the early-2000s. Her music industry career was legendary because most of her artists saw consecutive platinum success during the music industry's golden era. However, she had since moved on now that working in music didn't make the same money that it used to. Reality TV was her new hustle, and she was having even more success with that. These days, my experiences with people in this business, no matter what part of the field, had taught me to apply Q-Tip's infamous industry rule number 4,080 to *everyone,* because it wasn't just record company people who were shady. Speaking of, I must remember to thank my dad for playing A Tribe Called Quest like it was his religion when I was growing up.

"So, you're staying, right?" Mandy pressed again.

I looked at Reiko and Cookie, and they were looking back at me like hungry orphans in *Oliver Twist.* Oddly, I felt guilty for trying to do the right thing by leaving, but this was a shady situation, and I needed to teach Reiko a lesson about lying to me by omission when it came to stuff like this. I was tired of allowing myself to be forced into silly situations that weren't good for me. I grabbed my bag and stood back near one of the cameramen.

"I'll stay, but I'm not filming. Maybe Reiko will warn me next time cameras are going to be involved, and I'll *consider* shooting."

I gave them all a look that suggested they could try to get me to budge if they wanted to, but it wasn't happening tonight.

"Okay, fine," Mandy said, defeated.

I was surprised she let it go.

I watched Mandy hand Cookie some paperwork stating that appearing on camera meant she was signing her rights away for the purposes of this show. She wasn't getting paid for this since she was a secondary character; they could use her image however and for whatever they wanted, which probably also included frankenbites, meaning that all behavior and words could be chopped and screwed to suit their needs for the storyline or promotional purposes. I watched Cookie sign, admittedly curious about what this process would be like. The camera crew was fully set up a few minutes later, and they were being coached about how to ignore the cameras, and how to restart the conversation so that it translated well on TV. Basically, they were told not to speak in fragments, act as natural as possible, and also be turned up because you had to have more energy on camera so that it translated well on screen.

"So, are you joining me at Cynda's book release?" Cookie started.

"I'll be there," Reiko replied. "I don't like the bitch or her chickenheaded friends, but I want to see this fuckery for myself. I can imagine the self-aggrandizing speech she's going to give about her brand of fake-ass empowerment."

"That's true! Do you see how those women hang on to her every word?" Cookie said. "And people call *me* a groupie bitch! I was *never* thirsty. All my conquests came to *me*."

"It's that old cliché, though," Reiko said. "Men can talk about every chick they've bagged without consequence, even if they're lying, but when women do it they're hoes and attention whores. In your case, your unapologetic honesty *really* pisses people off because you're not ashamed of what you've done."

"Girl, you ain't never lied! Contrary to popular belief, I'm actually pretty good at keeping secrets and some people should be thankful that I only released fragments of what I know. People still try to paint me as some dumb video girl, but they forget that I had a nice little following from my podcast. And before that, I was on another morning show before I even started dating these celebrities. Underestimation fuels me, though. People can keep thinking I'm a dumb bird for now, but I won't hesitate to remind anyone that I know things that could destroy careers."

"SHOTS FIRED!" Reiko shouted. "I knew I liked you!"

They high fived each other and I just stared, still not sure what to make of this newfound camaraderie, but the one positive thing I could say here was that I got a glimpse of their frame through one of the cameraman's lenses, and they looked beautiful.

"Ooh wait. I got a Google alert for my bestie, Nyela," Reiko said. "Let's see what this is about."

"What!" Cookie said.

She snatched Reiko's phone and began reading aloud.

> *Our sources tell us that the identity of this "Fuchsia Girl" that Olu Major made a song about is none other than that brawling writer chick Nyela Barnes. You might remember her from past public brawls and maybe even some of her bylines, if people are even still checking for those anymore. Speaking of bylines, she wrote the recent GQ cover story on Olu and we're guessing that's when she snagged him. Looks like the timing is right for her because y'all know she got fired from Spark. Word is, she was such a hot head in the office that they just had to let her go. She's slumming it on a freelance budget and we all know the pack of birds she hangs out with probably ain't got no money either. Well, we thought Felani was doing well but based on that last outfit we spotted her in (click here) where she was looking like a homeless lady from the future, we're guessing Jigga ain't giving up that money just yet. But anyway, we reached out to Nyela's reps and Olu's respective reps but got no comment. Olu seems pretty laid back but it's always those types who like crazy bishes.*
>
> *--As always, Chatty Abernathy, the Gossip Slayer*

"WHAT THE FUCK!" I snapped, interrupting their scene.

"Hold on," Mandy said, signaling for cameras to stop shooting.

She stepped over to me.

"See, that's why we wanted you to shoot!"

"I'm not shooting."

"Can we at least have you over the phone? We can mic you up, have you step outside, and have Reiko call you and get your thoughts on this."

"Fine. I can do that," I replied.

"YAY!" Reiko shouted.

I got mic'd, signed a waiver signing my audio life away, stepped outside and waited for Reiko's call.

"Hey, girl," I said, trying to sound as normal as possible.

Reiko went over the whole blog post with me again. Still angry, I repeated my usual, "WHAT THE FUCK!"

"Right! First of all, you don't even *have* a rep like that other than your pen game being strong! And how could they straight lie and say you got fired?" Reiko said.

I started tapping my foot out of frustration.

"You there, Nyela?" Reiko said.

"Yes, I'm still here."

"Are you ok?"

"No, I'm not okay! Chatty Abernathy is always talking shit about us! He or she, no, *she*—I have a feeling it's a woman—makes dumb-ass false assumptions on one hand yet at the same time, a lot of it is surprisingly accurate. *Who is she?*"

"Nyela, I'm about to put you on speaker, Cookie has a good theory," Reiko said.

"You definitely know this person! No one connected the fuchsia dress you were wearing in that photo Olu posted to the song. If anyone had, they would have released that information as soon as they realized it," Cookie said. "Fastforward a couple of weeks to when your spot gets blown up at *Regality.* A couple of hours later you're on Chatty Abernathy first. Either someone you work with *is* Chatty Abernathy or they're friends with her."

"I told you she was a sharp Cookie, no pun intended!" Reiko replied.

"That's actually how I got the nickname. I was very inquisitive as a kid, and always knew things about other people that I probably shouldn't have. It got to the point where adults in the neighborhood would occasionally bribe me with treats and money so that I would spill the beans on their cheating spouses, or just to be nosey about other neighborhood people period. I've always been observant and into business I shouldn't have been in so it earned me the nickname, 'Smart Cookie.' Cliché, but true."

"Geez, I'm never going to get on your bad side, you might write a book about me or some shit!" Reiko replied. "In the meantime, why don't you help us get on the case and figure out who this Chatty Abernathy is?"

"Actually, I know someone who may or may not be able to do some extensive hacking."

"Is it you?" I said.

"I didn't say that. All I'm saying is if things get a bit too ridiculous, there are ways to uncover what's what."

I got it. She didn't want to further incriminate herself on camera. I quit my line of questioning because I might actually take her up on that offer and didn't want to reveal too much, at least for now.

"Good to know," I replied. "My thing is, I knew it would come out eventually, but I wasn't ready for it to happen this soon. How did I go from being one of the most low-key people in the fucking industry to fodder for idiot bloggers trying to paint me as a crazy hoodrat!"

"It could be worse. *No one* could be talking about you at all," Reiko said. "You know it's when they—"

"Yeah, I know. It's when they stop talking about you, yadda yadda, but that's not my fucking philosophy. I don't care about that shit! I like living in peace as someone who covers the scene from behind the scenes, not one who is in the motherfucking news."

"It's harmless. Don't stress about it just yet," Reiko replied. "If it's not interfering with your life in a major way, then let it fly."

"Nah, man. My patience is wearing thin."

"Like I said, if you need me on the case, I got you," Cookie said.

Cookie might actually have what it takes to be crew, but I still wasn't letting my guard down just yet.

We hung up and I stepped back inside to watch them continue their conversation, while not actually eating. They rambled and did retakes of the most important conversations—translation, the most potentially shit starting conversations—and did retakes if Mandy didn't like the way they phrased certain things.

I knew Reiko liked attention like this, but I couldn't fathom having cameras in my face for several hours a day clocking my every move. Just watching them and doing that phone call was exhausting. I gave them a little bit of what they wanted, but had Reiko not lied to me by omission I might have actually filmed with them.

I headed home after we finally wrapped our conversation, but Reiko and Cookie decided to go to some club, at Mandy's suggestion, for more party and bullshit.

#TheGreatest

I stopped paying as much attention to hip-hop sites as I used to since joining *Regality*. Their audience only liked *some* hip-hop, which was refreshing since I still needed to recover from my time at *Spark*, but today I checked out the Hip-Hop Slangaz's site because I saw people bickering on Twitter about the site's newly released, and always highly anticipated, top emcees list. Olu was on it, of course, but I almost spit out my oatmeal when I noticed that he was listed at number two, second to King Tootsie. Were they fucking serious? King Tootsie, who could barely string a sentence together, nabbed the number one spot. *King Tootsie*, who was known for ignorant party anthems, most of which consisted of stupid dances, talk about doing drugs, having as much unprotected sex as possible, and the same five words chanted throughout the entire song!

Hip-Hop Slangaz had long been known for its extensive knowledge of hip-hop. It was a site run by men who grew up on hip-hop in various cities around the country, with different tastes and interests in the genre, and not some trust fund babies who just got into it last year. To say that I was surprised, and not much surprised me these days, was an understatement. Then again, they had been slipping in judgment over the last couple of years. Ever since they joined the Heavy Weights

Blog Network and started making serious money, their content was starting to get a lot less honest and definitely more mainstream generic, or advertiser friendly. However, Olu was dope all across the board. He had current mainstream appeal, but with golden era hip-hop sensibilities, he produced, had a good musical ear, knew how to bend genres, played some of the instruments on some of the beats he created for himself *and* others, wrote fire, and basically should have been first on that list. I wasn't just saying that because he was my boyfriend, either! Any critic who was worth their weight would have put him at number one. I guess this decision was based more on industry relationships than anything else because I did notice that the site had been posting a lot of King Tootsie ads lately. I knew for a fact that these were ads that brought in a lot of money based on their positioning on the site.

I continued reading the list until I got to a video at the end. It featured a round table of all three Hip-Hop Slangaz, and a few more of the biggest so-called cultural critics in pop culture at the moment, from various outlets, discussing why they chose each rapper for their particular ranking.

Their criteria were lyrics, skills and social media presence, with the latter seemingly being the most important. Olu, who got nothing but praise on his lyrical skills, flow and songwriting ability from each critic had 100 fewer Facebook fans, 50 fewer Twitter followers and 10 fewer Instagram followers than King Tootsie at press time, so they placed him in the number two spot.

I got that these lists also had more to do with generating shock value than anything else, other than ad dollars, but this was the dumbest rationale I'd ever heard. Yet it wasn't the first time I had heard of numbers influencing decisions like that. Numbers was all they cared about at *Spark*, and pretty much every entertainment media company that I knew of. Quality be damned! As long as you had high numbers on social media, or high traffic, or whatever, then you were considered gold, even if you really didn't know what you were doing. Again, King Tootsie was barely even coherent when he rapped. I bet the only reason he had more social media followers was because people liked to gawk at the dumb shit he posted. From Instagramming post coital shenanigans with groupies, to the fact that he loved that his billions of baby mamas were constantly fighting over him, to generally tweeting dumb commentary—like the time he said that dark-skinned women were stalkers because no one wanted them—he was a living spectacle, and people loved drama.

My first thought was to reach out to Olu, but I decided against it. I'd let him discover it on his own. I knew he was going to be pissed, and

I didn't want to be the bearer of that news, so I'd take it from when he came to me about it.

The next news item I spotted made me thankful that I didn't hang out with Cookie and Reiko last night after dinner. I spotted it first on Jelly Bananas, the self-proclaimed "Gender Bending Gossip Queen," and the headline read: **"Reiko Rodriguez Involved in Brawl With Lady Blaq Widow's Entourage"**

At least this one wasn't from that Abernathy chick, although I was sure she picked it up along with the other vultures. I'd get there eventually, but first I had to read what damage Reiko and Cookie had done.

> *Oooh, honey chile...it's your honey pie Jelly Bananas...and Miss Honey Thang got the scoop on some mess that went down last night at a swanky club in NYC...You all know I was there on the seen so lemme tell you, them crazies Reiko Rodriguez and Cookie Clark got into some drama.*
>
> *By now you know that Reiko Rodriguez of NYC's Morning Riot has a thing for fighting chile. And you probably also know that she has a long standing beef with Lady Blaq Widow over some things she once said about the rapper last mixtape...Well Reiko...who formerly appeared on* The Bad Girls Club...*is currently taping a new show about hip-hop couples. Attention whore maybe? Anyway, she got some bad news about her current boo thang super manager France Deveaux and her nemesis. They've been messing around behind her back (but we already knew that France*

will sleep with anything) and it looks like Lady Blaq Widow is now pregnant. And get this! France has plans to take Lady Blaq Widow on his management roster claiming that he can help boost her already in the slumps career.

Word is...Reiko and fellow cohost Cookie Clark...you know the has been video heaux we know from writing that tell all about her days as an industry jump off...strolled into the club for a casual night out with cameras in tow...just in time for Lady Blaq Widow and France's show, allegedly unaware that they were inside celebrating France's new...uh...clientele additions.

When Reiko walked in and saw her man hugged up on Lady Blaq Widow, she went HAM...honey chile! She started screaming and carrying on and Lady Blaq Widow for once in her life backed down...I guess because she was protecting her unborn fetus but next thing I know Reiko started swinging on France because he jumped in front of his soon-to-be babymama and told Reiko to calm down. Then he pulled Reiko to the side where he dropped the news that he was having a baby with the chick. Ooooh, messy!

Well, Reiko spazzed out even more. She tackled him and tried to strangle him. Now ya'll know...Reiko is a little bit, she's average height for a woman at best...and France is damn near 7 feet. It took all the bouncers to pry her off of him. She was cussing him out and then let the cameras and producers have it too because she thinks they set her up to be there knowing what she was going to walk into. But doesn't Miss Reiko honey chile already know how reality TV works? Anyway poor Cookie was trying hard to get Reiko to calm down but she got sucked into the drama when some big husky chick from Lady Blaq Widow's entourage through a drink on her and all hell broke loose again. Eventually...bouncers pried the brawling women apart and no one was seriously hurt but I did see a nasty gash on some chick's forehead as security was escorting them all out. There's no word on whether charges will be pressed against anyone but y'all know the folks at high class clubs like that don't play with negro shenanigans my honey chiles...Just messy!

My editor's brain wanted to print this technically *and* editorially terrible story out, make edits with the reddest marker I could find and send it back to Jelly Bananas for a much needed grammar, spelling, and punctuation lesson, particularly with regard to his ellipses abuse, and the fact that he should have used "scene," and "threw," among other things, but there was no point since he obviously missed those lessons in grade school. Checking on Reiko was more important, but I got a call from Tina first, just as I unlocked my phone.

"Hi Tina." I tried to sound as cheery as possible.

"You didn't post at least eight stories yesterday," was her greeting.

"What?" I replied, seriously confused. I could barely remember what happened 10 minutes ago let alone yesterday.

"I counted. You posted seven out of your contractual eight stories, and we can't let this be a thing. Do you know how damaging that is to traffic?"

"Yesterday was a slow news day, so I didn't think posting seven out of the eight would be a big deal since you said we could post less if nothing of note really came in. How about I just post an extra story today to make up for it?" I replied, ignoring her nonsensical dig about traffic.

"You can do that, but don't make it a habit. It's important that you meet your exact story quota each day because the readers look for them. Also, you're not doing enough social media work to promote *Regality* online."

"But I share links all across my personal networks—Twitter, Facebook, Google Plus, and even Instagram and Pinterest occasionally, which all have a decent amount of followers."

"Yeah, but you have to do it from the *Regality* social media accounts."

"I never got any log in information for *Regality's* social media accounts, nor was I told that I'd have to socialize that way. Isn't there a social media editor who can take care of social strategy?"

"We don't have a social media editor. It has been interns lately, but we don't even have any interns at the moment, and we won't for another few weeks. But that's not the point! Why would we need a social media editor when you should be doing it anyway?"

"Because social media is a completely different job, an important job that takes intense focus on a different set of priorities."

"Well, we don't have anyone for it at the moment, like I said, so you need to get all our passwords and start doing it yourself."

"Will we all be doing this in shifts?" I tried to keep my voice as even as possible.

"*I* won't be doing that social media stuff because *I* need to focus on management, but I'm sure you can get with Kimmie and figure something out. The better the social media management, the better our traffic."

She didn't even really know what she was talking about. Getting traffic wasn't as black and white as she seemed to think.

"Um...*sure.*"

I had checked out on this bitch, but the good news was, at least she wasn't cursing me out.

"So, what's the strategy in place already?"

I knew there was none, but I was partial to being a passive aggressive jerk in situations like this. As shitty of a company as *Spark* was, they at least had a social media manager and understood the digital space slightly better.

"Just log in, tweet, and people will find you. It's not brain surgery! I need you to start as soon as we hang up, okay?"

Now I *definitely knew* she didn't know what she was talking about.

"Sure," I replied.

"Okay then, it's settled."

She hung up.

God forbid I missed one story. Oh no, the ground was going to open up and swallow us whole!

I was surprisingly apathetic about that dumb-ass exchange I just had with Tina. I guess I had gotten used to Type A lunatics and inane management.

I held off on calling Reiko long enough to check the text messages I ignored from last night, and noticed that I got some new messages from Olu, during my exchange with Tina, at what must have been 7AM his time in L.A.

Hey. Got a minute for FaceTime? I want to see that pretty face.

I could hear his sexy accent as I read the text to myself, but my moment of excitement was fleeting when I remembered that list. I hit the

FaceTime button, hoping he was still free. I still wasn't going to bring it up if he didn't, though.

"Nyela! Show me some titties, it's hard times over here!"

I let out a hearty guffaw.

"Well, that was smooth," I replied.

"I miss you."

"I miss you too. For real, though, lift your shirt up real quick."

"Down, boy! Maybe I'll Snapchat you a little something later."

He laughed. "How's work, though? I know you've been stressed."

"I should be asking *you* that, but I got some good news. I think I'm ready to send my screenplay to Nero."

"That's fucking amazing! I know he's going to like it."

"How's L.A.? What they got *you* doing out there?"

"You already know. I've been avoiding doing press for now, but I know doing interviews is inevitable, so that's whatever. And I'm putting the finishing touches on my album. I'm working on a joint with Pharrell that might be as big as 'Fuchsia Girl' is shaping up to be. Anyway, what are you doing Fourth of July Weekend? I want you to come out here for a few days to spend some time with me. I'll put you on the red-eye."

"I ain't doing shit! L.A. would be fucking amazing! Let me hit you back in a sec, though. My mom is calling me and I have to pick up this time, I've been ducking her."

"Actually, I have an audition and then it's writing and recording for the rest of the day, so I'll call you tomorrow to finalize plans.

"Sounds   good," I replied, surprised he didn't mention the list yet.

I wanted to believe that he was still blissfully ignorant, but that wasn't likely. He *had* to have known. I couldn't wait to see him this weekend, but I was anxious about how annoyed he was going to be when he finally addressed it. This would be my first test as the supportive girlfriend. Now it was time to deal with my mother.

"Hi mom."

"Nyela, what is this your father tells me about you dating some rapper? You know how I feel about that!"

"Mom, dad probably got whatever he told you from those stupid blogs. Speaking of, he could have just reached out to me!"

"But you get so busy that you don't like answering your phone, and let's not even talk about your timetable for calling us back, hmph!"

She had a point, which I was ashamed to admit.

"Sorry, mom. You know I've been working a lot more since I started freelancing."

"Yeah, but that's no excuse. Family first. You know your father and I support you and don't like to see you so stressed. Why don't you come help me with social media and PR at the fitness studio while you work on your screenplay."

"That's actually not a bad offer. I'll think about that and get back to you, but speaking of the screenplay, I completed a version that I like enough to shop around."

I felt it was best to leave out the fact that I now had a real relationship with Nero. If she hadn't brought it up yet, it meant she didn't know. Plus, she'd just ask me a billion more questions, and I wasn't in the mood.

"Oh, Dimple Doll, that's amazing! You must let me know what happens with that. I know you know a lot of people and you're talented, so you'll be fine."

"I hope so, but listen mom, I gotta go."

"Wait, we didn't even get to talk about you ending up on these blogs. And are you dating someone right now?"

I knew she was fishing.

"When do I ever tell you and dad about the people I'm dating? But since you're asking, and since this is actually something that I won't be able to hide anymore—"

"Are you pregnant?"

"Mom, no! I'm dating a rapper/actor named Olu Major."

"Oh, my goodness! Olu Major! Olu Mensah, right? Isn't he the one that that big time Hollywood producer once said was too young and ghetto to play James Bond! He is a fine chocolate young man, and talented too!"

"Ew, mom!"

I cracked up laughing, surprised that she was even familiar with Olu.

"How on Earth do you know who Olu Major is?"

"You know your dad keeps up with that stuff, but Olu is different! He's actually really talented. I liked him when he did some guest spots on that HBO series that I like, and your dad played me some of his music, even that 'Fuchsia Girl' song."

I laughed again, more hysterically this time.

"What's so funny, sweetie?"

"Mom that song is about me."

"Oh my goodness! So you two are serious?"

"Uh, it has only been about a month, but we do have a really strong connection. We could be going places."

"You know your father and I got married within six months of meeting. Sometimes, when you know you know."

"Yeah, but cases like yours are extremely rare."

"Oh Nyela, have some faith! When are we going to meet him? You're getting too old to be indecisive about settling down."

"Mom, I'm not even 30 yet."

"But you're close."

"Thanks for reminding me."

"Is he too big to come over for dinner? We could play some Fela and Roy Ayers. I haven't touched my sax or my piano in forever, it'll be fun. We could have a jam session," my mom said. "You should come over this weekend for the Fourth!"

"Um...I can't this weekend, but I'll think about when and let you know."

"Well you know your birthday is coming up."

"Yeah, uh, maybe we can come over then, but I have to go right now. I'll call you soon about my birthday. Love you, bye."

I sobered up from that amusing conversation with mom, thoughts of lover boy even meeting my quirky parents, and called Reiko.

"Heeeey girl," Reiko sounded 50 times happier than I expected.

"Why do you sound so chipper?"

"Oh, I guess you heard about the drama from last night too, huh?"

"Uh, yeah! Jelly Bananas said producers tricked you into going to that club. What the fuck was *that* all about?"

"I mean that's just how reality TV works, but it's cool. The show doesn't even air until the fall yet my online followers have tripled across all networks and I'm already lining up some potential deals like, a lipstick line, and a possible advice book! How dope is that!"

"Reiko, snap out of it! It's me, your real friend. Please tell me what's *really* up! I know you're hurting."

"There's nothing up, seriously. France is an ass and I was dumb for giving him another chance."

I decided against admonishing her with the usual, "I told you so."

"I hope this is the last time you do this to yourself. Like, for real, for real."

"He's already trying to get back together."

I sighed. "Please tell me you're not seriously thinking about going back!"

"It could be good for the show, but don't worry about me, girl. I got a plan."

I didn't know why I bothered with her sometimes.

"A *plan?* It's either you get back with the drama or you don't. Cameras or not, entertaining his bullshit is stupid."

"Nye, you know I plan everything when it comes to my career."

"What does this have to do with your career, though?"

I wanted to hang up because I hated when she got like this. Reiko was one of the most sensitive people I knew, so I *knew* she was hurting, whether she wanted to admit it or not. France was the only man that I'd seen affect her this way. I still couldn't understand what she saw in him. He had money, but that wasn't an issue for Reiko. He was just as much of a douche as King Tootsie, but surprisingly with no children that we knew of, except for the possibility looming in Lady Blaq Widow's womb, pending a DNA test. And aside from his height, he wasn't even that cute.

The fact that he got around so frequently should have been enough to dump him. He had even slept with or tried to sleep with some of her friends, myself included. Reiko knew this stuff already and she still put up with it. I was driving my blood pressure up just thinking about his nasty ass.

"Don't worry, Nye, I'm good; this will at least keep me interesting on TV, " she said. "Anyway, speaking of King Tootsie, did you hear his new song? I posted it up on my site."

I let her slide and rolled with her attempt to change the subject. I guess she'd talk to me when she was ready.

"I didn't hear the song," I replied. "Given his track record, I'm not in a rush to either."

"Girl, you ain't never lied! It's a mess."

I was over talking to her so I rushed her off the phone. "I bet it is. Look, I gotta get to work, catch you later."

"Wait! What are you doing this weekend? Want to come to the Hamptons with me and Cookie? One of Cookie's boos has an amazing house out there, and it's open to us."

"Nah, I can't, I'm spending the weekend with Olu in L.A."

"Ooooh, that sounds sexy. Don't come back knocked up!"

"Girl, bye! Seriously, I'm hanging up."

"Wait, before you go, we're still on for Cynda's book release next week, right?"

"Yup. I'll hit you up when I get back in town."

I headed to Reiko's website out of curiosity about how terrible this new King Tootsie song would be and once again, he out did himself in awfulness. The beat sounded like it was from a Casio keyboard-generated 1980s video game, and he didn't start rapping until after about a minute of that cacophony, if you wanted to call shitty adlibs rapping.

"Heeeeeeeeey I need me a poontang bitch! A poontang bitch! Hey! Hey! Hey!" was the just of the entire song, no joke, and it had been posted on every single music blog in my feed, a fact that made me want to curl up into fetal position and cry. I would take some cool points away from Reiko for posting it, but her redemption was that she actually included her real opinion in her posts, and she admitted that it was trash. Being honest sometimes got her in trouble in this industry, but I liked that she didn't care. Most of the other media personnel just posted one-liners like, "New music from King Tootsie," in the body of the post, and let it be terrible. Some even lied about it actually being a new smash. I believed that the best way to deal with terrible music was to stop letting publicists and politics coerce people into publishing it, but I was in the minority. People would post it and pretend it was good for the sake of being popular and keeping relationships, just so that they could keep getting invites to wack ass events—another reason I wanted out of this part of entertainment media.

What surprised me about music today was when genuinely good artists like Olu actually made it to mainstream success, especially in hip-hop.

I texted Reiko my disappointment in King Tootsie's song, and my confusion about how someone like Cynda, who pretended to be so empowering and refined, could represent an asshole like him.

I continued checking my text messages and there was another one from Sincere.

Hey you, I miss you.

I considered the possibility that he was dumb enough to text me instead of Netscape, or whatever her name was, since both our names started with the letter N, but I knew it was a stretch. In fairness, he was actually not a stupid man. I'd been good about ignoring Sincere these days, but I couldn't resist replying this time with hopes that I'd get the chance to gloat about Olu's awesomeness.

Um...did you mean to text me?

Yeah. I miss u girl. But I see you've moved on. I hope you and Olu find happiness. I really mean that.

But aren't you and Nasonex shooting a reality show about how in love you are?

Nasonex though? That's cold lol! Anyway, yes, we're shooting a show, but sometimes you have to move on to realize who you should have truly been with in the first place. But I don't have all that Olu money so I know I can't compete.

I surprisingly decided against offering tidbits about Olu's greatness because it felt like I had won. Not that I was competing or anything, but come on, an ex reaching out after you had finally moved on was the greatness equivalent to indulging in the first bite of a warm homemade chocolate chip cookie.

I left Sincere hanging form that point since I knew he was trying to bait me, and continued my work for the day proud of myself and excited about spending more time with Olu this weekend, even if he would be working through a lot of it.

#CyndaSchmynda

My Fourth of July weekend with Olu was even more amazing than I expected. He did have to work, but he specifically set aside the Fourth, which was a Saturday, for his family and I. It wasn't my first time in L.A., but it was nice to be there with him. I arrived on Thursday morning and stayed his room at the Peninsula for the weekend, though we weren't in the room much. Although we didn't have a lot of time, we got a lot accomplished. In those short few days, I rolled with him to shoot a commercial for a major headphones brand, put the finishing touches on a sexy song he recorded and co-produced with Gary Clark Jr., screen test for a guest spot on *Empire,* and we went to lunch with one of my good friends from college, who was now a wardrobe stylist and costume designer in the movie world. On Saturday, we went to his paternal aunt and uncle's house for a cookout. His family seemed to like me, and it was fun to watch him interact with them.

He and his cousins even taught me how to azonto, a popular Ghanaian dance that I couldn't wait to show my mom. I didn't leave until Sunday night, so we spent the morning looking at a condo he considered buying, and then we browsed some of the streetwear stores on Fairfax. I refused his offers to buy me anything for the most part, but then we got to the Melody Ehsani store and saw that she had released a new sneaker collaboration with Reebok. He wouldn't take no for an answer, so I got some cute colorful snake print kicks, plus a couple of pieces of M.E. jewelry out of the deal.

Parting was bittersweet, but of course we did our usual routine on Facetime and Snapchat throughout the week, and I took solace in the fact that I'd be seeing him again soon. I made it to Thursday without any major incident, but the day isn't over. I committed to going to Cynda's book release party tonight, and I was pretty sure there would be fuckery afoot.

Reiko and I got to the party together, and I was glad there were no plans for her to tape her show. Cynda secured a private loft with a rooftop for her event. I noticed, when we stepped off the elevator, that most people were outside enjoying the weather.

I scoped our surroundings as we made our way outside, and I had to admit, Cynda had a good eye for décor, but the luxe surroundings weren't enough to distract me from shitty, pretentious people. This revelation reminded me that I really missed Olu even though it had only been a few days since I last saw him. Luckily for me, he'd be back in NYC in next week, just short of my birthday. I hadn't planned on celebrating, but I figured my birthday would be a good day to hang out with my kooky parents and have Olu join me for the fun.

"HEEEEY WARRIOR DIVAS!"

It was Nefertari Isis from Warrior Divas, "The number one source for all things Fierce, Fab and Feminism." She greeted Reiko and I respectively with that kiss on each cheek thing that Europeans do—but this chick was from The Bronx.

"You ladies look fab! Let me take some photos of you for my street style section!"

"Since when did you have a street style section?" I asked.

"It's new. I decided to start showcasing all the beautiful sisStars of the world since we are constantly marginalized by the mainstream. We gotta keep it fierce, fly and feminist! Smile!"

Reiko drew me closer to her side and we smiled through gritted teeth. Ideally, this should have ended once we approved our photo, but that wasn't realistic. Instead, Nefertari decided to pry.

"So, no fuchsia dress today, huh?"

She winked at me.

"Girl, what?"

"Don't act like we don't know who your new man is! I hope your influence on him will inspire him to continue being a positive example to the rest of these brothers out there. They, too, must learn that it's okay to be in love and sing the praises of their queen! We must overcome this pathological misogynoir perpetuated by these Ashy Ankh Hotep Niggas!"

"Um, yeah, okay, gotta go!"

I grabbed Reiko and dashed off.

"Nice girl, but she's so ridiculous," Reiko said in a low conspiratorial tone.

We cracked up laughing, but sobered up as we spotted Cookie and Cynda, and realized they were engaged in a heated conversation. They were off to the side, presumably trying to keep the discussion away from the party, but Cookie was extremely animated. Despite speaking in hushed tones, she was making aggressive hand gestures.

"That conversation doesn't look too inviting, but let's overstep our boundaries anyway," said Reiko, and I was definitely here for her suggestion.

We continued eavesdropping on their exchange, unnoticed, and discovered that Cookie was confronting Cynda about some behavior that wasn't in alignment with her female empowerment shtick.

"Cookie, I assure you this wasn't my doing. I mean, our ideas were similar anyway and I guess I pitched mine better," Cynda said.

"That's bullshit! You got that idea from me! I explained it to you over brunch and you took notes claiming you wanted to pitch it for me as my manager!"

"I never said I…"

Cynda finally noticed us.

"Welcome ladies, I hope you're enjoying the party," she said in a faux cheery tone. "In case you didn't know, you're welcome to all the champagne and cupcakes you can eat, right on the other side of the room."

"Sure," I replied, stifling my laughter.

She was seriously trying to pretend like she didn't know we had caught part of her conversation with Cookie. Naturally, Reiko and I stuck around.

"You aight, Cookie?" Reiko said.

"No!"

"Oh, it's just a misunderstanding that we're working through," Cynda replied. "Business stuff."

"I'll drop this for now, on the strength of the fact I've decided not to ruin your party," Cookie said.

"Ooh look, there's Miriam and Princess," Cynda said, as if she didn't even hear Cookie, and pranced away.

"What the fuck happened?" I asked.

"I'll explain eventually, but right now I need a minute alone," Cookie replied, before storming off.

"I told you Cynda was shady," I said, as Reiko and I continued to the terrace.

"Yeah, but Cookie plays hardball too. Whatever is going on probably isn't going to end well for Cynda."

"If you say so."

"Trust me. Get that popcorn handy because Cookie *will* handle this, and it's going to be entertaining."

We finally got to the rooftop area and noticed there was a red carpet set up on one side where Felani was posing for photographers, dressed nothing short of a lunatic.

"I thought Felani was recording tonight?" Reiko said.

"I thought so too, but apparently she found time to dress like a scorpion and head to this party."

Actually, she looked like the offspring of a scorpion that mated with Homey D. Clown. She was wearing a pink Afro wig styled into two Afro puffs, rainbow platform moon boots, and a neon yellow pleather unitard with a long black stinger sticking straight up.

"Reiko, I hope you know this is our fault. She obviously took our style badgering to heart."

"No it's not! We told her to step it up, and *she* was the one who mentioned having all these hush-hush dynamic plans to get people talking about her style. This is *not* what we meant!" Reiko shouted. "Now let's go see what the fuck is going on."

We got to Felani just as she finished up her last few photos.

"OH MY GOD! IT'S MY BOOS! GET OVER HERE!"

She was obviously excited to see us, but her tone of voice was different.

I had never heard her say "Oh my god" out of excitement, and there was something a lot less Brownsville and more Kim Kardashian vocal fry about her tone. We joined her on the carpet for obligatory photos.

"These are my girls right here," Felani said, as she and Reiko made gratuitous duck faces and hugged each other ad nauseam for cameras.

I tried not to roll my eyes and forced a smile, despite feeling awkward.

"Nyela, where's Olu?" yelled one of the photographers.

"Working," I replied.

"My brother Olu is out there working hard! He's tryna get her that rock!" Felani said.

"So you guys are getting married?" said another photographer.

"No! Felani, what the hell!"

"Girl, you know he's about that life. He loves him some you."

"Nyela and Olu sitting in a tree..." Reiko chanted.

"K-i-s-s-i-n-g..." joined Felani.

"Forget ya'll!" I replied and stormed off.

Damn attention whores!

"Aw, Nyela we're sorry we blew up your spot!" Felani shouted after me gleefully.

She and Reiko obviously thought fanning the fire for these non-reporting ass reporters was cute. I got that *they* wanted to promote themselves, but I didn't want to be apart of their shenanigans.

I headed to the other side of the terrace, as far away from the red carpet as possible, and took in Midtown's beautiful skyline as I took deep breaths and calmed down. I could still see Felani and Reiko from where I was and watched them mingle with the crowd. I settled onto a couch and prepared to tweet my whereabouts just for the hell of it, but peace was hard to come by at events like this.

"You're Nyela, right?" said a familiar voice.

I looked up to find Miriam towering over me, trying horribly to pretend like she didn't know who the fuck I was.

"Yup," I replied, staring back into my phone's screen.

"Mind if I sit down?"

That was a rhetorical question because she abruptly plopped down next to me before I even answered.

"So, you and Olu, huh?"

"Me and Olu what?"

"That's your man now, right?"

Why the fuck was she asking questions she already knew the answer to?

"Yup."

"Wow, you must be special. I only got a song *after* the break up, and definitely not for wearing a dress," she said looking me up and down. "He did always like heavier women, though."

I ignored that last bit of shade because one, I was a toned Coke bottle-shaped size 6, which wasn't heavy in real life, and at an average body fat percentage according to my doctor. Two, I'd be mad too if I were built like a string bean.

"Mmhmm," was all I mustered in reply. I didn't make much eye contact during the whole exchange, hoping she'd pick up on my disinterest and leave me alone with my phone and Twitter, but nope that was never how situations like this worked.

"So, what's he like now?"

I got an e-mail message from Nero just as I was about to tell her to fuck off, so I used that instead as an excuse to remain silent and scooted a few feet away from her. She was still close enough to make me sick, but I figured that with my back turned to her I'd get a few moments of fleeting solitude.

"Did he just text you?" she said, slightly louder than her previous tone since I was a little farther away from her.

I shot her a, "Bitch please!" side eye, proceeded to read my message, and almost fainted.

"OH MY GOD!" I shouted, just as Felani and Reiko rejoined me.

"Do we have to take the trash out?" Felani said with her natural Brownsville accent back on as she eyed Miriam.

I wanted to laugh at Felani despite the palpable intensity of her rage. I didn't care how tough she was. She still looked ridiculous.

"No, I got some good news..."

I started to blurt out what I had just read, which was that Nero loved my script and he wanted to help me see the film become a full on production after I made a few edits to the screenplay. He wanted to give me that bit of news personally, but moving forward, I had to schedule a meeting with him through his assistant so that we could talk in depth and make sure we were on the same page. However, I figured it would be best to keep that news to myself for now.

"…I'll tell you what it is later."

I could barely breathe from excitement, and Miriam's presence no longer mattered.

"I was just leaving!" Miriam said as she waved us off and stormed away in a huff.

"Bye bitch!" Reiko shouted after her. "I hope your baby daddy isn't somewhere expanding the world population again with his crowd sourced dick!"

Our collective fit of laughter raged so loud that it startled people, even over the music. But jokes aside, I needed to know what the fuck was up with Felani's outfit.

"Felicia Simpson," I said, noticing her cringe, which she always did whenever someone said her real name. At least she knew I was serious, though. "With all due respect. What the entire fuck are you wearing?"

"And what the fuck have you been wearing lately!" Reiko added. "I've seen you up on these blogs and even in *PEOPLE* magazine a lot lately for your fashion choices, and that's not a good thing. You were supposed to turn things around for the better. You got some explaining to do!"

"Well, you and everyone else were right about me needing to switch up my style, but I decided to go in a slightly different direction. I discussed it with my team and we decided it was best that I hire a stylist who can help me get more cross over attention. We wanted people to look at me more as an avant-garde artist than a rapper from the hood, so that's what I did and you bitches are *still* complaining."

"We didn't say to dress like a Killer Klown From Outer Space!" Reiko replied.

"But I'm getting attention that I didn't used to get. You said it yourself, you saw me in *PEOPLE!*"

"Not all attention is good attention, though," I replied.

"I'll take whatever I can get while I'm still on the come up. Once my numbers and endorsement deals get to where I want them then I'll flip another switch and make my style more classy and grown up."

"But you're already crazy popular! You're in talks with MAC for a line!" Reiko said. "What you've done already ain't so bad for a girl from the hood."

"Don't get me wrong, I'm proud of and love where I'm from, but this is what I have to do for more crossover love for now," Felani replied. "Speaking of, I finally got my first official single and my debut release date straight."

"CONGRATULATIONS!" Reiko and I screeched in unison.

"I can't say too much just yet because I'm still putting the final touches on the single, but I'll keep you posted. Y'all know I'm gonna need your help!"

"We got your back, girl!" Reiko replied, drawing Felani in by the waist for a side-hug.

I spotted Cookie headed in our direction with a facial expression similar to what I'd imagined she'd look like if her wallet had been stolen.

"I want to rip that bitch's head off, but I'm not going jail for her!" she said.

"But what did she do exactly?"

"She stole my fucking idea! She was supposed to be pitching my next book as my manager, but pitched it to *my* motherfucking agent behind my back, as if it were hers, and now she has a deal to write *my* book!"

Me, Reiko and Felani just stared at her at a loss for words.

"Mind you, I mentioned the idea to my agent before Cynda ever came into the picture, but she was reluctant due to my reputation from my first book."

Cookie briefly gazed at the skyline with watery eyes but managed to continue without crying.

"They basically want me to keep playing the whistle-blowing video hoe role, even though I told them several times that I'm off that. My next idea was more motivational, but using my experiences in the industry as anecdotes. Cynda somehow convinced my agent that she'd be a better fit to write the book."

"How do you know that's what she did?"

"Because my bitch-ass agent told me so, after I confronted her. She's a fucking coward, and she knows that what she did was wrong so she told me the truth, more so in an attempt to make Cynda seem like the bad guy who bullied her into this deal. No one pressures an agent into doing anything!"

We were used to hearing stories like this. In this industry, people didn't bat an eye when they fucked you over, especially when it came to jacking ideas, even people who pretended they would never do such shady things.

"Okay, so now what?" Reiko said.

"You want me to get some goons to go fuck that bitch up?" Felani added.

"I don't know yet," Cookie replied. "I'm going to enjoy my pre-birthday trip next week, have my birthday bash when I get back, and then I'll figure things out."

As if on cue, Cynda headed to the DJ booth to prepare for a bullshit speech.

"Attention ladies!" she said as more people started spilling out on to the terrace.

She was wearing a silver cocktail dress with puffy shoulders straight out of the '80s. She seemed to be channeling Dominique Deveraux from *Dynasty* and actually looked nice, although still ridiculous given that it was the 21st century.

"I want to thank you all for coming out tonight in celebration of my book, *Work Diva! How to Become an Alluring Woman and Attain Everything You've Ever Wanted in Your Entire Life*. Soon, you will benefit from my nuggets of wisdom and learn how to live a fabulous life with or without the man of your dreams. I have been living by the mantras and advice in my book my entire life, and it's exactly why I stand before you today with a successful career that spans multiple industries and with multiple lucrative income streams. Follow my advice and you will also be on course toward ruling the world."

Cynda's minions—a.k.a. most of the crowd—erupted into raucous applause and I even heard a few, "Go girls!" being shouted.

"Settle down ladies. There's more. I just landed a publishing deal with Simon & Schuster for my next book! I wasn't supposed to announce that news just yet, but I'm just so happy, and those of you who follow me on social media know how important I feel it is to wallow in your blessings. Yaaaaaasssss hunties!"

I didn't clap, but I did want to vomit.

"But back to today's news," she continued. "I never would have been able to release *Work Diva! How to Become an Alluring Woman and Attain Everything You've Ever Wanted in Your Entire Life* if I didn't believe in myself enough to publish it on my own. Those of you who pre-ordered will all get 30% off a coaching session with me. It is my honor to continue serving as your inspiration. Now that the formalities are aside, let's get back to the party!"

Cynda took a sip of champagne and started two-stepping, joined by her crew on stage.

"I'm done for the night. See you ladies later," Cookie said before making her exit.

I watched her vanish into the crowd, surprised by how much restraint she practiced, and still wondered what the hell she was planning to do to Cynda. I sensed it was going to be epic.

#MeetTheParents

I had been really intentional about never dating or sleeping with any actual celebrities throughout my entire career. I had also been really diligent in my general dating life about never bringing anyone home, not even Sincere. My parents may have heard a name or two when it came to my boyfriends, and there weren't many, but they never actually met any face to face because I never felt that any were *really* ready. Yet here I was, giving Olufemi Mensah a tour of my home after dating for a short while. It was surreal, but it felt right.

My parents embraced Olu with ease as soon as we got to their place. They treated him like he was any ol' body because as far as they were concerned, *he* was auditioning for *them*. When we first arrived, my mom badgered me about the fact that it was mid-July and I hadn't seen them since Memorial Day, which was embarrassing since I didn't live far from them, but other than that I was happy to be home and that Olu could share this experience with me. Surprisingly, Olu seemed comfortable and even wanted a tour of the house because he was fascinated by New York City brownstone architecture.

"Okay, Olu, I've saved the best for last," I said, leading him by the hand into my childhood bedroom, which was kept exactly how I left it before leaving for college. "This is the space that cultivated my imagination."

"This is exactly what I imagined your old bedroom would look like," he replied, picking up and examining one of my old pointe shoes.

The walls were covered in posters, particularly black memorabilia that commemorated some of my favorite moments in performing arts history, and ran the gamut from film to hip-hop.

"Yeah, I guess my design aesthetic is pretty much the same, but more grown up now," I replied, while unsuccessfully trying to snatch my pointe shoe from him.

"Hold up! Let's take these with us, we can do some things with these!" he said, toppling on top of me after nudging me on to my old bed. "I'm picturing you naked, with these on, doing some sexy contortion shit on top of my piano. Ooh, we haven't actually done it on my piano yet."

I melted for a moment as he started planting soft kisses on my neck and we then began making out, but I caught myself once I got the urge to undo his belt buckle. It was starting to get too steamy.

"Not here!" I said, gently pushing him off of me. "Get an eyeful of my room and let's get back downstairs before my parents come looking for us."

An impish grin spread across his face. "You think they'd notice if I gave you a hickey?"

"YES!"

I was so turned on that I contemplated giving in, especially when his impish grin turned into a devilish laugh.

"I dig that Josephine Baker poster," he said. "Let's get you one of those banana skirts, you know, for research purposes."

"Oh my God, Olu! Let's go!" I snapped, amused.

I wasn't about taking that risk after all. There was no coming back from parents catching you having sex, and this was my first time bringing a man home, like I said, so chancing getting caught in the act was a no go. I started to make my way out of the room, but Olu gently pulled me back.

"Okay. I'll chill out for now," he said. "But I do want to give you your gift before we go back downstairs."

"Gift? Olu, I—"

"I know, you told me not to get you anything, but I couldn't resist."

He handed me a small white box with a tiny fuchsia bow on top. I opened it and revealed a gold nameplate necklace that said, "Nyela."

"What the fuck!" I said joyfully.

Once again, I told him in random conversation about how I had broken my previous nameplate necklace, which was one of my favorite pieces of jewelry, and that I eventually planned to get another one, and here he was coming through with a new one.

"Believe it," he said, making a move to drape the necklace around my neck.

I lifted my twists to assist him, and that was exactly when my mom called us downstairs to eat. She prepared a vegan soul food spread of raw collard green salad with peanut vinaigrette, candied yams, grilled barbecue tempeh, and red beans and rice.

"I see you've got a new piece of jewelry, Dimple Doll," my mom said, as we joined she and my dad at the table in the backyard.

"Yeah, it was my birthday gift from Olu."

"How did you manage to get her to put it on," my dad said. "I *know* she told you no gifts."

"DAD!"

"Yeah, she did. I'm learning how stubborn she can be," Olu replied.

"Sounds like someone else I know," my mom said, playfully glaring at my dad. "Those two are two peas in a pod when it comes to being stubborn. I've never seen anything like it."

"But I see Nyela gets her stunning looks from you, Mrs. Barnes," Olu replied. "You two look like twins."

My mom was a rich almond-hue of brown and obviously couldn't blush, but I could tell she was flattered.

"Oh, stop it, and call me Harriet!"

My dad kissed my mother's hand. "She gets even finer as time goes by! If y'all make it, you'll have a lot to look forward to young man."

"Ew, you guys!" I said.

"I love this. How long have you been married?" Olu replied.

"32 years," my dad replied. "And I still can't believe she's mine."

"I didn't give him a hard time either. He captivated me right away," my mom replied. "I didn't plan to pursue what I was feeling because I wanted to focus on my business, but apparently, he felt the same way."

"It might sound cliché, but this was one of those situations that when you know, you know," my dad said. "I was fresh out of law school and sitting on that stoop out there, writing the business plan for my company. It was summertime, so sundresses were in season, and I got a glimpse of this beautiful brown creature filling out a yellow dress with that dance body, and fell in love on sight."

"So, it wasn't just me," Olu replied, laughing.

My dad smiled, pulled his chair closer to my mother, and then nuzzled her cheek with his nose.

"Dad! Continue the story, please!" I snapped, not as grossed out as I pretended to be. They were actually really cute.

"She was new to the neighborhood, so I started asking around about her and come to find out, she was the owner of the new dance studio everyone had been buzzing about. I needed some work to hold me over until I got my business going, so I went to see if she needed help, and she actually needed another djembe player for some of her dance classes," my dad continued. "I started the next day. We went on our first date the following week. Within a month, I helped her launch djembe classes for drummers in training, and six months later we were married."

"Wow, so that can actually work, huh?" Olu said. "My parents, as traditional and conservative as they like to pretend they are, got married because my mom got pregnant with me after a year of dating. They at least still like each other, but there's definitely no spark like what I'm seeing here."

"It can work, but don't get no ideas," my dad replied, winking.

"He was the finest man I had ever seen, and there was just something about his spirit that felt right," my mom said. "We moved faster than most, but I think one of the best things for us was that we waited a few years before having Nyela, so we got to know each other through amazing conversation, travel, getting our businesses off the ground, and really just cultivating that connection we felt. Marrying Josiah is still the best decision I've ever made next to having Nyela."

"I see why Nyela is so amazing," Olu said, grabbing my hand.

"What about you, son?" my dad said. "I know who your parents are, so how the hell did you become a rapper? I did read the story my Dimple Doll wrote about you, but nothing beats hearing it from you in the flesh."

Olu went into the story we're familiar with by now, about how he had been a rebellious soul his entire life, and took us through how he ended up in the United States starring on *Lockers*.

"Dimple Doll, I like him. I like that he's not like a lot of those other rappers," my mother said.

"Um, so, Olu, in case you couldn't tell, my mom isn't quite the hip-hop fan. I know I've mentioned this, but I can't stress it enough."

"My parents aren't either," he replied. "They've lightened up on me now that I've started to make money, but I still don't think they've even heard one song of mine. They think most hip-hop promotes negativity and that music or anything in the arts can't be a real career, but what's funny is, my dad was in a high-life band when he met my mom, yet they seemed to have forgotten that life."

"That's too bad," my dad replied. "You got some real talent, and you actually have something to say in your music. I like how versatile you are, too. I managed to get Harriet here to appreciate the musical value and lyricism in your work."

"I appreciate that, Mr. Barnes. I can't always be as musical as I'd like to be since I do have to go for a more commercial sound on occasion, but I'm all about lyrics when they count most, music theory, instrumentation, and talking about my personal experiences and observations, none of that fake stuff. That's why I like performing with live bands."

"Oh really?" my mom said.

I saw her brain working and had an idea what she was thinking. We had finished dinner by that point, so I figured she was preparing to spring a plan for what we were going to do next. It definitely involved the djembes, piano and saxophone set up in the living room, which served more decorative purposes lately.

"As you saw, we have a nice array of instruments set up in the living room." She got up and motioned for us to follow her.

My dad followed swiftly behind her. I grabbed Olu's hand and followed my parents. What followed became an epic jam session. My mom started out by playing the opening saxophone riff to Fela Kuti's "Water No Get Enemy." Olu joined her on the piano, and my dad added some improv on the djembe. I don't sing much, but I can hold a note, so I lent my vocals here and there. We laughed and jammed to various popular songs, even some we created.

Eventually, my mom brought out a surprise birthday cake, even though I *definitely* told her no cake, and they serenaded me on being another 365 days older. I was usually at a party or out of town on my birthday, but the simplicity and genuine love that I felt here was everything. I was a little freaked out about my age since I wasn't quite where I wanted to be just yet, but I was thankful for another opportunity to get it right, and hopeful about what was coming. With the recent events that had been unfolding, it looked like I was finally starting to head in the new direction that I had been praying for.

Part III

#SOBs

I didn't realize how long it had been since I actually attended a show at SOBs until I stepped out of the Houston Street station and the memories starting flooding back. Back in my intern days, I was out and about as much as possible fraternizing with people I thought were movers and shakers at various shows and open bars. I was at SOBs for a show every other week. That was back before I knew what bullshit awaited me. However, despite my jadedness, I still enjoyed supporting genuinely talented artists, especially if it was my boyfriend who happened to be headlining, which was a concept that I was still getting used to.

I couldn't believe that I was sulking over douchebag Sincere just a couple of months ago, and that I was in love—though we hadn't said the L word to each other yet—with an unexpected man who seemed to be authentically good. It still tripped me out how grounded he was. I was still learning to just go with it, but the cynic in me still wanted to count down until he started acting an ass.

I entered the venue just as Olu finished his sound check and wanted to scream like a toddler because we could spend some more time together, even if it was just a few hours before the show started. Instead of screaming, I kept my spaz more silent by rushing him for a hug. I hadn't seen him since my birthday celebration almost two weeks ago.

"I missed you too," he said, catching me as I jumped on him and wrapped my legs around him.

His grip around me was firm, and I nuzzled his neck so that I could take in that cologne that I loved. There was something about the way it blended with his pheromones that made me wish I could bottle it up just for myself. By the time he put me down, I collapsed onto his chest until he was the only force supporting me, and I closed my eyes as we kissed.

"Let's go get some grub!" he said, pecking me on the lips one more time.

He led me to a greenroom downstairs where there was pizza and arugula salad topped with fresh shaved Parmesan cheese waiting for us. I was surprised that we were entirely alone, at least for a little while.

"No manager or publicist?" I said.

"They're around, but I told them to give me at least until 7 before they barge in with work."

"Speaking of work, how out of the loop have you been?" I said.

He still hadn't mentioned that Hip-Hop Slangaz list, but surely he must have felt some type of way about it.

"Probably very out of the loop. I've checked the web here and there, but I've been kicking it with you when I could, and getting this money so that our future kids can be straight."

He winked at me and I emitted a low quick laugh, not knowing how to reply to that.

"You're cute when you feel awkward," he said.

"Who said I feel awkward?"

"That laugh did. I know you, Nye."

"WHATEVER!"

We both laughed.

"There's something I've been dying to tell you, but I wanted to wait until we got face to face," Olu said.

"What's up?"

"As you know, 'Fuchsia Girl' is getting nuff love everywhere, so the label wants to shoot a video. As a matter of fact, the label wants to do a video for each song on my album to be released exclusively when the album drops."

"NICE! What directors will you be working with?"

"The creative direction is on my terms since I'm paying for it, so I've enlisted Nero to direct exclusively, and he wants you to help him write the treatment for 'Fuchsia Girl,' and star as my lead. I told him not to tell you because I wanted to be the one to see *that* exact look on your face."

"Are you fucking serious!"

"You heard me, love. It's yours if you want it."

"Of course I want it! First the screenplay, now this! Hell yes! But wait, co-writing is cool, but *me* as the lead too? Isn't that a bit much? I'm no actress."

"Nothing's a bit much unless you think it is. You deserve this. Plus, I'd rather not hire an actress or model since they're not you. You know the concept of my album is basically about my journey from London to the United States, and I need each video to reflect that as much as possible. Who better to do 'Fuchsia Girl' than you—the woman who inspired the song?"

The rascally smile he flashed as he pulled me closer to him didn't leave my internal critic with much functionality. Actually, I wanted to jump his bones, so turning him down was obviously impossible.

"Good point, babe. I'll do it!"

Admittedly, I would have gotten jealous if he got to work with some impossibly beautiful woman who was playing me. Any other song would have been fine, but not this one. He was right. It was better to have the real thing. I was no actress, but with all the theater training in my past, I wouldn't be half bad with a little more work. Plus, it wasn't like I'd have lines like that. This was more about the music and the visuals that complemented the song. The writing part of this was what I was *really* excited about, though. This was going to be an awesome step toward the career direction that I really wanted. However, I knew that I'd have to tough it out at *Regality* for a little while longer since I hadn't talked specifics about *my* screenplay with Nero yet. His schedule was so jam-packed lately, but I was still excited about what was coming—a feeling that I missed feeling about my career, about my life.

We noshed on our pizza and chatted as usual. He told me about more travel he had coming up. I shared with him about how bitchy the women at *Regality* were, but I also gossiped about the drama between Cookie and Cynda since I hadn't gotten a chance to tell him, and I was dying to tell someone who wasn't involved. That was when Olu revealed that he also didn't trust Cynda because she tried to seduce him back when he was head-over-heels for Miriam, despite the fact that Cynda and Miriam were supposed to be so-called best friends. Of course, this further confirmed my theory that she was really an evil genie disguised as a debutante!

Our playtime was interrupted when Olu's manager, Fish, walked in with new information about last-minute show adjustments. I stepped outside to avoid the business chatter, opting instead to see what guests were starting to arrive.

It was about 7:45 and the show was scheduled to start at 8:30, so people were starting to trickle in. I saw a few familiar faces milling about, but none that I knew very well so I kept my distance. Reiko didn't give me an arrival time, but I knew it would most likely be after the show started, and Olu mentioned that Felani was going to perform her verse on one of his mixtape classics, a new song, and do hype woman duty, but she hadn't arrived yet either, so I made my way back to the greenroom before I got trapped in a random conversation with anyone, but it was too late.

"Nyela, hold up!"

I heard the signature baritone voice first and then felt the firm grip on my arm from behind. It was France. In all the years that I had known him, he may have actually acknowledged my presence twice in public, so why the fuck was he grabbing me?

"Hi," I said, not sure what to expect.

"Have you seen Reiko?"

"Not yet."

"Is she coming?"

"She said she was, but I haven't spoken to her since this morning."

"Damn. Okay."

And with that he took off to the bar. He only got like this when Reiko pretended to be adamant about not wanting to speak to him anymore. Like I said, I was used to their drama over him fooling around with hoards of women, but this Lady Blaq Widow thing was the worst. I was reading some story just the other day where France said he was convinced that it was King Tootsie's kid.

"Ooooh is that you Miss Nyela? I been looking for you, honey child!"

This time it was Jelly Bananas, the gossip blogger with all the sass of Madea and an affinity for androgynous clothing. Today, he was wearing a button down white shirt with a bowtie and cummerbund, black tuxedo pants, and some six-inch classic black Louboutins. He was wearing Ruby Woo on his lips, winged black eyeliner, and his hair looked luscious and healthy in a shoulder-length bob with a neatly trimmed goatee framing his face. He *looked* fly, but he was annoying as fuck. I cursed under my breath.

"You were looking for...*me*?" I replied.

Neither of us knew the other well enough for him to have been "looking for me." Something was definitely up.

"Ooh girl, honey child. Where is that man of yours, girl? He's about to get into something deep!"

"*What?*"

"Girl, yes honey, lemme tell you girl, honey child. Your man started some drama when he was over there in L.A. doing interviews."

"Please explain what you're talking about in straight sentences without all the honey boo boo effects."

"Sista girl, I can't not have effects. It's what Miss Jelly Bananas Does, honey! But before your man came back from L.A., he made a stop by the top morning show out there, and he finally addressed the fact that he's not happy about that top emcees list, and now the clip is circulating all over the internets. He don't want to be number two behind no King Tootsie, and I can't say that I blame him. Girl, yo' man talked real greasy about King Tootsie, but you know Tootsie finna come for him, right?"

Like I said, I purposely didn't bring up the emcee list stuff with Olu because I wanted him to tell me in his own time. He was selective about the interviews he did, which was why it probably took him so long to finally get around to addressing it publicly, and now here I stood, before this Bananas character, who was fishing for information and also trying to stir up more drama. We all knew that Olu should have been number one, so why wouldn't he be upset? Olu was extremely honest and direct, but it wasn't his style to trash talk in interviews, though. I knew that Jelly Bananas was prone to exaggeration, but I was curious about what he was talking about.

I finally made it back to the green room with the intention of asking Olu about these so-called crazy interviews, but Fish was still there and now so was Emma, Olu's publicist. I'd rather not have this conversation in front of them, but they were his staff and I figured it was now or never, or at least now or not for a while, and my curious mind needed to know *now*.

"What happened during your interviews before you left L.A. this last time?"

"I talked to them about my projects. You know, interview stuff."

"Cute, but why did Jelly Bananas tell me that you were talking smack about King Tootsie being number one on the top emcees list?"

"Of course I'm tight about that list! That was the first interview I did since it happened, and I talked about it because they asked me about it. Everyone has been trying to get me to talk about it. I knew it was something that needed to be addressed, so I finally did and it wasn't that deep. I stated my position, which was that I felt like I should have been number one, and that the judges failed by using social media over lyrics and sound quality as one of the determining factors—nothing more, nothing less, just my truth. You know how these online personalities blow everything out of proportion."

"Yeah, but Jelly Bananas is pretty big," Emma said. "Let's look into this because if you're on track for a public beef, then we have to position it so that we can maximize your visibility and favor."

She pulled up Jelly Bananas' website on her phone and found a video snippet of the interview. At this point it had gotten more than one million views. The reception wasn't good enough for us to play the video without interruption, but there was enough of a description under the headline for us to get the gist of what was being said about it. In true to blog journalism style, the inflated headline read: **"Olu Major Slams Top Emcees List and Goes in on King Tootsie."**

> *Honey Childs lemme tell you. That foine specimen of a rapper Olu Major is doing all that promo stuff for his upcoming album and ya'll know them Hip-Hop Slangaz done made him number two on their top rapper's list. And behind none other than King Tootsie at that! Say what honey girl? Yes child! That non-rapping midget with a thousand babymamas! Y'all know everyone has been saying Olu Major was the golden child of hip-hop and all that but he is not feeling being number two. He went on the LA Stunnas Morning*

Show and let errybody have it behind that poor judgment call! You can find the video clip below but in case you don't feel like watching here's what he said:

"It's unfortunate that a decision about something that should be about skills and talent boiled down to the amount of Twitter followers one has. Tootsie and I are two different types of rappers and if you look at what I represent based on the fundamental principals of hip-hop and musicality then it's obvious that I should have been number one on the list. The truth is, I have better rhyme skills, beats, and a musical ear, and I still know how to make a good commercial hit. Anyone worth their salt in critiquing hip-hop or music in general as an art form knows that I'm the better choice, but again, it depends on what elements you're looking at because he and I are apples and oranges. It's cool. It's not gonna stop me from doing what I need to do, and it's not going to stop me from reaching the people who continue to rock with me."

"That's all you said?" Emma said, disappointed.

"Yup," Olu replied.

"I shoulda known that damn Jelly Bananas was exaggerating," I added.

"So we can all move past this now, right?" Olu said.

"You do realize that you're not going to be able to move past this as easily as you'd like to, right?" Emma said.

"But it's not that deep," Olu replied.

"Be prepared for the majority of every interview you and Tootsie do respectively, from now on, to consist mostly of questions to one about the other about this situation," I said. "Every single outlet is going to want some sort of exclusive quote and try to create more hype so that they get traffic."

"She's right. What you said wasn't bad, but it's not favorable, and people, especially you rappers with your fragile egos, are sensitive and always looking for a way to get attention, and the media is going to continue blowing it out of proportion," Emma said. "The nature of this beast means we're sitting on a potential fire storm, but that's not a bad thing."

"This is a good time to get eyes on you," Fish said. "Your album is finally dropping in September, and we're about to shoot major visuals. As long as we're prepared, this works in our favor."

"We haven't heard any King Tootsie interviews in response yet, so let's not get ahead of ourselves," I said. "He surprisingly doesn't do too many interview either, but I'm pretty sure it's coming. Olu, you better get that diss track ready, or at least think of some memes you can create about him just in case!"

"A diss track from King Tootsie? I'll body that dude! I hope he's smart enough to know that he don't want it!" Olu smirked.

"Tootsie isn't a bars trading type of dude. His music speaks to that point very well," I replied. "Most likely he'll fire back in an interview or on social media because he's basic like that. But you releasing a diss track would slaughter him, especially since people don't really do diss tracks anymore. If you come with the ether he'll become the laughing stock of #BlackTwitter and *they'll* handle the memes and jokes for you."

"To your point about King Tootsie, releasing a diss track might be a bit much. We can have it ready just in case, but we can start strategizing how we're going to engineer our own social media tactics if memes and hashtags is the route he chooses," Emma said. "It's as simple as a 'fuck King Tootsie' hashtag as a way to direct Olu's fans to his timeline with a barrage of insults. The man is a ratchet meme personified. There's so much material we could come up with! This could be good."

I headed back upstairs to see if there was any more buzz going on about this and I literally almost ran into Sincere on my ascent.

"Oops, I'm sorry," I eeked out before realizing who it was.

"Damn, girl. I see *you've* been doing well." He looked me up and down.

I didn't respond and continued walking.

"So you just gonna keep ignoring me?"

I kept walking with no particular destination in mind. SOBs wasn't that big so there weren't many places I could go. I spotted the only familiar face in the room that I actually didn't mind talking to near the bar, and headed in her direction, but Sincere stayed on my heels.

"Nyela, wait!"

He grabbed my arm and I wanted to slap him, but kept it cool. I took a breath and turned around.

"WHAT!"

"Well damn, I missed you too."

I glared at him.

"Damn, okay. I see everything's been good with you and Olu, but I wanted to make you an offer that will make life even sweeter."

I continued glaring.

"Cynda just took me and Nasreen on under her management and PR roster, and you know we're taping the same reality show that your girl Reiko is doing. I was wondering if you'd be interested in taping with us too."

"Why the hell would *you* be asking me to tape a reality show with you and your girlfriend?"

"Here's the thing, and I'm not gonna lie about this, I miss you."

"We're done!" I tried to storm off again, but he placed another firm grip on my arm, and this one hurt.

"Sincere, you already know I will fight you if I have to!"

"I'm almost done!"

I tried to yank away, but he was too strong for me, so I relented to avoid making a scene. I didn't think he'd actually hurt me, but I'd scream if necessary.

"Look, Nasreen mentioned the other day that I seemed distant from her. And honestly, I have been distant because I feel bad about the way I treated you, and I think there still could be something between us. But it wasn't until I had dinner with Nasreen and Cynda the other night, where they helped me realize the issues Nas and I have been having need to be addressed on camera and with every party involved. So, with Nasreen's support and Cynda's encouragement, I was wondering if we could play this out on TV. All you'd have to do is tape a couple of meet-ups with me where we talk about this and I'll explain how I think we could still be together. I think you myself and Nas make the perfect triangle."

This dude was really fucking serious.

"So, basically, you want to pretend that you might still be in love with me on camera for the sake of creating a storyline?"

"Well, it's not exactly pretending. I mean, I care about Nasreen and all, but you're not easy to forget. I'm a celebrity blogger because of you! It would be so cool if we played this out on camera leading up to the big talk that Nas and I had recently about where our relationship is going, and you and I can play up the tension that we both know is still there. It's an epic love story that will be a good look for all of our brands, and your little boyfriend can make an appearance too. Maybe he can get caught up in the triangle. I mean, who'd be happy about losing their girl to her ex-boyfriend, right?"

"Are there cameras on me right now that I don't know about? You've fucking lost your mind!"

"I'm very serious. There aren't any cameras on now, but trust me, if you do this, we all win."

I snatched away from him and walked off laughing, headed to my original destination, which was to chat with an old co-worker from *Spark*. My phone vibrated when I got to the other side of the room and I checked it, thinking it might have been Reiko or Felani, but it was from Sincere.

You'll be sorry if you don't go through with this.

We've long established that Sincere was a bastard, but *threats?* That was new. He was probably just being a spoiled baby because he wasn't used to being rejected by me, and I gave zero fucks. He'd just have to figure out another way to spice up his dumb-ass storyline.

I focused my attention on the stage where Morena was testing the mic in preparation for her hosting duties. If she was here then Miriam and Cynda were probably nearby, but I claimed no drama tonight. Hopefully the universe worked accordingly.

I headed back downstairs after Morena announced the first act because I didn't dig sitting through a million bad openers, and spotted Deion D and France at the bottom of the landing, engaged in a shouting match. Reiko was sandwiched between the men, trying to get them to stop.

Normally I'd just go back to Olu's green room and wait for Reiko to tell me what drama her affiliation with France hath wrought, but I watched the commotion this time because their shoving match was blocking my path. Reiko finally spotted me and eased from in between the near-brawling men, just as bouncers stepped in to separate them, and stepped toward me.

"Girl, how crazy is this!" she said, kissing me on the cheek as if this entire situation were normal.

"Yo, Reiko, you know where to find me!" Deion D shouted as he brushed past us on his way back upstairs.

"Okay!" Reiko replied.

She and I made our way back to the green room, but by this point most people downstairs had congregated in the small hallway, trying to figure out what was happening.

"Can you believe they're fighting over me?" Reiko whispered to me right as France grabbed her arm.

"Let's go!" he snarled.

"No! Get off of me!"

"I need to talk to you."

"Oh, so now you want to talk to me! Nah, go play with your babymama and tell her I said to literally break a leg on stage tonight."

"Why are you so mad at me! I told you that ain't my baby!"

I noticed Lady Blaq Widow making her way toward us with Cynda and Miriam in tow, right on cue.

"Oh look, there she is," Reiko said. "I'll make sure to send you guys a gift."

Reiko grabbed my arm and dragged me along as she stormed past Lady Blaq Widow and company to head back upstairs. I looked back and caught eyes with Olu who mouthed the words "what's going on," and just shook my head and shrugged. I could tell he got it based on the look he gave me. He had a show to prepare for so it was probably best that I left him in peace anyway. I went with Reiko's flow and followed her upstairs.

"He wanna be mad now that I'm rolling with the next dude, but I'm done giving him chances," she said as we landed.

"Wait, you're dating Deion D like, for real, for real? When did this happen? I actually like Deion, you could have told me!"

We continued our conversation as we positioned ourselves near the front of the stage, but off to the side so that we could see the show without being trapped by the crowd.

"We kinda just fell into it when I decided that Deion was sexy, into me, worth my time, and that I need to stop settling for France's bullshit."

"Works for me, but is it true that King Tootsie could be the father of Lady Blaq Widow's baby?"

"I don't give two flying fucks. France wouldn't be caught up in that type of bullshit situation if he kept his dick in his fucking pants, or at least wrapped it up!"

"Can't argue there," I replied, deciding to drop the conversation since there was nothing new to offer.

The only thing that could make this night more explosive was if King Tootsie showed up. From his speculated beef with France for possibly knocking up his jump off, to instigating bloggers and reporters who'd ask mischievous questions about Olu's overhyped commentary about that damn list, chaos was almost unavoidable if he came.

Reiko and I eventually drifted toward Deion, who was chatting with one of the up and coming rappers scheduled to perform tonight. After about another hour of enduring opening acts, it was finally time for Olu's set, but he hadn't stepped on stage yet. Instead, I saw Felani grab the mic.

"Yo, yo, yo!" she shouted as the crowd roared. "It's your girl Felani, the Queen of Lyrical Homicide."

I was trying to figure out how and when she arrived without anyone noticing, because she looked, um, interesting, once again. This time she was wearing a red Diana Ross-style curly wig flowing down her back, a black halter top with white polka dots all over it, a red sequined mini skirt and leopard print Jeffrey Campbell Night Walks.

"I know y'all wasn't expecting me tonight, but my brother Olu asked me to do him a solid with the hype woman duties. Only for him, though! Yo DJ, you ready?"

The music started after Felani's prompt and it was a new joint entitled, "Party High," which conveniently featured an opening verse from her. It was my first time hearing the song, but it sounded like Olu's typical style. However, Felani's flow was different from what I was used to from her. Gone was the hardcore Brownsville girl. Instead, she was rapping in some sort of Japanese anime schoolgirl accent. The beat was lively, and Fel continued rapping in this new persona that she eventually referred to as "the living doll," before her verse was over.

Her verse wasn't terrible, but she was definitely not pandering to her typical audience. However, admittedly, the anime doll baby stuff was catchy. Olu finally stepped out and started rapping as Felani took the reins on her hype woman duties by keeping everyone energized, and the crowd loved it. "Party High" was definitely going to be another smash. Olu's set was so good that I didn't notice how fast the time passed. He did a few more of his mixtape classics, and then it was time for the finale—the fan favorite, "Fuchsia Girl," of course.

"Aight, y'all. We're about to get into my last song of the night," Olu said as the crowd cheered. "Y'all know this one, but I need some help from my inspiration. Come here girl."

I had succeeded in being low-key throughout the night for the most part, and now here was this bullshit! I told that man *not* to drag me on stage, but like me he was hard headed.

"Girl, you better get up there and be with your boo," said Kimmie from *Regality*, nudging me on the back. I didn't even know she was here, let alone near me.

Reiko acted as an accomplice and nudged me too. "You better get up there!"

I surprised myself by heading toward the stage. Fuck it, everyone knew about us anyway. I was happy, and happy people liked to dance. Felani made her way over to help me up as I got closer. The next thing I knew I was on stage with Fel dancing around me and playfully bumping me with her hips.

"Clap it up for my new sister," Felani said to the excited crowd. "Take notes ladies, she probably gonna get that rock soon."

WHAT!

I looked at Felani, horrified. There was never a conversation about nuptials and Felani knew damn well that you couldn't say shit like that to people, especially not this crowd. Where did she get this crazy talk all of a sudden?

Olu made his way over to me, grabbed my hand and guided me closer to him as he rapped his verses and two-stepped around me. I started to sway and got used to the idea that this was happening. Olu's presence always calmed me, and it was hard to see into the crowd, but I did catch glimpses of all the phones and cameras that were recording. I started to play along just in time for Olu to start rapping the chorus again. He hugged me from behind and towered over me as we swayed in unison. He occasionally ditched the mic since the crowd knew the words well, and let them take over as he rapped verses into my ear.

Shit, as nervous as I was at first, this definitely felt good as fuck. I smiled harder realizing that I was finally starting to get out of my head. I did say that I wanted some new excitement in life. Man, did I ever get it! We rocked out until Olu's set was over and ended the night on a high note, no pun intended.

#WhyTheFuckYouLyin

I got home the night after all the fun at SOBs at around 8pm. I went home with Olu, but left him this evening on his way to the airport for another work-related weekend trip. He had a series of college shows in the New England area and wanted me to come, but I had some work of my own to do and needed to focus. I hadn't blogged in days and I had been half-assing my *Regality* duties. I decided to check my phone first since it had been going off non-stop all day, more than usual. I noticed about ten back-to-back missed calls and a couple of voice messages from Reiko, and a voice message from Tina. I tackled Tina's message first. Reiko probably wanted to chat about more of her self-imposed drama with France, which could wait, but Tina called me a couple of times *and* left a message. She often worked late, and sometimes contacted me at odd hours, but the fact that she left me a message this time was odd.

"Nyela, why is it that we have an inside connection to Olu through you, but everyone else got to know how he felt about his number two spot on the Hip-Hop Slangaz top emcees list except for us? This is just unacceptable and I need you to know that you've cost us some valuable traffic. Please call me immediately."

This bitch was actually serious. Why would I give *her* the scoop when *Regality* was a girlie magazine that didn't really cover hip-hop news like that, especially not in the realm of beef, and *especially* not the top emcees list? Man, it was Friday night! I decided we'd talk about this when I got to the office on Monday. Fuck her!

I moved on to my text messages and felt overwhelmed by how many there were, which made me nervous. I tried to be positive and convince myself they had something to do with last night's show, so I went through them just to get them out of the way, starting with Reiko's texts. She was a drama queen, so I reluctantly opened her messages. After a string of texts like, "Where are you?" and "Please call me, this is urgent," I finally got to the crux of what she wanted, and immediately got the urge to toss my phone out the window after reading the text.

Nye, I'm sorry to keep blowing you up, but have you seen Sincere's latest post?

I didn't reply to that one just yet because I knew it was going to get worse. I continued scrolling my text inbox for more and noticed that it was all messages to the same tune from various people, even people who I never really talked to like that asking if I was okay.

I faced the inevitable by pulling up the post, and there was my mug shot with the following headline: **"When Psycho Exes Won't Quit."**

I felt the rage bubbling, but kept my composure so that I could get through this foolishness:

> Sometimes you gotta keep your exes in pocket and mine—y'all know her—the writer broad that's holed up with that emo British rapper straight up groupie style. I've been nothing but nice to her, even after I cut her off, but I ask for one favor and she wants to act all stuck up like she don't know me anymore.
>
> I know you're wondering why I would need a favor from my ex, especially when I've moved on to a new, badder bitch, but me and that writer broad were still cool. I had her back and I thought she had mine but I guess I thought wrong. She overstepped some boundaries that I won't get into right now, so I have to bring her back down to Earth. Let this be a lesson to all my male readers. You have to assert your dominance and keep these chicks in check. They love a man who exercises his natural right to be a leader. So to that point, I gotta let her know that she's not as high and mighty as she thinks she is.
>
> When we first got together, I accepted her for all her flaws even though she admitted that she was a psycho, hence the mug shot. Back in her college days she caught some battery charges aka, she stalked some poor dude who got caught up in her fat ass and pretty face. I can't front, she looks good as hell, and that did influence my decision to still accept her for her past yet fast forward to today when we were supposed to be looking out for one another, and she couldn't even do one favor for me. Her head got a little big since she's been hanging out with that rapper, but this is how you bring chicks back down to Earth, especially

when you knew them when they weren't shit. So,
all my dudes reading this: Don't let these women
get too big for their britches, especially if you
made them who they are. I encourage all of you to
share this story and that mug shot as a cautionary
tale. By the way, she's still sexy in that mug shot,
though, right? LOL.

I stared at the screen for another 5 minutes, shaking. I was angry enough to storm over to his apartment and beat the shit out of him, but that wouldn't accomplish anything except prove his case. Rarely was I at a loss for what to do, even if those choices weren't always right, hence the mug shot. When I thought back to that day, I realized that I could have handled the situation better, but even then I had problems removing myself from obviously bad situations despite the fact that I knew better. I often allowed things to get crazy just to see how far they'd go. It happened when I was bored or flustered, but I was actively trying to better manage that part of my life and personality these days, and I refused to let some asshole try to shame me for a past that I owned, and that made me stronger.

That mug shot situation stemmed back to my first boyfriend in college, Marcus Quimby. He was gorgeous in a cliché kind of way—you know, smooth brown skin, an athletic build, and he was ridiculously tall.

He also had the sense of entitlement that typically came along with gorgeous men, and the charm too.

I didn't want to admit it when I was paired with him for our first group assignment in Intro to Documentary Making at the beginning of sophomore year, but I was a goner the moment he said hello. Over the course of the semester we had to gather news stories in our campus community and create docu-shorts while alternating roles between writer, producer and camera operator. I didn't think I had a chance with him because I didn't think I was his type, but he eventually began showing interest.

My intuition told me that he'd introduce me to a world of heartache and I didn't listen, of course. He seemed nice at first, which led me to believe that the rumors weren't true, and my ego hit the mesosphere because he found me attractive. So, I did what any woman who told herself she wasn't going to fall for the ladies man's advances did—I lapped it up like a starving puppy in one of those save the animals commercials. Before Marcus, men labeled me as the little sister type or the best friend. I was a late bloomer, but *he* saw me as *foine.*

We started off strong. He was sweet and romantic. I even gave him my virginity. Despite occasional reports that he had been spotted canoodling with the next chick, I deluded myself into thinking that I had found *The One.* After about six months of blissful courtship—in my mind—the rumors picked up in frequency and I got to the point where I began checking his phone, emails, and social media profiles obsessively. I was typically very laid back and thought snooping on your partner was silly, but I could no longer deny what people were telling me, so I snooped until I unfortunately found what I was looking for.

I often confronted him, and he always had excuses. They were his cousins, or they were "groupies" who pushed up on him because he played basketball, even though he told them he had a girl. And then there was the, "Nyela, you're crazy," Jedi mind tricks. He convinced me that I was an insecure loon who was imagining things, and I believed him. I believed him when he convinced me that I needed to lose weight despite that fact that I was a size 4 and at 20% body fat then since I danced with the school's dance company. I believed him when he told me I needed to write his English papers, and by the end of sophomore year—because I put up with his bullshit for *that* long—I believed him when he told me that his math teacher was stalking him, so I offered to start picking him up from that particular class since it was a night time class. He told me that his teacher sometimes wouldn't let him leave and that she'd find all kinds of excuses to keep him longer. He claimed that she kept him in class after the other students left because he was failing, so that she could "tutor" him, but that she always ended up sexually harassing him. He agreed to let me pick him up, and I knew better when he was unusually insistent that I waited outside. Sometimes the delusion of happiness was easier to deal with than reality. He always came out almost an hour after class was allegedly over, and I dutifully waited for him like the willful dumbass that I was. We kept up this schedule for a couple of months. He texted me a few hours before class so I'd know what I needed to do.

However, there was one day that I hadn't heard from him at all. I reached out but got no response, so I initially left it alone thinking that maybe he wasn't going to class that night. I checked his dorm and his roommate informed me that he had gone to class, so I headed over anyway but parked in a discreet location where I could still see the building. Eventually, I spotted Marcus and his teacher holding hands and flirting with each other. He even patted her butt as they hopped into her car.

I followed them to her apartment complex, saw them making out before going into her apartment, and immediately began cursing Marcus out. The ruckus that ensued was epic. My fists flew at Marcus, who tried to restrain me, but his teacher-girlfriend surprisingly charged at me— then again, what would you expect from a married middle-aged, college professor who was foolish enough to engage in a sexual relationship with a student in her class? Anyway, some of the following events were hazy, but Marcus egged the fight on between his teacher and I. Yes, that fool actually stood off to the side and encouraged us to throw hands shouting, "Winner takes all!"

Her neighbors called the police and we were broken up. I could have just gone home without further incident, but I managed to break free from the officer's grip. I charged toward Marcus and almost successfully choked him out. My adrenaline was in overdrive. I was hurt, angry and humiliated, and to make the situation worse, Marcus pressed charges against me for battery.

The charges were eventually dropped. Marcus later told me that he was just trying to make a point because I needed to learn a lesson about my crazy behavior, but really it was because he was a manipulative cunt.

Sadly, the mug shot remained public so anyone could take bits and pieces of actual facts and twist them around. I never hid the fact that this happened, but I also didn't go around broadcasting it. I wasn't proud of it and have made an effort to do better. Yet here we were again, where someone I once trusted was using something against me in an attempt to make me look like the monster that I wasn't. I knew people could be foul, but this was lower than a snake's belly.

I made the tragic mistake of reading some of the comments and of course, people that didn't know anything about me had everything to say. I got called a "star fucking bitch," but that was dumb considering the fact that the only famous person that I had ever slept with was Olu. There was also the other derogatory stuff calling me a "hoe," "trick," "slut," 'THOT," "the destruction of the entire black female population," "the destruction of the entire black race," and the like. I wasn't usually one for revenge, but Sincere had it coming, and I knew exactly how to fix him.

Reiko called me for the umpteenth time while I was in the midst of ruminating on my revenge. I didn't really feel like engaging anyone in conversation, but I decided to pick up anyway.

"JESUS, NYELA! I'VE BEEN CALLING YOU ALL DAY!"

"Where are you, it's crazy noisy in the background?"

"Out and about. Anyway, I've been worried about you since I couldn't get in touch. Are you okay? Do we have to start kicking doors in?"

Surprisingly I laughed and my anger subsided for a moment.

"Girl, no need to kick in any doors. I got something that will fix Sincere's dumbass."

"Okay, but what about King Tootsie?"

"What do you mean what about King Tootsie?"

"Oh…so…you haven't heard the latest?"

My stomach dropped.

"Heard what?"

"You know how people started blowing Olu's reaction to the Hip-Hop Slangaz list out of proportion? Well, King Tootsie was on the *Moo Moo and Juice Show* about 30 minutes ago and went on a tirade against Olu, calling him wack, gay and all the typical stuff that rappers say when they want to get at each other, but he also released a diss track where he said he slept with you."

"WHAT!"

"Yeah, girl, and you know they asked him about it in the interview and he basically said you threw yourself at him that time you did that feature on him for *Spark*."

I paused, trying to process this.

"Nyela, you still there?"

"YES, I'M STILL HERE!"

"Did you sleep with King Tootsie?"

"I didn't sleep with King Tootsie! I wouldn't sleep with King Tootsie if we were humanity's only hope for survival, and I had a remote controlled clone of myself to do the job for me! Are you fucking nuts? I'm hurt that you would ask such a thing."

"Sorry. I *had* to ask, just in case. A lot of us have those industry skeletons that we're not proud of. You just never know sometimes."

"You're about two more sentences from me hanging up on you."

"My bad, Nye. Does Olu know?"

I remembered that Olu was supposed to let me know when he got to his destination, which should have been about an hour ago by now. It was odd that I hadn't heard from him yet.

"Olu is en route to a show. I'm not even sure where he is right now."

"Do you need me to come over?"

"Not now, Reiko. Enjoy your night. I just need some time alone."

"Well, if it's any consolation, King Tootsie's track was awful. Probably some of his worst work yet, which says a lot."

"Talk to you later, Reiko."

I hung up and started trolling the web for clues. The story was on every urban website in different variations of the same headline: **"King Tootsie Smashes Olu Major's New Boo Thang."**

I chose Chatty Abernathy as my poison, since she seemed to have it out for me the most.

Nyela Smashed the (Not so) Homie

Y'all know that THOT writer Nyela Barnes, right? Well, looks like all isn't lovey dovey for Miss Fuchsia Girl and her new man, rapper/actor Olu Major. King Tootsie was on the Moo Moo and Juice Show just a few moments ago and said that not only is he not feeling Olu for his recent comments about the Hip-Hop Slangaz top emcees list, but that he also smashed Nyela a while back and that this is probably where all of Olu's hate is coming from.

According to our sources, this happened back when Nyela wrote a feature story on King Tootsie for that major magazine she just got fired from. King Tootsie not only rapped about it in his new diss track aimed at Olu entitled, "Shots Fired," but he also spoke about it in the interview. This is what he said:

"Y'all already know what it is, mane. These broads ouchea can't keep their hands off me. That's why I got so many kids, ya dig? It's natural. But for real though that Nyela chick, she fine as hell. And you know what happens when two fine motherfuckers get together. We met at the interview and she showed me some love. She was tryna hide behind the professional persona like she wasn't a fan, but really, once she got a little comfortable she started throwing herself at me, so I did what any man would do when ass gets tossed in his direction. I smashed."

When he was asked about Nyela's psycho status, because y'all now know about her stalker incident stemming from back in her college days, and how she attacked Sincere McDonald's new piece once he kicked her to the curb, King Tootsie kept it coy:

"I mean, y'all know I put it on her. She texted me here and there, but she ain't get too out of line or nothing like that. Y'all see she ain't my next babymama yet!"

Well, y'all know how angry birds can get, especially industry chicks who are supposed to be professional but use their jobs to get close to the stars so they can play in the golddigging olympics. We guess Nyela is just looking for the right come up. All she has to do now is drop a baby for the right rapper and she's financially set at least for 18 years. Speaking of golddigging, her chicken coop of friends have been quite busy lately too.

We spotted Reiko of the Morning Riot gallivanting with millionaire Hip-Hop Slangaz co-owner Deion D, even though she's supposed to be France Deveaux's girl and they're taping that reality show. Also, make sure you click here for photos of Reiko's co-host, Cookie Clark – yeah, the one with the slorey reputation who wrote that infamous book – on a pre-birthday getaway in St. Barths. She's lounging on a yacht with Shane Miller, the pasty comedian and TV host who has a thing for chocolate. Y'all know Miller likes those stripper types anyway. I guess hoes be winning.

--Chatty Abernathy, the Gossip Slayer

I clicked on the link for Cookie's photos, hoping I'd be calm by the time I was done gawking. The photos featured Cookie frolicking on a yacht and canoodling with Shane. I tried not to gag because Shane was at least 60, but not a sexy 60, dad 60. I mean, if he were older man hot

354

like George Clooney then I'd understand, but she seemed into him so whatever.

My thoughts drifted back to rage, revenge, damage control strategies and the fact that I hadn't heard from Olu yet. Did he know? Was he foolish enough to believe it? Even worse, was he avoiding me because he believed it? *Fuck!*

The next logical step was to troll Twitter and as predicted, my feed was full of insults. Most people, complete strangers, were @'ing me about how much of a whore I was. There were people making references to me in jokes and @'ing me despite the fact that they weren't talking directly to me. There were the disingenuous people who actually did have my real contact information, but were making a public show of asking me if was okay on social media just so they could be involved in the spectacle instead of privately reaching out. People were also @'ing me in their tweets publicizing the erroneous stories they had written about me, and I also made some stupid website's asinine list of "Most Trifling Industry Chicks Volume 1." Mind you, not one of these so-called reporters reached out to me for comment.

Finally over the Internet carnage, I mustered up enough gumption to call Olu. After what I had seen on Twitter, including his back and forth with King Tootsie that took place not too long ago, he obviously knew.

"Yo," Olu said.

His tone was strange. It was as if we weren't familiar with each other.

"Since when do *you*, 'yo,' me?"

"Make it quick, I got a show."

"Whoa! Based on that attitude I'm going to assume you heard, but—"

"You were honest with me about how you got your mug shot. But Tootsie? You purposely kept that information from me."

"Olu, it's not true and I can't believe *you*, of all people, would believe that shit."

"Maybe if that shit hadn't happened with Miriam I'd have an easier time with this, but I – look, I know that everyone has a past, but this isn't something I can handle."

"YOU CAN'T BE SERIOUS! I DIDN'T TOUCH THAT MAN!"

We got locked in an awkward moment of silence.

"You there?" I choked.

"I'm here."

"You can't be fucking serious! He's upset with you! All beefing rappers go for the girlfriend or even the wife! It's the most cliché thing ever and you *know* King Tootsie has no imagination!"

"Nye, I gotta go."

I held the phone to my ear for a good thirty more seconds after Olu hung up on me and stared out the window unsuccessfully trying to fight back my tears. It was foolish of me to believe that this thing with Olu was actually destined for greatness.

Unable to move, I found myself watching a stray cat rummage through my neighbor's trash across the street. It was the only sign of life on my block at this time of night, but it wasn't enough to distract me from my thoughts about what just happened. I kept asking myself why people were so incredibly shitty to each other, especially online. I knew the answer, though. The anonymity that the Internet afforded made cowards feel like they had power.

I circled back to the fact that I didn't know who Chatty Abernathy was, and the fact that this stupid rapper lied about having sex with me, and a new wave of rage overcame me. Exacting revenge was petty, but if I remembered *The 48 Laws of Power* correctly, then sometimes it was a necessary part of life, especially in this industry, where people were *always* testing your limits. Apparently I was seen as a weakling. That worked to my advantage, though, because they wouldn't see my retribution coming. It would be swift and definitely not anonymous. By the time I was done, they'd know that I wasn't to be fucked with. I had shit on almost everyone, and if I didn't have dirt, I could get it easily.

#ShadyBoots

I didn't do anything over the weekend but sleep and watch TV. Olu didn't call or text, but he did release a diss track reply to Tootsie. I didn't listen to it, though, and I resisted the urge to check up on him, or anyone on social media. It felt good unplugging from the digital world, but it was Monday, so I had to jump back down the work rabbit hole again. At some point, I had to figure out a new plan of action for how I was going to clear my name with the King Tootsie situation. I had an idea of what could be done to teach Sincere a lesson, but for now I had to deal with the day-to-day freelance bullshit for the sake of my bills. My meeting with Nero wasn't for another couple of weeks due to his schedule being so crazy and all over the place, so I couldn't make any moves there just yet. I sent out a few emails, checked in with other companies that I had done freelance jobs for that owed me money, and just as I prepared to hop in the shower, the phone rang.

"Nyela!" was Tina's choice greeting.

"Hi Tina."

"We will no longer be needing your services at *Regality* magazine effective immediately."

"Wait, what?"

"We've decided that we would rather not have a woman of your caliber associated with our illustrious brand. I'll have Amy mail out your last check."

She basically said she was firing me because I was a hoe.

"Are you guys seriously letting me go based on hearsay?"

"Hearsay or not, you obviously did something to get accused of less than ideal behavior for a *Regality* woman, and we just can't deal with that."

"But—"

This bitch hung up! It crossed my mind that I could possibly sue for unlawful termination and that I could have my dad look into this matter. No company wanted a lawsuit that petty, especially not a company that was supposed to be about legacy and sisterhood.

Then again, I hated working with them anyway. I had worshiped *Regality* magazine and what I thought were the amazing women behind the brand for my entire life. But in reality, they were all just the same catty bitches I had encountered everywhere else in this industry—male and female. To fire me based on hearsay without any proof was bullshit, and I refused to put up with that type of stupidity in my career ever again, so, fuck 'em! My site was finally starting to bring in enough revenue to at least earn a part time salary. I had some other freelance writing projects lined up, and I had enough savings to get me through at least six more months. I also didn't think Nero would let this bullshit cloud his judgment in terms of working with me. *My* screenplay was one thing, me writing the treatment for 'Fuchsia Girl' was something I was willing to lose if Olu didn't want to have anything to do with me. For once, I had managed to silence my cynicism and assured myself that I'd be fine once I got over this hump.

For the first time in a long time—probably ever, actually—I decided not to stress things that I couldn't control. With no man and no job, I could focus on my site earning more money and create more video content before I started seriously working with Nero. I just hoped that Nero really was different. So far our meeting hadn't been cancelled and no one mentioned anything about me being off the 'Fuchsia Girl' shoot, which was still pending scheduling, but I'd find out soon enough.

I put the King Tootsie matter on hold for now since it was his word against mine. Most people, especially in the entertainment industry, would unfortunately always believe the man, especially a rapper, no matter how trite it was to claim to have slept with a woman because he was beefing with her boyfriend, but back to Sincere; I could definitely teach him to keep my name out of his mouth and off his blog for good.

Back when we still hung out sporadically around the time he first started acting like a dick toward me, I knew something wasn't right, but I initially ignored that feeling—it was that pesky delusion once again—don't judge me. I had good reason not to trust him, but I second-guessed myself because he always tried to make me seem like I was crazy whenever I questioned him about his behavior, so I started snooping. Does anyone else hear *The Twilight Zone* theme playing? Talk about déjà vu!

Anyway, I surprisingly didn't find any of the raunchy photo messages from random chicks that I expected. Instead, I found some gems from the time he pledged a fraternity in college. He once mentioned in passing that he got hazed in undergrad, but that was the extent of the conversation. He always got uncomfortable to the point of anger when I asked him about what he went through, especially after discovering that his chapter had been suspended from his campus the year after he graduated. It piqued my curiosity, but I dropped it because I didn't like seeing him upset. However, for someone who was allegedly so smart, he was also incredibly careless. He left photos from the experience on his computer in a folder entitled, "The Pledge Years," right on his desktop.

I discovered that he wasn't physically abused like a lot of hazing reports that I've heard about on the news. Instead, he was forced to dress in drag and pose like he loved it in front of a popular gay club and various other places, wardrobe changes included. From the looks of the photos I found, he might have actually enjoyed the experience. My favorite photo was the one where he was wearing booty shorts, fishnet tights, a wife beater, five inch heels, and a full face of make up making a duck face. There was another one where he was bent over as if he were twerking and some of his frat brothers were smacking his ass.

I had a feeling the photos might come in handy one day, so I transferred them to my portable flash drive. I then contacted an old pledgee who Sincere mentioned had defected before crossing over, and pretended to be a reporter doing a story on hazing. He was disgruntled and willing to tell me anything I wanted under the condition that I kept him anonymous, and I got all the information I needed for my back pocket. Sincere wanted to be a part of this frat so bad that he was literally willing to do anything for it. On the surface, this could be considered viewed as typical frat boy foolishness and not so bad considering what it could have been. However, in the Internet world where people struggled with contextual thinking, comprehension, and fact checked nothing, Sincere, the beloved macho "relationship guru" dressed in drag, plus *my* slightly fabricated version of events, would make him the butt of many jokes for a while. I could picture the memes now.

I called Reiko to explain what I had been sitting on all these months and she convinced me to meet her along with Felani and Cookie for dinner, no cameras. It would be good to get out of the house and take my mind off the drama, but I was nervous about seeing Felani. For all I knew, she might actually believe the rumors and try to fight me.

#SquadGoals

I was the last one to arrive at Olive Tree and found the crew tucked away in a booth, noshing on an order of pita bread and hummus.

Surprisingly, Felani seemed a lot more receptive than I thought she'd be. Actually, she was acting normal toward me.

"How's it going?" I said.

"We should be asking *you* that question!" Felani replied. "Why the hell do you look so dazed and confused?"

"I thought you'd be mad at me."

"Mad at you for what? I know gotdamn well you didn't have sex with that ass hat King Tootsie! Come on, son! The first thing male rappers do when they beef is pull the, 'I fucked you girl' card. I know you better than that!"

"That's what *I* said, but apparently Olu doesn't seem to know me at all."

"That's that ego shit! He's too blinded by the Miriam shit that happened with Tootsie, so his rational thinking skills got fucked up for a moment. He's caught up in the idea of being seen as a punk and what this looks like for his brand, but I told him what an ass he's being!"

"He should still know me better than that. Miriam acted like a bird from day one. She and I are worlds apart. What pisses me off the most is the fact that I have no proof, and as a woman *no* one is going to just take my word for it."

"Trust me, he knows. He definitely still loves you. If anything, he probably hasn't reached out and apologized yet because he realizes how dumb he was acting and may be trying to figure out the best way to approach you."

"I guess. He was uncharacteristically cold to me the last time we spoke, so I don't know if I want to hear from him right now anyway. But I did hear that he replied to King Tootsie in a diss track. Was it any good?"

"WHAT! ARE YOU KIDDING ME! OLU MURDERED KING TOOTSIE! WHERE THE FUCK HAVE YOU BEEN?" Felani replied.

"Um, I've been in a hole, working and getting over a broken heart."

"Girl, go on Instagram and look up #OluVsTootsie!" Felani said.

I obliged, and the memes that I saw were hilarious. King Tootsie was definitely the laughing stock of #BlackTwitter.

I cracked up laughing at all the clever memes that I saw. It appeared as if Olu had won, and I wasn't surprised.

"I guess I'll get around to listening to Olu's track at some point."

"Please do, it was epic! People are already playing it at the club and it's in rotation on the radio, " Reiko said. "And for what it's worth, Olu comes to your defense in the song. He actually states that you wouldn't be birdbrain enough, like Miriam was, to go there with King Tootsie. That wasn't the line verbatim, but it packed punch and it was smooth."

As mad as I still was, it was nice to know that Olu may have had some ounce of sense left.

"Did I really miss *that* much?"

"YES!" replied everyone at the table.

"A week in digital might as well be 10 years. Anyway, we did *not* come here to talk about that. Y'all know men ain't shit!" Reiko said. "Look, I gathered all you ladies here because Cookie and Nyela both have some important news to share. You go first, Nyela, since we talked about this earlier."

I pulled up Sincere's photo shoot on my iPhone and handed it to Reiko first. I decided against texting or emailing it to her before tonight because I needed to see her reaction in person.

"Are these the actual, wait, OH MY GOD, THEY'RE WORSE THAN I THOUGHT!"

Reiko screamed so loud that even strangers in our vicinity paused for a moment to stare at us.

"Reiko, you're so dramatic," Cookie said, grabbing my phone.

She realized, in the following few seconds, that she underestimated what she was about to see. She affected her own version of dramatics by grabbing her heart and feigning a heart attack.

"I'm coming, Elizabeth! This is the big one!" she yelled.

Laughing hysterically and with tears in her eyes, she shoved the phone in Felani's hand.

"NOOOOOOOOO!" Felani screeched.

She tossed herself on the floor and cackled uncontrollably. By this point, patrons in the restaurant had started ignoring our antics.

"Can you please explain why the fuck we're looking at your ex, Mr. A Real Man Knows How to Control His Chick, in drag?" Cookie said.

"That's what I wanted to talk to you ladies about. This is my revenge," I replied. "This is from some hazing incident that he endured while pledging in college."

"How did you get the pictures?"

"I stole them." I rehashed my Inspector Nyela shenanigans.

"You are my kinda woman," Cookie said. "I think you should unveil them at my birthday bash."

"But that night is all about you. And how do you even know he'll come?"

"True, the night *is* about me, but this is how I want to put on a show. I've got plans of my own, that I know you're going to love, that will work in tandem with yours. Plus, Sincere is an attention whore scenester. He'll be there. I've already confirmed with Mandy that her cameras will be rolling."

She started rubbing her hands together for emphasis on her master plot.

"There's more. One, I know who Chatty Abernathy is. Two, *she* actually masterminded that lie King Tootsie made up about sleeping with you."

"HOW THE FUCK DO YOU KNOW THAT! WHAT'S THE CONNECTION!" I yelled.

Cookie smirked, but didn't continue. We stared at her momentarily trying to process why she was being silent.

"So, what the fuck! You want us to beg you for the information?" Felani said.

"Maybe."

"Don't do this to us, bitch!" Reiko chimed in.

A devious smile spread across Cookie's face, making her resemble a sexy version of Harley Quinn.

"You're cute when you're being an evil mastermind," I said. "Now spill it!"

"Chatty Abernathy is, drumroll please…"

She started banging on the table.

"SAY IT!" Reiko yelled.

"Cynda Bently."

"CYNDA BENTLY!" the rest of us echoed in unison.

"Yup."

"Get the fuck outta here!" Reiko said.

"I'm as serious as those pictures of Sincere in drag."

We all laughed.

"I started spying on Cynda so that I could figure out an appropriate dose of karma for her stealing my book idea, as you all know. You also know by now that I went on vacation with Shane Miller. However, what you don't know is that Shane is best friends with, well, I won't put his name out there, but he's a billionaire technology genius—"

"I think I know where you're going with this, and I love it!" I interjected.

Cookie started with the sneaky smile again.

"Shane loves showing me off to his friends so he invited some of them over to his yacht for lunch in honor of my birthday. They got shitfaced drunk. I was the only sober one for pretty much the entire trip, which is what I was banking on. I charmed Mr. Billionaire Genius by feigning interest in his smarts and company, and naturally he wanted to show off for the pretty girl—"

"So he got the goods on Cynda?" I jumped in, too excited to contain myself.

She smiled again, but this time in an attempt to feign innocence.

"The next thing I knew, there was a sort of hackathon and we ended up in Cynda's email, and on the backend of all of her social media profiles. Let's just say, she's a conniving bitch. Breaking into her email easily led us on a trail of all her digital deceit. I'm impressed by how slick and ballsy she is, but she's sloppy. The Cynda I knew back in college was low-key and frumpy, but the grownup version is quite the megalomaniac."

"So all those years of being a bum bitch took its toll on her psyche and she gave herself a makeover!" Reiko said.

"Exactly, but I think there was always a bit of crazy there even then," Cookie replied. "The level of fuckery I discovered didn't just pop up overnight."

"I *knew* it! I knew I was right not to trust her," I said, still processing the discovery. "Did you get any dirt on her from when she was married?"

"She was married?" Cookie replied.

"Hold up! Before we go there, I want to hear the rest of what Cookie has to say about what she found," Felani said. "You know we get sidetracked easily."

Cookie stopped with the creepy smile effects and took a sip of water before locking eyes with me.

"Her clients don't even know that she's Chatty Abernathy, except for Tootsie.   That little piece of shit knows about and supports her shady endeavors. He gets a percentage as a silent partner, pays for her hosting and design needs, and occasionally feeds her rapper tea," Cookie said. "She gets most of the information on her own, but the site makes them both a nice bit of money."

"Holy shit!" Reiko said.

"There's more. In addition to this double life she lives, she's obsessed with Olu. I mean like, it's not a psychotic obsession, but it's still bizarre. She keeps a private online journal and has devoted several blogs to her fascination with him—"

"Hold up, Olu told me she tried to sleep with him on more than one occasion back when he was with Miriam. He never told anyone until me. And just so we're clear, he didn't go there, ew."

"Ain't that about a bitch! Meanwhile, Miss Girl Power over there is going around claiming that she and Miriam are like sisters," Cookie said. "It's all in that diary, which surprisingly doesn't mention anything about her marriage, so I'm guessing the time period for the diary was after the nuptials. Anyway, she was jealous of Miriam's relationship with Olu and hated how Miriam treated him. Actually, she's jealous of anyone with a vagina, so if you have one of those and just so happen to get close to Olu or anyone she crushes on then she *really* has a problem with you. She's extremely insecure, but good at hiding it."

"Inferiority complex, much?" Reiko said.

"Or just pure concentrated evil," I replied. "But how did *I* get on her radar so early? She started talking shit about me right after the fight with   Sincere."

"Um, word about the *GQ* story had started leaking by then, and she probably saw Olu all up on you at Felani's party that time," Reiko said.

"People with hate crushes find a way to be all up in their object of non-affection's business as much as possible, just so they can hate more."

I scrunched up my face and shook my head at the ridiculousness, but also truth in Reiko's theory.

"There's definitely some extreme narcissism going on. It's like she gets off on being the puppet master to make herself feel in control," Cookie said. "Not only did she convince King Tootsie to lie about sleeping with you, but she also urged Sincere to get back at you for not complying with that dumb request to be a part of his love triangle on his reality show. She really thought you'd agree to getting involved with that stupid plot, and hoped that it would create friction between you and Olu because she thinks everyone is stupid. So, when that didn't work out so well she convinced him that airing out your dirty laundry was a good way to shame you into going along with his plan. She's big on chess, and *The 48 Laws of Power*."

"But she's doing it all wrong!" Reiko said.

"Most people aren't *really* about that life. Out here fronting like tough guys and shit! Hell, my dad effectively applied and remixed the 48 laws back in his dealing days," Felani said. "I *definitely* know how to use it right."

"My dad is a judge. My mom is the vice president of a top financial firm. I might be small and cute, but I learned from the best growing up," Cookie said. "Power moves are in my blood, so we're going to serve this revenge, but we have to strategize, especially given this new information about Cynda having been married. How did you know about that?"

"It was something Morena drunk babbled to me in passing at an event once. I think she and Cynda had a brief falling out, so she let it slip out to me in complaining about her. She said something along the lines of, 'That's why her ex-husband doesn't even want her crazy ass back,' and once I got wind of that, I tried pressing her for more information, but that sobered her up and she immediately started begging me not to say anything about it," I replied. "Apparently, the marriage phase is a real sore spot for Cynda. She tried to shade me at an event not too long ago, and when I asked her how her ex-husband was, she looked like she had seen a zombie. She was shocked that I knew and immediately stopped antagonizing me. I've been trying to figure out who her mysterious ex-husband was ever since because I'm just nosey like that, but so far I haven't gotten any leads."

"Oh my god! I think I know who her husband was," Cookie said. "Like I said, she was low key in college, but I do remember that she was engaged by our senior year. She got engaged to a popular football player and went around bragging about it to anyone who would listen. Shit, this is getting good! Nyela, I'm going to send you more info about who I think her ex is, and then you can do what you do best."

"Oh, I'm already crafting my fake reporter story in my mind!"

"Perfect! And I'm going to meet up with King Tootsie. I need to steal his phone," Cookie replied.

"Steal his phone!" the rest of us said in unison.

"But you've already implicated him in Cynda's lie," Reiko said.

"That's not enough. I need to forward emails and probably text messages too directly from his phone, which we can put on display. I don't want to reveal that we were made privy to this info by hacking, but getting his phone should be easy as long as he thinks I'm going to have sex with him. I'm not, by the way. I don't even plan to get that close, but knowing him, the fact that I asked him to hang out probably already has him gassed like he's about to get some."

"Damn girl! You're crafty as fuck!" Felani replied.

"Yup, and Sincere's photos sweeten the deal, I'm thinking we could do something in homage to what Jay Z did to Prodigy at that epic Summer Jam."

"My plan was just to leak Sincere's photos to as many gossip sites as I could with a made up story," I said. "But Cookie, I like the way you think."

Typically, this was not the type of behavior I would entertain, but the concept of classy mature Nyela long went out the window. I was not the iron bull that I pretended to be, especially when my reputation and career were at stake. At the moment, everyone thought I was some sort of hotheaded industry groupie. True, it was all based solely on speculation and *I* knew who I was, but that shit still hurt my feelings, and the other reality was that perception was starting to cost me my livelihood. I'd be damned if I sat around and let people think they could keep targeting me and ruining my life in the process.

#TeamPetty

It was the night we served revenge at Brooklyn Bowl, the perfect place to make a spectacle. It was the second Saturday in August, and the end of the first full week of the month, which meant it was still summer, but we were nearing the end so it was best to enjoy everything you could now. Translation: The industry cool kids, scenesters and wannabes were *definitely* going to show up to Cookie's party. Her parties had a reputation for being epic, but no one realized what they were going to get tonight.

I decided to look the part of the she-devil by wearing a red tank top and red high-waisted short shorts, which emphasized my slightly more exaggerated curves due to my stress-related 10 lbs. weight loss. A text message came in as I rummaged through my jewelry box trying to figure out how I'd accent today's ensemble. Thinking it might be one of my girls on the way to pick me up, I looked at the phone only to see that it was another text from Olu.

"You know you can't ignore me forever right? I'll be at Cookie's party tonight, hope to see you there."

Olu had been texting, calling and leaving apology voicemails incessantly for the past few days. I missed him terribly and liked the idea that he realized what an ass he had been, but I was still sorting out how

I felt. I got the whole rapper ego thing and how crazy it would have looked if I actually had slept with the same man who his previous girlfriend left him for *and* got knocked up by. However, the fact that he took outside word over mine out of fear of embarrassment hurt. We have had so many conversations about not letting the ego interfere with progression and judgment, yet he *still* allowed it to happen.

On one hand, I hoped we could fix this, but maybe love didn't always conquer all, as that saying went. I tossed my phone in my black Vlieger & Vandam Guardian Angel clutch, slipped on some leopard print pumps and adorned my neck, ears and wrists with turquoise jewelry for a pop of color, just in time for Reiko's call for me to meet the girls downstairs.

—

Reiko, Cookie, Felani and I pulled up to Brooklyn Bowl fashionably late, of course, and the venue was swarming with people as expected.

"Let's do this, ladies," Cookie said as we congregated on the sidewalk and waited for the reality show cameras to get situated.

For once, I wasn't annoyed by the presence of cameras. Felani led the pack as we posed on the red carpet on our way inside. Posing for photographers would always feel strange. I was used to documenting people on red carpets, not actually walking them, so this already nerve-racking experience felt even more awkward times ten. Every other person I made eye contact with—mainly reporters and influencers that I knew from the scene—asked me about the Tootsie situation, but I just played coy. They'd get what they were looking for soon enough.

Brooklyn Bowl was packed. The mammoth space, which probably used to be a warehouse, consisted of a bowling section on one side, the eating area on another side, a stage, dance floor and DJ booth on another side. It was sensory overload.

"Give a shout out to the birthday girl who just stepped in the building! Dirty 30!" shouted DJ Blackenstein.

The crowd started cheering as Cookie began bouncing and waving her hands in the air on beat to Beyonce's "Flawless," her requested entrance music. She continued dancing forward while mingling with familiar faces, accepting gifts and soaking up the attention.

We descended upon a booth reserved for Cookie and company. It was festooned with hot pink balloons, gold confetti and bottles of every cliché alcohol known to man, and we weren't the first guests to arrive. Mandy, Shane, who was holding a bag of presents, and Nero, of all people, were already engaging each other.

None of us sat down, but we all started engaging the pre-existing group and the party in general. I loved the fact that the music switched to a '90s hip-hop set. DJ Blackenstein was on an A Tribe Called Quest kick.

"Good evening ladies, you all look fabulous!" Mandy said, greeting Reiko and I with respective hugs and kisses on the cheek.

"So do you! But you always look good!" Reiko replied. "Anyway, how's that release form business coming along?"

"Fabulous thus far. This place is already packed and no one is giving us any trouble with signing."

"No blurred out faces, huh? Now *that's* what I like to hear," Reiko said, sneaking a wink at me.

"I've been following you around long enough to know that you got something good for me, Reiko. Spill it!"

Reiko grinned so hard that her already small eyes, inherited from her half-Japanese mother, disappeared leaving nothing but eyelashes.

"I can't say just yet, but you'll love it when you see it."

"You never disappoint so I'll wait, but I do need you to tell me where you got that dress!"

I felt a hand lightly tap my shoulder just as I started to feel left out of the conversation between Reiko and Mandy. It was Nero.

"Nyela! I haven't seen you in ages!" he said wrapping his arms around me in a tight hug.

"I've been laying low. I'm surprised *you're* here though! I thought you were booked up for the next couple of weeks."

"I snuck away. I needed a break, but I head back to LA in the morning. Are you ready for 'Fuchsia Girl,' and moving on to the next phase of launching your project?"

"Absolutely! I'm definitely excited about my screenplay. But, uh, you still want me on the 'Fuchsia Girl' project?"

"What do you mean do I still want you on 'Fuchsia Girl?' Of Course I do! We're actually shooting all the videos for Olu's album in L.A. in early September. It works out perfectly anyway since you and I are meeting around then too. My assistant will be contacting you to coordinate details by end of the day Monday."

"Wow. I didn't think I'd still be on board for the 'Fuchsia Girl' video."

"Why the hell wouldn't you be?"

"I mean, I know you know—"

"That you and Olu aren't speaking? So what!"

"Yeah, but that's like, one of your besties."

"Listen, Olu, even if he's upset with you, would never block you from achieving your dreams. He's also a smart guy and realizes how stupid he has been. You'll talk to him soon, though, and you'll work things out. Until then, I'm minding my business if it's not about the video shoot or screenplay business."

I let out a sigh of relief knowing that Nero wasn't affected by all of this, which meant that he *was* truly professional, and as real as I thought he was. I even started to give more in to the idea of actually talking to Olu again.

"Is Olu here?" I blurted.

"Last I heard he was nearby. Shane was right about this being a party not to miss. My dear Nyela, I must go mingle with more familiar faces."

He winked at me and then walked away. I watched him disappear into the crowd, amused, once again, by how quirky he was.

I glanced around and noticed Reiko still chatting with Mandy, Felani was taking usies with random fans and Cookie was sitting in Shane's lap canoodling, so I decided to walk around.

I didn't get far before I finally spotted Olu, who was flanked by Tina and Kimmie from *Regality*. The latter two thirst-buckets seemed very passionate about whatever it was they were talking about as they made googly eyes at him. Olu, who despite his disinterested facial expression and vacant head nodding, didn't seem to mind that Tina was rubbing her hand up and down his forearm during their most likely stupid conversation. What the fuck was *that* about?

Olu caught my gaze just as I was about to go back to the booth and sulk, and motioned for me to come over. Tina and Kimmie didn't look too thrilled. I was not in the mood for cattiness, so I decided not to play and headed back to the booth anyway.

The scene at the booth was the same as it was moments earlier. I heard the same conversations and saw the same canoodling. I nestled into the booth next to Shane and Cookie's spit swapping session, still wondered what she saw in him, and hoped that he was at least genuinely nice to her.

"So, Miss Nyela, am I ever going to get my cameras on you and Olu as a couple at some point?" Mandy said. "You guys would be so good on TV. I can feel it."

"Did somebody say my name?" Olu replied, appearing out of nowhere.

What the fuck! Did he teleport?

He slid in the booth next to me and I tried as hard as I could not to be turned on or give off even one iota of I-give-a-fuck, but I got a whiff of that Issey Miyake cologne and started to feel myself fading. No one else seemed to notice or care about the awkward severity of this situation, so I climbed over him and headed back into the sea of dancing human beings, but he followed me, of course.

"Where you going, love?" he shouted over the music.

God. It was that sexy accent again. But I just kept walking, not sure where I was headed. Olu carefully grabbed my arm in an attempt to draw me closer to him. I turned around and scowled at him, hoping my eyes would shoot telepathic darts.

"That face, you're breaking my heart and turning me on at the same time."

"OLU, THIS ISN'T FUCKING FUNNY!"

I yelled loud enough to startle people around us including Olu, and even myself. He deserved it.

"I'm sorry, Nyela."

"Yeah, me too!"

I yanked my arm away and started to walk away again.

"I overreacted!" he shouted behind me, still trailing me. "I should have believed you, but I let my pride got the best of me. I *do* know you better than that."

"So you're just gonna keep following me?" I stopped to face him. "*I* thought I knew *you* better than that, but I guess not."

He started kneeling and grabbed my hands as if he were going to propose. "I know I fucked up but…"

"Olu, get up! People are staring."

"Fuck 'em. I'm here for *you.*"

"OLU! GET UP!"

I noticed cameras flashing and people starting to record us.

"Nyela Sojourner Barnes, I'm sorry I acted like a wanker."

"GET! UP! OLU!"

"I'll get up if you promise not to be mad at me anymore, or at least work on forgiving me. I can't lose you."

He handed me a small piece of a napkin with a handwritten note that read:

"Nyela, I love you, will you be my girlfriend again? Check yes or no."

It was juvenile, but funny. We shared a silly sense of humor. I watched that impish smile that I loved spread across his face, and felt myself giving in, but decided not to be a pushover. I grabbed the piece of paper and tore it up.

"Ouch," he said, sounding somber and a lot more serious than he had before.

I continued serving him stoic face until he finally stood up and grabbed both my hands. He started caressing my hands as we stared at each other. I could tell he was trying to find the right words, which usually wasn't hard for him.

"Well!" I said.

"Remember the time you spent a week at my place, and you made me watch every season of *A Different World* on Netflix because you were appalled that I had never seen it before?"

"Uh, yeah. I told you it was mandatory viewing for Black America, even black immigrants."

"Is that a smile?"

"No!"

I sobered up, but he drew me in closer to him anyway and I relented a little.

"Remember the episode when Whitley was about to marry Byron, and Dwayne Wayne ran down the aisle and asked her to marry him, and then he said, 'Baby, please!'"

I started smiling again. Olu remembered that that was one of my favorite episodes of *A Different World*. Something about it reminded me of how crazy my parents were about each other and what I ultimately wanted for myself one day.

"Yes, I remember."

"Well, I'm feeling like Dwayne Wayne right now. I don't know what else to say, but I know that I want you. I *need* you, Nyela. If I have to let you go then I will, but just know that I will storm into your wedding a decade from now and yell, 'Baby, please!' just like Dwayne Wayne. We could be epic. I know it. I knew it when I first met you. As cheesy as that sounds, it's true. I've never been so sure about anything."

I smiled harder, and probably looked like a doofus.

"I really am sorry, Nyela, and I need you to tell me how I can make it right. How can I earn your trust again?"

One thing I liked about Olu was that he didn't mince words and was never afraid to let anyone know exactly how he felt. If he wanted something, he was persistent and direct about getting it, which usually worked well for him. I knew he was sincere, no pun intended. I could feel it.

"I'm still hurt, but I do want to work this out," I replied. "I've fucking missed you like crazy. Let's talk later, away from this party, please."

"Okay, as long as I have your word that you haven't given up on me yet."

"*You* gave up on me, shit!" I replied.

"Nah, that was my ego. I'm smarter than that, though."

He slid his hands down to my butt while making our embrace tighter. I was on my tippy toes, trying to get as close to his neck as I could so that I could take in that intoxicating smell of his. We momentarily forgot where we were, and I started to feel right again, you know, that boneless feeling that I got whenever he held me.

"Aaaaaw, now that's what I'm talking about! Black love!" Sincere said, slow clapping like a walrus with Nasdaq in tow. "Nyela, I'm so glad you found someone who is stupid enough to put up with you."

Olu nearly pressed himself chest-to-chest with Sincere, who was slightly shorter and definitely a lot less accustomed to the gym. "You not gonna talk to her like that, mate!"

"I'm sorry. I must have touched a nerve," Sincere replied. "I wrote a blog dishing advice for pussy-whipped dudes like you. I might turn it into a book, so I suggest you check it out now and get some of my advice for free before I start my lecture tour and start charging!"

"Fuck you! I got your advice!"

"Aw shoot! This emo, singing-ass dude must be feeling froggy," Sincere added, faking a terrible English accent. "Is that what you all say across the pond, ay? Froggy?"

Olu backhanded Sincere and almost knocked him to the ground. I recalled the private mixed martial arts lesson he and I once had as a date and how impressed I was with his skills. Nasdaq, and now King Tootsie, who seemingly appeared out of nowhere, caught Sincere before his ass connected to the floor and helped him regain his bearings.

"Fuck you too!" Olu yelled, charging at King Tootsie who was diminutive, but not afraid to fight.

Fish appeared and nudged me out of the way as he pulled his client/friend out of the scuffle. I'd never seen Olu without Zen-like patience for people's fuckery, but then again, look at the people we were dealing with. Sincere and King Tootsie was a combination that could even make the Dalai Lama gouge someone's eyes out. I heard King Tootsie and Sincere yelling threats over the music as Fish and I dragged Olu back to our booth.

"What the fuck, yo! How you over there fighting alone, son!" Felani shouted.

"I'm good, Fel. Drop it," Olu replied.

"Nah, yo, I'm going to snuff at least one of them niggas!"

Felani started making her way to the other side of the room, where Sincere and company were situated, but her mission was aborted when Olu grabbed her firmly. Her resistance was futile.

"Chill, Felicia. I'm good."

"That's right, yo! You ain't gonna fight nobody!" Reiko said playfully as she made her way back to our general area along with Deion D.

He walked behind her with his arms wrapped around her waist.

"Um, is France going to be okay when he sees this?" I said.

"FUCK FRANCE!" Deion replied.

"Mmkay. But no more fights until we do what we came here to do."

"I like how you think," Cookie said, wedging herself between Olu and I and wrapping her arms around our waists. "You lovebirds okay?"

"Yes," Olu and I replied in unison.

"Good," she replied, turning her attention to Deion and Reiko. "Nyela and I have a wonderful vision for tonight so I have to agree, no more fighting with anyone until we set this thing off!"

"What is she talking about?" Olu said in my ear.

"I don't know. That girl crazy."

He shrugged, but I could tell he was skeptical about my response despite leaving it alone. We watched Cookie make her way to the stage and the crowd started cheering when she picked up the mic.

"Aw, you guys are so sweet," she said and curtsied. "I just wanted to thank you all for coming out to my birthday celebration. I know that many of you could have been anywhere in the world, but you chose to party with me and that really means a lot."

"I love you, Cookie!" shouted an intoxicated Shane from the front of the stage.

"Babe, get up here! Actually, I want all my people to get up here. Nyela, Reiko, Felani, Olu too! Get up here! Cynda, you too! Join me on stage."

"What's going on?" Olu said.

"Be patient," I replied.

"Oh, Sincere and King Tootsie, too? Where are they? I want to make sure the entire roster of Cynda's PR Associates is represented,"

Cookie said, peering into the crowd. "There they are, put a spotlight on them."

Sincere was in a corner with Nasdaq, King Tootsie, and Miriam, nursing a bloody nose, but still trying to look cool, especially since there were eyeballs on him now. He was so predictable.

"Sincere, I know we haven't *really* spoken in a while, but I have to say, your blog held me down when I first got to New York and started trying to navigate the dating scene. I hung on to every word you said until I met you."

Sincere temporarily removed the bloody tissue from his nose. The flummoxed looks on he and his crew's faces were hysterical.

"Here's the thing. I'm curious about how someone who is so easily manipulated could fool as many people as you have," Cookie continued.

I handed Olu my phone and told him to record because I wanted to document this for my personal stash. He obliged, but I also noticed, based on his facial expression, that he was still trying to figure out what the fuck was happening.

"I know. Everyone's wondering what the hell I'm talking about. Well, I'm going to let my girl Nyela take it from here. She knows you better than most people in here."

Cookie handed me the mic.

"Sincere, it was, um, interesting watching your devolution from Wall Street to relationship blogger. You started out as such a seemingly nice guy, but the blogging fame went to your head. I let a lot of bullshit from you slide, particularly the whole trying to make me look like a psycho thing, but since we're blowing up spots and digging shit up from the past, what kind of psycho ex-girlfriend would I be if I didn't show the world these photos I stole from your desktop!"

The crowd erupted into raucous laughter as the TV screen behind us began playing a slideshow of the photos of Sincere in drag.

"Can you give me some makeup application techniques?" Cookie shouted. "You should totally be a beauty guru. Eyebrows on fleek!"

I had tears in my eyes from laughing so hard. I caught eyes with Olu who was also cracking up.

"WHERE DID YOU GET THOSE!" Sincere yelled, attempting to push his way to the stage, but his nose was still leaking, which hindered his mission. Nasdaq and King Tootsie were close behind him.

Cookie nudged me.

"You got this girl," she said before finally giving in to another convulsive fit of laughter.

"My dearest Sincere," I said, totally winging it. "Remember all those subtweets and passive aggressive blog posts that you wrote about me? Remember how you leaked my mugshot from that unfortunate college experience that was a misunderstanding, and generally mislead everyone into believing that I'm crazy and desperate? Unlike you, I own my mistakes, and learn from them. I mean...I would have expected the fine media personnel in this room to have actually done their research about what really happened, especially since many of you know me, but I guess my hopes were too high. I get it; it's more fun pretending that I'm something more egregious for the sake of page views."

"What the fuck are you talking about!" Sincere snapped, still trying to play dumb and still holding his nose.

"Shhhhhh."

I pointed at the slideshow, which then changed from images of Sincere in drag to screenshots of the most recent messages he had been sending me.

"It's quite interesting that you tried to make me look like *I* couldn't let go of *you* as if it wasn't really the other way around. I mean, it's not like I don't have any text messages from you as recent as a few weeks ago." I cleared my throat and prepared to read from the screen. "Nye-Nye, letting you go was a mistake. It's not working with Nas and I need you back. We can even film this for my show. A love triangle would be the perfect storyline. I know I came on strong, but you really should think about it."

I paused and watched as Nesquik, or whatever the fuck her name was, tossed a drink in his face and stormed away. The crowd wailed an, "Oooooooh," and I continued my speech.

"It's not like you're an attention whore enough to try to arrange a love triangle for the sake of a reality show, right? *Naaaaah.* Oops, my bad, I was supposed to keep that to myself."

"WHAT! THE! FUCK!" he shouted, still unsuccessfully trying to charge forward to the stage with a bloody nose.

I glanced at Olu, who was staring at me nodding his approval, still laughing and recording. Most people in the crowd were still cracking up because the slide show started looping those goofy photos of Sincere in drag again.

"So, yeah, Sincere...eat a dick, if you haven't already!"

The audience burst into more uproarious laughter.

"Cookie, what is this!" snapped Cynda, who was a few feet away from me.

She tried to snatch the mic from me, but I yanked my arm away and glared at her, and Cookie stepped in between us prepared for a fight. Cynda backed down.

"Hi Cynda!" Cookie said in an overly chipper tone of voice.

By this point, I gave in to my own desire to laugh harder.

"What are you doing?" Cynda said. "This is unacceptable! A lady must be classy at all times!"

"You're right," Cookie replied. "You're the queen of class acts, aren't you?"

"That's...that's right."

Cynda looked pleased by the obviously disingenuous compliment, but also puzzled because she wasn't as dumb as the rest of her buddies. Cookie and I exchanged glances and I began speaking again.

"So, Cynda, please explain this..."

A photo of Cynda's mugshot from back in the day popped up on the screen and everyone gasped.

"I spoke to your ex-husband. Joshua Stephens, right? Since I'm so psycho, and all, I called him and explained that I was working on a story about men who had sole custody of their children, and exploring the deadbeat mom phenomenon, and he was more than eager to give up the goods on you. I guess you left a bad taste in his mouth. He told me how abusive you were during your five years of marriage, and not just to him, but also to your daughter. He also told me how that beautiful mug shot of yours was from his last straw with you. You know, from the time you tried to knock him out with a bat in an argument over who'd get custody of your daughter after the divorce. Remember the restraining order and the many violations that followed? Yup! Joshua told me you finally disappeared after losing custody. You thought moving to New York and reinventing yourself as this relationship guru under your maiden name was going to help you erase your old life. But I heard you're about three months behind in child support."

The photo on the screen then changed to a photo of Kermit the frog sipping tea and I heard more laughter.

"I don't know what you're talking about," Cynda replied.

"*We* know what she's talking about, though," Cookie said. "Let's also not forget about that time you were caught throwing a brick through his new girlfriend's car window."

"And how many times have you been engaged?" I added. "Based on my research, you have a history of abuse and dysfunctional behavior on your track record."

"And let's fast forward to more present day and talk about how you tried to sleep with Olu while he was with Miriam, or how you stole my book idea. Facts are facts, and all your female empowerment talk is bullshit," Cookie jumped back in. "You had many of us fooled with your grand ideas, and the fact that you hold down a billion jobs successfully. I actually admired you for a hot second."

"But I...what are you talking about?" Cynda was insistent upon still playing dumb.

I jumped back into the conversation.

"We're talking about you and your exceptional talent of fooling people. Aside from pushing up on your friends' boyfriends, and stealing book ideas and agents, there's one job that you don't really publicize much," I added.

"What's that?"

"You're the puppet master."

"I don't understand."

"Cynda, I know you put King Tootsie up to lying about having sex with me."

"I did no such thing!"

"I figured you'd say that," Cookie chimed in. "Hey Tootsie, heads up!"

She tossed an iPhone to him, and he caught it with ease.

"What the fuck! How did you get this?" he shouted.

"Yeah, so, remember that date we went on the other night, and you thought the waiter stole your phone and had a fit? I may have accidentally knocked your phone in my bag and forgot, oops. You should really try setting a less predictable password next time."

The next slide on the projector was the start of a series of slides depicting the following text exchange between Cynda and Tootsie, where she convinced him to go along with lying about sleeping with me and outed her self as Chatty Abernathy:

Cynda: *So, are you going to do it or nah?*

King Tootsie: *Why u want me 2 lie on that chick like that?*

Cynda: *She's just a casualty. Remember, you have to get back at Olu for talking shit about you. That's just how it is. What better way to do that than by dropping a diss track, since no one really does those anymore, and then going the classic route by lying on his girl? Do you know how epic that would be? Shit! People still don't know whether Tupac was telling the truth or not about sleeping with Faith. This could be amazing! You'll make history and keep people buzzing.*"

King Tootsie: *U do have a point.*

Cynda: *I know I do! Duh! My sneaky mind is how we've made so much money under the Chatty Abernathy brand for so long, and exactly why you're a partner! Making a scene is the only way to get eyeballs on you. Attention can mean money if we play it right. I don't know why I always have to go through this with you.*

King Tootsie: *Tru.*

Cynda: *Speaking of, I just want to thank you for being so loyal to me all these years. You could have been blown up my spot about the blog, but never did.*

King Tootsie: *No doubt. I mean, I do own a piece of that pie, but I also ain't not snitch, shawty. I also owe u for keeping my baby mamas in pocket on that child support shyt and u been helping me get this money. I do owe u, but u gotta admit u don't like Nyela just as much as you want me to get at Olu. U know how you is wit dem females.*

Cynda: *Ugh. Did you have to even type her name?*

King Tootsie: *My bad. Look, if Olu don't want u like that, u already know I'm down for the cause. U sexy as shit.*

Cynda: *Boy, bye! I'm never going there with you, but for real, I just don't get what he sees in her. I mean, I tried to be there for him after Miriam. Hell, I tried to warn him about Miriam, and he still shut me out.*

King Tootsie: *Miriam needed a nigga like me. U do too.*

Cynda: Ugh, I told you to stop coming at me like that!

King Tootsie: Aight, Imma stop 4 now. I think u should let that shit go, but who knows, u might have another shot after we pull this stunt.

Cynda: Perhaps. Anyway, when can we meet to discuss how we're going to roll out this plan of action? You should also start recording that diss track. We need to get it out before the week is over.

"Ok, that's enough," I said, signaling to end the slide show. "So, as you all can see, Chatty Abernathy, I mean, Cynda, gets a rush from drama and manipulation."

I paused for dramatic effect, looked around and made eye contact with Olu, who mouthed the words, "I'm so sorry."

I gave him an affirmative nod, smiled, and then caught a glimpse of Mandy, whose eyes were as wide as Gollum's when he was holding The Precious.

What her cameras captured was reality TV gold. I could see it now. Some website would eventually incorporate this in a list of the most epic moments in reality TV history. This moment would definitely be ranked in the top ten if not number one.

"So, there you have it ladies and gentleman. Is this the woman you all trusted for empowerment and guidance?"

"I HATE YOU!" Cynda screamed.

She lurched forward in an attempt to get to me, but Cookie jumped in between us, so she wrapped her hands around Cookie's neck instead, causing them both to topple backward as Olu yanked me out of the way.

Felani and Reiko descended upon the skirmish. Felani began punching Cynda while Reiko surprisingly tried to pry the brawling women apart. I was calm, but still prepared for a fight. However, I couldn't move anyway because Olu had a firm grip on me and telepathically communicated that he wasn't going to allow me to jump in. Cynda managed to break free from the fight and charged toward me like a wild bull, but Reiko caught her leg and she toppled forward. She fell just short of my feet, and that's when Olu let me go, lunged in between us, and hoisted her in the air as she flailed hopelessly, screaming at him to put her down. That was the most action she'd ever get from Olu in her life. King Tootsie then jumped in and began trying to pry Cynda away from Olu, which sent Olu into a rage. He let Cynda go and began pummeling King Tootsie. Cynda charged toward me, and I finally managed to get some good punches in before Reiko, Cookie and Felani caught up with her again. I knew my parents wouldn't approve of this behavior. I mean, sure, I wasn't brought up this way, but man, Cynda deserved this, and it felt good.

Mandy's security team *finally* started breaking up the melee. The fighting parties were pulled apart, and I caught a glimpse of Felani brandishing a large chunk of Cynda's weave as one of the reality show's security guards had a grip on her. I peered into the audience and noticed Miriam leading Sincere out of the venue. Cynda was still clawing at and cursing out anyone she could, but her attempts were pointless because security had a good grip on her too. King Tootsie had calmed down again, but security also held him in place. The latter two parties were being dragged toward the exit. Cookie, who had composed her self, picked up the mic as if nothing had happened and finished her speech.

"Well that escalated quickly. Security, get these grimy motherfuckers out of here!"

#Epilogue

Charlatan Business Woman Cynda Bentley Spotted Out and About in A New City

I laughed out loud after stumbling upon yet another post-Cookie's birthday bash headline in my story feed. It was two weeks after party-gate and folks were still going in with the jokes. I opened the post and found shots of Cynda brunching with a group of women—none of whom looked familiar—in LA.

The story read:

> *Publicist, manager, author, alleged life coach and formerly anonymous gossip blogger Cynda Bentley seems to have ditched her New York home base for L.A. She was spotted out and about with a group of women, brunching and partying around the city. One of the girls with Cynda is said to be up and coming singer/socialite and former star of the hit reality show* Basketball Groupies, *Cherry Hepburn.*
>
> *You know the industry is small so clearly they've heard about her by now, but I guess they don't care. These days, it pays to be famous for more negative things than positive, and if you saw Cherry in action on that reality show, then you know she and Cynda are definitely angry birds of a feather. Plus, Cynda probably needs as much money as she can*

get since she's being sued for back child support for the daughter that no one even knew she had until her spot got blown, and she hasn't updated Chatty Abernathy since she got outed as the scandalous blogger a couple of weeks ago at Cookie Clark's now infamous birthday party.

That was an event that will definitely play out on cameras this fall on VH-1's forthcoming reality show Love and the Industry, *but our sources tell us that Cynda will be starring in a forthcoming episode of* Iyanla Fix My Life, *where she will be forced to confront her crazy behavior stemming back to her marriage. Our sources tell us that Cynda believes she can start her career over in L.A. We're not sure how she's going to pull this off yet though because her old fans have demanding their money back from coaching sessions and that first book she self-published. She was dropped from the company that was going to publish her second book too, so we'll see how this plays out. At the moment, ratchet rapper King Tootsie is the only one who is really still in her corner. According to our inside sources, the two were spotted making out at an L.A. club, and seen holding hands and feeling up on each other all over town, which is trifling because Cynda used to be best friends with King Tootsie's last babymama.*

Speaking of King Tootsie, he finally started tweeting again. Y'all know he went ghost from social media for a minute after Olu Major's second diss track, which was released the day after Cookie Clark's epic party, made #BlackTwitter drag him even more than they were before. I still can't get enough of all the memes I saw. Anyway, that's all I have for now, but it seems like Cynda and King Tootsie were made for each other, and they're definitely still as messy as ever over in Tinsel Town. Tisk. Tisk.

I chuckled at the irony of this situation. Cynda wanted to be famous so bad that she went about it the wrong way yet she still seemed to be headed toward the path that she wanted in the first place. If the reports about she and King Tootsie canoodling were true, she might end up another one of his babymamas, which is karma enough. Perhaps that visit from Iyanla would actually help her, though. Hell, if she played her cards right, she could probably get a spinoff show about starting over, even if it would most likely be disingenuous, but I could care less.

I've finally learned that it wasn't for me to understand why people loved and rewarded drama so much. From now on, I would make a concerted effort not to let what other people did bother me, and I'd be more disciplined with myself about not getting dragged into nonsense. I'd rather be positive, productive, and make myself, and my parents proud, so that's what I'd focus on moving forward.

The next story I found was also hilarious. The headline read, *"Radio Personalities and the Whipped Men Who Love Them."*

This one was a pictorial of Cookie, Shane, Deion D and Reiko frolicking on Shane's yacht somewhere tropical. There were various shots of each respective couple being amorous, and being besties with each other. There was even a brief blurb about Shane and Cookie making appearances on *Love and the Industry* as an official couple, as well as Deion, who was now officially Reiko's boyfriend—much to France's chagrin.

Speaking of France, the next story I came across was about how King Tootsie admitted that there was truth to the rumor that Lady Blaq Widow may actually be pregnant with his baby and *not* France's. We still had a few months until the baby arrived, so we didn't know for sure just yet, but France was still messy, so I hoped Reiko had him out of her system for good. Although Deion started as a revenge date for Reiko, he was a much better fit for her.

I glanced at the time and realized that I had about 20 minutes to finish packing. I'd been a procrastinator since birth, so it was no shock that I left so little time to get myself together before the start of my whirlwind few weeks ahead, but I just *had* to read this one last item first.

The next headline read, **"Olu Major and Nyela Barnes Marriage Watch Update."**

> *There's still no word on when raptor Olu Major and Nyela Barnes plan to get married. But several eyewitnesses did see him down on one knee copping pleas at Cookie Clark's blow out birthday party that was full of drama.*
>
> *It's not audible what Olu was saying in the video footage that we obtained and there was no ring, but sources close to us say that it was an informal proposal and that the two plan to elope before his* International Rights of Passage *tour starts in a few weeks. This story is still developing but we'll keep watch because you know we love a good wedding.*

I laughed out loud at the absurdity of that story. All of those people watching us that day and no one could actually hear what was being said or figure out that it wasn't a marriage proposal? Logically, I wanted to find that hard to believe, but then again I'd learned the hard way that what people read and believed versus actual facts rarely matched.

There was no point in getting flustered about this, especially because as the girlfriend of one of the most popular men in the world right now, I was going to be blog fodder much more than I'd like to. It just was what it was, and that was okay.

I used to think all that new age-y bullshit about your life becoming a product of your thoughts was, well, bullshit, but after the past few months that I've had I was willing to ease up on my cynical stance. Sometimes you just had to laugh at people's shenanigans because most of what they did, if not everything, stemmed from some kind of personal issue, and in the case of my industry, it was usually the desire for power or attention that was the driving force.

I never wanted to be famous, but even in my new direction toward becoming the successful screenwriter that I had always dreamt of being, fame was something that I'd probably just have to deal with. I did say that I was bored with my life and it definitely got more exciting. I was now headed to L.A. with Olu where we'd shoot the video for "Fuchsia Girl." Nero and Olu loved my *Coming to America* meets *Black Cinderella*-themed treatment, so that's what we're going with.

"Fuchsia Girl" is the first video to be shot, but since Olu is shooting a video for each song on his album, we're looking at about a week in L.A. on a tight schedule. I won't be involved with shooting the other videos because Nero wanted me to focus on some meetings that he set up for my lawyer and I with regard to my screenplay. I've completed another round of edits as he and I discussed, and he has decided to become executive producer of my project. Did you fucking hear me? Nero is going to finance my screenplay under his Oscar-winning production company, and we're working on a Netflix streaming deal for its release! I've signed a contract with Nero, so our partnership is official! Not only that, but I'll also be meeting with potential directors, and it's looking like Issa Rae is a frontrunner! Awkward. Motherfucking. Black. Girl. I promised that I wouldn't die before I saw my screenplay actually play out as a movie, but thinking about how fast my life had suddenly shifted for the better made me breathless, like I could die any moment and be completely satisfied.

"NYE! COME DOWNSTAIRS!"

I rushed to my window and found Olu standing outside.

"Why didn't you just call or text me?"

"I wanted to take it back to the old school," he quipped. "You ready?"

"Uhh…kind of."

"I knew you'd bloody procrastinate! Do you need help?"

"Ten minutes, Olu! I'll be right down."

Olu and I were in a great place now. He was releasing his debut album, *International Rights of Passage,* in three weeks. It was remarkably already at 950,000 digital copies pre-ordered, and fans weren't even aware yet of the videos he was going to add. That was great news, but it also meant a tour and whirlwind promotions for at least six months. I understood it as a career woman, so I had to brace myself, but at least I had Olu to myself for now. My phone rang as I scrambled to toss my last few items in my carryon bag.

"I'm coming!" I put the phone on speaker.

"Hurry up, love. We're going to be late."

"But isn't it different if the plane is chartered?"

"You know there's still scheduling and air traffic stuff that needs to be accounted for, right?"

He mentioned that we'd head to London after we got done in L.A. because he wanted me to meet his family. After London, we were going somewhere tropical to wind down for that final week before the madness *really* started. He refused to tell me where we were going, but I did mention to him that I had always wanted to stay at the Sandy Lane in Barbados. We've already established that he was a great listener, so I was pretty sure I wouldn't be disappointed.

"I'm coming right now!"

"Good. The faster you get on with it the faster we can get this trip started, the faster we can get our work done, and the faster we can get you across the pond to meet my mum. I think she's going to like you."

I swept the apartment one last time to make sure I had everything. The last thing I did was shut my laptop down and slid it into the laptop compartment of my carryon.

"Your mum, huh?" I replied in the worst English accent ever. "I like the sound of that."

Acknowledgements

Thank you mom! You are the best support system anyone could have. Thank you Donya, for listening to my complaints about all the crazy people and abuse. Thank you Shannon, for understanding my cynical observations about life. Anslem, thank you for editing that one particular scene that I struggled with, and thank you for being an amazing man, even when you drive me nuts (lip curl). Aunt Shira, Aunt Ricki, Aunt Millie, Uncle Red and Uncle Keith, you are the coolest! To my favorite cousins, Warren, Donald, Sharina, Tee Tee, Kadeja, Lauren, Drake, Troy, and Devaughn, love you to pieces! Love you Johari and Kalila! Paris and Shanna, you already know what it is! The Nouveau Clarks, thank you for good energy, company, and industry talk, love you two! Malik, Indigo, and Tiffany J., thanks for listening and encouraging me. Redhead, thank you for listening, and for enjoying my probably mean jokes about people that I keep offline! Suezette, thank you for the encouragement, for being down-to-Earth and a really great spirit! Jessica (Likkle Bit), Aura, and Eb, thanks for the industry tea and ki ki's! Leesa Davis, love you! Shanelle, Taj, Kela, Nekia, Shayna D, and the whole Cancerian brunch crew, thanks for getting me.

Stephanie Vaughn, you are the best, and if anyone understands the dark places I have been mentally, it's you. Thank you for listening, non-judgment, and for understanding my anger, and thanks for sharing with me, now take care of yourself, please. Matthew a.k.a. "Nukirk," thank you for the support! Trudy, thank you for holding me accountable, for believing in me, and for being someone that I can learn from once I organize my business life and get my marketing skills together lol.

Rakia Clark, you are thorough, girl! Thanks for handling my edits gently.   Anyone else that I may have left out, I hope there's no love lost. Charge it to my head and not my heart. I purposely made that last line sound like the thank you's in all the '90s album booklets.

Made in the USA
Charleston, SC
17 March 2016